Only
A Fisherman's Daughter.

BY

MARIA
(STATIA M. ENGLISH)

Entered according to the Act of the Legislature of
Newfoundland, in the year 1899, on behalf
of the author, at the Colonial
Secretary's Office.

PRICE 50 CENTS.

MANNING & RABBITTS, PRINTERS

Library and Archives Canada Cataloguing in Publication

English, Anastasia. 1862?-1959
Only a Fisherman's Daughter / by Anastasia English; edited by
Iona Bulgin.

First ed. published 1899. Includes bibliographical references.
ISBN 978-0-9809144-4-3

    I. Bulgin, Iona   II. Title.
PS8509.N48O54 2009   C813'.4   C2009-901766-0

Newfoundland
Labrador

We acknowledge the financial support of the
Government of Newfoundland and Labrador,
through the Department of Tourism, Culture
and Recreation, for our publishing program.

Cover design by John Andrews
Cover photo by Sheilagh O'Leary (Bridget Wareham, model)
Layout by Granite Studios

Published by Boulder Publications Ltd.
www.boulderpublications.ca
11 Boulder Lane, Portugal Cove-St. Philip's, NL A1M 2K1

Printed in Canada

A NOTE ON THE TEXT

This edition of *Only a Fisherman's Daughter* is based on the original edition printed in St. John's in 1899 by Manning & Rabbitts. Simple typographical errors such as misspellings, redundant quotation marks, and transposed letters have been silently corrected. I have tried to eliminate errors from whatever source, except for those that have a bearing on the text. Any substantive changes or additions have been signposted in endnotes.

I have modernized the spelling of older hyphenated words and, where other inconsistencies of spelling occur in the text, I have regularized these. Punctuation has been altered where the sense is difficult to comprehend. I have not corrected the author's grammar or her rendering of Newfoundland dialect. Song lyrics and poems, including titles, quoted in the text remain as the author quoted them. One problem in this text is the inconsistent and often confusing use of quotation marks, both single and double, to indicate when a speaker ends and another begins, or to show dialogue within dialogue. I have silently corrected these inconsistencies. I have occasionally broken up extremely long paragraphs into shorter ones where such a change aided clarification.

I have used italic type to indicate names of newspapers and ships, which differs from the double quotation marks used in the original. Other instances of italic type reflect its inclusion in the original text.

Where I have found sources I have identified them, except for a few that proved impossible to find. Fragments of songs have been identified where possible.

— Iona Bulgin

And we want to recover
    our foremothers'
    navigations.
But where are the signposts,
    the keys, the legends,
    the scales for reading their experience;—
Where do we find the markers of their efforts?
    Without maps,
    We stumble,
    Or ask—
Stop someone along the way, and say:
Can you help me to find –?–

                Jo Gates, "Without Maps"

ONLY A FISHERMAN'S DAUGHTER: A TALE OF NEWFOUNDLAND

By

ANASTASIA ENGLISH

Edited by Iona Bulgin

for Dr. Elizabeth Miller
who mapped the landscape

CHAPTER ONE

"Yes, Mrs. Hamilton, I should break off the intimacy immediately if I were you. Nora Moore is no fit companion for your refined little girl." And the aristocratic Mrs. Brandford emphasized her words with a slow, knowing shake of the head.

"But why?" asked Mrs. Hamilton, the doctor's wife, who had only lately come to the village which we will call St. Rose. "I have seen a great deal of Norrie since coming here. She is certainly wild, careless, mischievous even, but I've seen nothing either low or vulgar in her. To tell the truth, I like the child. She interests me. She and Lucy are very fond of each other, too."

"But, my dear Mrs. Hamilton, she is an imp, a real imp; even her own friends will tell you that."

"I thank you, Mrs. Brandford, for taking such an interest in Lucy, but I could not forbid the intimacy without having some just reason for doing so."

"Just reason? My dear lady, do you require more reason, when I tell you that she is the idler, the mischief maker—well, in short, the terror of St. Rose? Did anyone tell you that it was she who put that lump on poor Jerry Malone's head a few years ago, that she has chased the magistrate's little daughter with a dead muskrat 'til the child ran screaming through the house, frightening into convulsions the sleeping infant, and she has actually dared to pelt me with snowballs?"

Mrs. Hamilton found it difficult to keep the smile that was lurking round the corners of her mouth from going further, not that she approved of Norrie's misdoings.

"That was very rude," she answered, but not looking at all as shocked as Mrs. Brandford wished. "I shall watch them closely and should I see anything that would justify me in forbidding their friendship I shall certainly do so."

Here, Mrs. Brandford adjusted her gold-rimmed glasses, and rose to go, saying, "Of course, Mrs. Hamilton, I only warn you for your child's good. If you do not think her an unfit companion for Lucy, and I can see you don't, I have nothing more to say." And she drew her stately form to its full height, wished Mrs. Hamilton a cool good morning, and departed, anything but pleased with the result of her visit.

Mrs. Hamilton was a good woman in the true sense of the word. She was one who always took care to hear both sides of a story before she passed judgment. She sat in deep thought for some time after Mrs. Brandford's departure. "How hard she is on the poor child!" she murmured. "The little thing has neither father nor mother to guide her, and I am sure those relatives of hers do not understand her properly. That there is nothing bad or vulgar in her, I am sure. I shall tell Lawrence when he comes, and he will know what is best to do."

Lawrence is her husband, Doctor Hamilton. They have but one child, Lucy, the idol of their hearts. She is about twelve years of age, a delicate child, small and fairy-like, with flaxen hair, large blue eyes, but rather pale face. It was mostly on her account that Doctor Hamilton had settled for an indefinite period at St. Rose, for he was a gentleman of unlimited means. "The fresh sea breeze and continual contact with pure country air will improve the child's health," he said, "and make her a strong woman." Everyone who knew Doctor Hamilton loved and respected him; he was the friend of the poor, the adviser of those in trouble, the consoler of those in sorrow. He was a man who had little patience with the haughty ones who draw aside their skirts lest they should come in contact with those of their humbler neighbours and, on this account, was unfortunate enough to get into the bad graces of the dignified Mrs. Brandford. He was a plain-spoken man and had a habit of driving home unpleasant truths to those who deserved it. He met the aristocratic lady on the way home from her visit to his wife.

"Now," she thought, "I will open the doctor's eyes to the danger he is running in allowing his child to associate with that little imp, Nora Moore." "Good morning, Doctor," and she stood before him, as he, raising his hat with a polite bow, was about to pass on.

"Good morning, madam. I'm pleased to see you are taking advantage of this beautiful day by enjoying a constitutional walk."

"Yes, it is a magnificent day, but it is from a sense of duty that I've taken a walk this morning, and I fear I have failed in my object."

2

"I'm sorry to hear this, Mrs. Brandford. In what way have you failed?"

"Well, the fact is, I'm just returning from a visit to your wife. I thought that perhaps you are not aware of the kind of girl of whom your little daughter is making a companion."

A humorous smile appeared in Doctor Hamilton's eyes. He had heard all about the snowball business and knew to whom she was alluding, but feigned ignorance. "Oh, I daresay Lucy has quite a number of companions. She meets them at school, you know."

"Oh, yes, I know she meets Nora Moore at school. That is the girl I speak of. But she is constantly in her company outside of it, and, really, Doctor, it would be a wise thing for you to stop the intimacy at once. I have been trying to impress the fact on your wife this morning, and it is the object in which I fear I've failed. But perhaps I may not be so unfortunate with you, Doctor."

"And what has little Norrie done this time, Mrs. Brandford? Been into mischief again, has she?"

"Been into mischief?" she echoed. "When is she out of it, I'd like to know? She is a low, impertinent, vulgar girl without a particle of refinement."

"Oh! I think you are making a great mistake, Mrs. Brandford. Norrie is not by any means as black as she is painted, and she is anything but low or vulgar."

"But you certainly cannot forget, Doctor, that she does not belong to our class at all. She is but the child of fisher parents and cannot help being ill-bred."

"How do you explain this, madam?" And the doctor put on his severest aspect: "Why, because she is the child of fisher parents, must she be ill-bred?"

"I wonder at your asking such a question, Doctor. The utter absence of refinement and education makes them ill-bred."

"I am surprised, Mrs. Brandford, at your ignorance of such matters. The absence of education does not, by any means, necessitate ill-breeding, else how is it found, I am sorry to say, so often amongst what is called the higher classes?"

"You do not mean to tell me, sir, that ill-bred people are ever known in our class?"

"I do, most assuredly, madam. I've met them time and again. I call people ill-bred who criticize the doings of others and pry into their private affairs, who look with scorn on their humbler neighbours, and magnify their little faults and follies into vices; paint, in the most glaring colours, their little shortcomings and then hold them up to view, while their own far more serious ones are safely hidden by the mantle of refinement that is supposed to envelop them. These, madam, are the true offspring of ill-breeding. Little Norrie Moore is simply a wild, impulsive child, brimming over with fun and merriment. She is truthful and honourable as it is possible for a child to be, and I do not, in the least, fear for Lucy's morals in associating with her."

Mrs. Brandford put on her haughtiest air and said in an injured tone, "Since I cannot convince you, Doctor Hamilton, of the risk you are running in allowing your child to keep company with a good-for-nothing ill-bred idler, I will wish you good morning."

"Good morning, Mrs. Brandford. I thank you for troubling yourself so much in Lucy's behalf, but it is quite unnecessary. Perhaps you think you are right, but Mrs. Hamilton and myself think differently."

Mrs. Brandford could have cried[1] with mortification during the remainder of her walk. She had rejoiced when she heard of the popular doctor and his wife coming to St. Rose, as they would add to the few whom she thought good enough to be her friends. And the knowledge that she had failed to impress them with the weight of her superiority was certainly very trying. She was a widow. Her husband had made a large fortune by supplying banking schooners[2] for the fishing season. He had had several branches of his firm in different parts of Newfoundland. He had been a fair and lenient merchant, and all in his employ had trusted him. The present Mrs. Brandford had been his second wife. There was one son, Harry, a lad of nineteen, to whom the house and property belonged exclusively, while a yearly allowance was settled on his stepmother and, as she had great business tact, her husband left her in control of all 'til his son was of age.

The house was large, well built, and magnificently furnished, with meadow lands and gardens attached. Harry had, only a few weeks ago, arrived from college, where he had received a good education, and soon he took upon himself the whole management of the firm. Mrs. Brandford was only too glad to have the responsibility lifted from her shoulders while the proceeds were pretty well at her control. She had no great love for her stepson; it was not part of her composition to love anyone. She was proud of him, tho', as well she might. He was what is generally called a straight-goer and, like his father before him, honest and upright in his dealings with everyone. Judging from the seriousness of his manner and appearance, one would take him to be much older than his years.

CHAPTER TWO

We will leave Harry Brandford for the present and direct our attention to the heroine, Norrie Moore.

When Doctor Hamilton had arrived home, he related to his wife what had passed in the meeting between himself and Mrs. Brandford. "I think I have offended her beyond pardon," he said.

"I feel rather anxious since her visit, Lawrence," she answered. "I wonder if we are wise in allowing Lucy so much in Norrie Moore's company."

"You need not worry in the least, my dear. I'm not a bad judge of character and, hearing such terrible accounts of Norrie's escapades, I've made a study of her, watching her when she did not know it, and, you may take my word, she is just as innocent a child as Lucy herself. Her faults are all on the surface, poor child, and that is why she gets into so many scrapes. She is heedless and reckless for herself where danger is concerned, but she is always most careful over Lucy. I've often seen her carry our little girl across pools of water, fearing she would get her feet wet. You need not be at all uneasy. Let her romp away with Norrie over beach and stones, through wood and bramble. It's just what the child needs to make her strong and healthy."

Yes, it was true; poor Norrie's faults were magnified into vices by a great many. She had a dim recollection of being held in her mother's arms one night as her father kissed her goodbye to go to the fishing grounds. It was for the last time. He, together with other brave men, met a watery grave near their own shores. His wife did not long survive him. She died one year after, and little Norrie, then but five years old, was left to the mercy of her nearest of kin. These were her late father's cousin and his wife. They were childless, and had prim notions and old-fashioned ways which did not at all suit a child of Norrie's temperament. They were not unkind, and intended doing their duty by their kinsman's child.

If she had been of a quiet, yielding disposition, she would have fallen into their ways and lived their plain humdrum life. But this was not Norrie. She was a child overflowing with fun, mischief, and buoyancy of spirit, ever gay, ever light-hearted. She could no more resist the impulse to play pranks on people than she could help being alive. It seemed sometimes as if she could not give vent enough to her high spirits. While a mere child, she could row, swim, catch squids and tomcods,[3] jump as high as any boy, and whistle better.

One day, when in her tenth year, she had been sent to the top of the house in punishment for some slight fault, but she managed to steal downstairs and out without being seen, bringing with her a bowl of water and a sponge. The house was not far from the beach, where men, women and children were engaged in spreading fish.[4]

On this beach was a large store, and into it Norrie crept, climbed up a ladder to the top loft where there was one small window, and here she amused herself by squeezing water from the sponge on anyone who came near. Now, working at the fish was Jerry Malone, as original an individual as ever one met with. He was quite alone in the world, made no friends, and did his work talking to himself; meanwhile, he looked at the sea and sky. He could foretell rain forty-eight hours in advance, and he was seldom wrong in anything he said about the weather. When he was a few times mistaken, he did not at all like being reminded of it. He was ill-natured, ill-tempered and disagreeable in every way.

On this particular day in the month of August, the men had asked Jerry if it would be safe to spread the fish, as it seemed a little cloudy. Jerry happened to be in one of his better moods and grinned from ear to ear as he said, "No rain today. Any man knows dat." And leaning against the store, took off his hat to cool himself.

"I dunno den, Jerry. I felt a few drops on me head a wile a gone," said one man.

"Begob, so did I," said another.

Norrie was in fits of laughter as she heard them. She knew Jerry's weak point about not liking to be at fault in anything he said about the weather, and determined to keep it up.

Jerry, tho' not an old man, was slightly bald, and, as he leaned against the store, there came drop, drop, drop on the bald spot. He looked at the sky dumbfounded, saying to himself, "Dat's quare. Never seed rain afore from a sky like dat." But he put on his hat and went to work again.

A few minutes more and another cry is heard. "Hello! Dares more drops comin'. Yer out in yer reckinin' dis time, Jer. I don't tink we ought to spread de fish ta-day, boss."

"Jerry," roared the boss. "What are you thinkin' of, tellin' us it's not goin' to rain, and the drops comin'? I felt them meself as I came out of the store there."

Jerry leaned against the store again and took off his hat, when drop, drop, drop splashed a second time on his head.

"'Tinks 'tis out o' de store 'tis rainin'," he grumbled.

Norrie was enjoying herself immensely, but, alas, her pleasure was soon cut short. She was shaking so much from laughter that her arm knocked against the bowl laid on the ledge, and down it came, water, sponge and all, on Jerry's head. This, of course, led to an investigation of the store and there they found the culprit, not hiding away in fear, but screaming out in merry laughter, "Oh, my, such fun! I never had such fun in my life," as she was led forth by one of the men.

"You little hussy," said one. "You young imp," said another. "I'll walk you straight up to your uncle's (she had been taught to call her guardians Uncle and Aunt), and get you a sound trashin' for makin' us lose our mornin' dis way." While Jerry grumbled, "Saucy little ting, nearly broke me head."

The next unpardonable act was throwing the snowball at Mrs. Brandford. It was Christmas time and there had been a heavy fall of snow—much to all youngsters' delight. Norrie, together with five or six others, were at it in full swing, sliding, skating, jumping and snowballing; Norrie, of course, leader, as she always was of everything, when Mrs. Brandford appeared in sight, giving a disdainful glance at the children as she swept past them.

"I bet you," said one youngster, with a grin on his face, and his hands in his pocket. "Nera wan o' ye id fire a snowball at her," nodding in Mrs. Brandford's direction.

"Well, what do we want to fire one at her for?"

"I bet ye yer afeard now wid all yer bravery, Norrie Moore."

"I'm not afeard, but I won't do it."

"'Cause she'd wring yer ears if ye did."

"Would she, indeed, wring my ears? I'd like to see her try it. You just shut up now, Tommy Brown, or I'll throw a snowball at you." She had a very large one in her hand at the time.

"Yer afeard of me, too," said Tommy, and he ran off, as fate would have it, in the direction of Mrs. Brandford.

Norrie followed, but she must have used more strength than was necessary in the throwing of a snowball, for it whirled past

Tommy and, horror of horrors, came down with full force on the lady's bonnet, and fell in a shower about her neck and shoulders.

All the children ran except Norrie, who stood where she was, watching the injured lady as she approached her.

"'Twas she as done it, Norrie Moore, ma'am," said mean Tommy, who was in reality the culprit.

It would be impossible to describe the rage and indignation on Mrs. Brandford's face as she said, "You low-born little fisher girl. How dared you throw that snowball at me?"

Norrie was not at all frightened, and did not look it either; but she was about to apologize and explain when the words "low-born fisher girl" fell on her ear, and she remained silent. It was one of her peculiar habits that she often would not justify herself when accused of something she did not do.

"Only that I would not soil my hands, I would box your ears, you bold, impertinent tomboy," went on the indignant lady.

"She desarves it well, mum," said Jerry Malone, who happened to come along at the time. "She slapped down a heavy bowl on top of my head last summer and the lump's dare still." (Of course Jerry never believed it was an accident.)

Norrie stood watching her accusers in silence, with large, fearless brown eyes.

Mrs. Brandford said no more, but walked on to Norrie's home and told her story, which resulted in the poor child being kept indoors for the remainder of the holidays, to card and spin wool[5] all day.

Shortly after that came the falling out with the magistrate's little girl, Eva Fenton, when Norrie followed her with the muskrat, which was the cause of putting the infant into convulsions. Many such complaints were made against her, 'til at last there was nothing thought too bad for Norrie Moore to do.

CHAPTER THREE

It was at school, when in her twelfth year, that Norrie first met, and fell in love with, fair-haired Lucy Hamilton. The latter was not long in returning the attachment, especially when Norrie had warmly espoused her cause in some little disagreement amongst the children, and saved her from the persecutions of those who take a delight in teasing a new pupil.

There was only one school at St. Rose; its teacher, a lady, Miss Bryant. Norrie, in her twelfth year, was taller than Lucy, her form more rounded. She was lithe, active, much improved in rowing and swimming, and took as much delight in fishing for tomcods and jigging squids as she did two years before.

She was graceful in every movement; her head a mass of dark brown curls; her eyes large and of soft brown, with a gleam of mischief, merriment and candour in their depths; cheeks and lips the picture of health. Her skin was tanned to a dark brown from constant exposure to wind and weather.

On this particular day near the end of August, she stands bareheaded, on a large stone, her hat swinging in her hand. She has a foot on either end which, being a little rounded at the base, she rocks up and down. A true child of nature she certainly looks. There is an extra degree of mischief in her eyes today and anyone who understands her would know she is up to something.

A few days previous, she and Lucy had arranged a little party of seven or eight girls, besides themselves, to go on a rambling picnic. They meant to go away out to the extreme end of a large beach which led to the sea, and there have a nice lunch, which Norrie and Lucy had prepared, and this was the day set down. But it also happened that 'twas just the kind of day suitable for hay and fish making,[6] so that whilst the men and women worked on the beach at the fish, the boys and girls were expected to go in the fields turning hay.

The system on which they worked was, the children of the neighbouring houses would work at one man's field, then his boys and girls would help them in turn. So, when Norrie and Lucy came around, bearing a large basket filled with currant and buttermilk buns, bread and butter, cake, and plenty of milk, they read the story in the sad, tearful faces of the children, that hay making, not picnicking, was to be their occupation. Unfortunately, the field of Tommy Brown's father was to be the scene of their labour, and thither Norrie went with them and begged Skipper Brown to let them off this glorious day, and they would do twice the work tomorrow, and she, Norrie, would help them.

"Faix,[7] I cannot," said this industrious individual. "We're some time lookin' for this kind of a day, and the hay wants it. Ye'll have plenty of time for picnics when it's all med. And, indade, 'twould be better for John Moore to find somethin' else for you to do; but it's a hard time he got wid ye, ye idle little runabout."[8]

"I think it's Uncle John's business, Skipper Brown, what he finds for me to do, and it would be no use for him to find anything for me today for I wouldn't do it, because a promise is a promise, no matter who it's made to, and we all promised each other to go off today over the hills and marshes and out to the sea. And I wish we were all gone before you came with your nasty old hay making. If I was them (Norrie's grammar was often at fault), I'd break all the hay prongs on purpose, so I would."

"Is it puttin' them up to yer own mischievous tricks ye are? Get out of my field, Norrie Moore. It's all very well for the doctor's little girl. She's a born lady and will have nothin' else to do all her life, but you ought to be earnin' yer bread."

"Oh! keep on your wool!"[9] said Norrie in an undertone, as she took Lucy's hand and turned to go.

"She says to keep on your wool," roared Tommy of the snowball, who happened to be near and caught the words.

"What's that, ye saucy little faggot,[10] if I don't complain ye to yer uncle. Wen and ware did ye larn that word?"

"The only one I ever heard saying it then is your own mean tattletale Tommy, when he came home from St. John's last spring. 'Twas 'keep on yer wool,' 'keep on yer wool,' if anyone looked crooked at him. I suppose he was tryin' to show off what he learned while he was there."

"Oh! Skipper Brown, do let us go!" cried all the children, in a chorus, for they knew if Norrie went without them their last chance was gone.

"Nera wan o' ye 'ill stir from dat hay dare; if it's fur nothin' else but that young imp's sass, an' I'll go straight to John Moore's an' tell him about her."

Norrie and Lucy were outside the field by this time, and the disappointed children went at the hay, but their hearts were not in their work, and they gave angry scornful glances at Tommy. Not one girl would work near him, for Norrie was a favourite with them all, and they only wanted her now to urge them on to rebellion.

"Oh, Norrie!" cried Lucy, with tears in her eyes. "Must we give it up?"

"Not a bit of it. Do you think, Lucy, I am going to look at the poor little things working at the hay, and we going off on a picnic? And, besides, we would have no fun with only two of us."

"No, indeed, we would not," said Lucy. "But what will you do, Norrie?"

"I'll just keep out of the way. And, Lucy, will you keep the field in sight? He won't suspect you. You're never up to mischief like me. And as soon as old Tom Brown starts for Uncle John's to complain me, I'm off for the field, and see if I don't bring them all out of it with me."

"But, oh, Norrie, what will they do to you when we come home?" said Lucy, clasping her hands and looking with admiration at Norrie.

"Oh, I don't care. The picnic will be over then. Now, Lucy, I'll stand here on this stone and you come and tell me when the coast is clear."

So there she stood playing wady-buckity[11] 'til she saw Lucy running towards her.

"Oh, Norrie, he's gone right up to your house."

"Very well," she answered, as she started for Tom Brown's field. "I was just going to give him a chance. Now if he didn't go to complain me I would let them alone at his hay, and have the picnic another day, but he'll have to put up with the consequences now."

When the children saw Norrie and Lucy appearing in their midst again, they surrounded them.

"Oh, Norrie, he's gone to tell on you," they all cried.

"Well, let him," she said. "I'll be even with him. Where's that nasty little tattletale Tommy?"

"Oh, he had to make himself scare. We smothered him with hay and tripped him with our hay prongs every time he came near us. He took all the boys with him, too."

"Well now," said Norrie, as she straightened herself and moved a little distance off, so as the eloquence of her persuasive powers might have the desired effect on her auditors, "if you have one spark of independence in you, if you have the likin' you all talk of for Lucy and me, if you want to punish that mean little brat Tommy Brown, and, last but not least, if you want to have one glorious, jolly day,[12] drop your hay prongs, and we'll run as fast as our legs can carry us to the hills."

The children looked spellbound with eyes and mouths open for some time.

Then one said, "We'll be killed when we get back."

"I'll take the whole blame for everything. I'll tell Skipper Brown and all your mothers that I made you do it."

"That's fair, anyhow," said another. "I tinks Norrie is very good-natured and we would be mean not to go."

"But, Norrie, you'll be skivered[13] altogether."

"Never mind me. I'll be kept in for a week whatever way it goes for tellin' old Brown to 'keep on his wool,' so perhaps the week 'll do for all. And just look at the nice lunch Lucy and me got, lots for all of us, so run while there's time. When Skipper Brown comes in sight, our chance is gone."

The tempting lunch settled it. The children's appetites were already sharpened from work in the bracing air and with one accord every implement for hay making fell to the ground, and away they flew after Norrie, who dragged Lucy by the hand, and not 'til they were far from sight of the houses and fields did they pause to take breath.

"Oh," cried Norrie, laughing and clapping her hands, "when I think of the way ugly Tommy Brown and his cross daddy will look when they go to the field and find us gone. Oh, how I would love to be able to be ahide somewhere and watch them."

All unpleasantness was soon forgotten, for Norrie's merriment was infectious. They wandered on 'til they came to a long sandy beach where the sea rolled in, in big white waves. Here they sat and took their lunch, all (even Lucy) with keen appetites.

Then they left the seashore and crossed a small river over a kind of impromptu bridge, consisting of a narrow plank one end of which rested on a pile of stones so as to bring it on a level with the river's bank at the other side. They had to go one by one, it was so narrow. Norrie and Lucy, of course, went together, Norrie holding Lucy's arms round her own waist as she kept her close behind, and making her shut her eyes fearing she would feel giddy.[14] Then, away over hills and valleys, eating berries as they went, 'til their lips were blue. At length they sat on top of one of the highest hills to rest.

Norrie, with all her reckless ways, was a dear lover of the beauties of nature, and the scene now presented to her enraptured gaze was certainly enough to arouse the artist's soul within her.

A beautiful sky of cloudless blue met the sea of a deeper shade on one side as it sank into the horizon. On the other, hills red with berries of different descriptions, and interspersed with little rivers, brooks and ponds, with beautiful white water lilies gleaming on their surface, and, further off at sea could be seen the spires of the distant lighthouses, rising tall and straight to the sky, and the neighbouring hills looking blue in the distance.

"Norrie, what are you looking at?" asked Lucy, as she took her hand to rouse her from her reverie.

Norrie turned towards her with a sigh and a serious face, two things foreign to her nature. "Oh, how beautiful it all is, Lucy!"

"All what?" she asked.

"All this," answered Norrie, taking it all in with a sweep of her hand. "There are people who paint these things, aren't there, Lucy? I was reading something about them one day in a book that Eva Fenton lent me, but Aunt Bridget made me give it back without finishing it; she said it was all nonsense and not fit for me."

"Oh, yes, I was learning drawing and painting in St. John's but of course I could not paint all this. They are called artists, you know. I expect when I go away to school I will learn to paint well, but I hope that will be a long time coming, for I don't want to go at all."

"Oh, Lucy, what will I do when you go? I will be more lonely than before you came. You know I like the other girls, but I can't talk to them like I do to you."

"Oh, Norrie, if you could only come with me, I would not mind going a bit."

"If I only could," said Norrie, clasping her hands. "I'd study all day and all night, too, to paint places like these, and play and sing, and learn history and grammar and geography, and all about the great men who wrote all the beautiful poetry. I don't give much time to my lessons now because I'll not be let go to school long enough to learn all I'd wish to, and then I don't care. I heard Aunt Bridget say to Uncle John the other day that she would soon have to keep me home to help her at the carding and spinning, and he said, 'I think about another year will finish off what larnin' she wants' (that's the way he says it, but I always try to speak the way Miss Bryant tells us, and the way you and your father and mother speak)."

"Perhaps," said Lucy, "when the time comes for me to go you will be able to come, too."

"I don't think so, Lucy," she answered, shaking her head, and then her serious mood was over. "Let us go down to that little river," she said, "and catch some prickleys.[15] I think the other girls went that way."

They descended the hill, but on arriving at the bottom they saw on the other side of the river a young gentleman, fishing.

"Who is it?" asked Lucy.

"It's Mr. Brandford," said Norrie. "He is only home a short time from college."

"I suppose he has learned everything," said Lucy.

"Oh, I daresay," answered Norrie. "He could play the fiddle[16] (that's what the men here call it) before he went away at all. I often stole up under his window to hear him."

"Is he nice, Norrie? Do you like him?"

"Not much, though he is nicer than his mother. She hates me, you know, since I spoiled her bonnet with the snowball, but she is not his real mother, only his stepmother."

"How handsome he is, Norrie!"

From where the children stood they had a good view of Harry Brandford, and handsome he certainly was, tho' it is not this fact that impresses you as you look at him. His is a face that would attract attention anywhere. One looking at him would be sure to look a second time. He is tall, straight, and manly looking for a lad of nineteen, with dark brown wavy hair, a broad high forehead, well cut features, and clear dark grey eyes, a square determined chin, the mouth beautifully shaped and firm, tho' yet possessing almost womanly sweetness when it smiled, and a slight, dark moustache. There is a look of seriousness almost amounting to sadness in the face, but this disappears instantly in a bright kind smile, as his eyes rest on the two girls opposite.

The river was so narrow at this spot that, by raising their voices a little, they could be heard speaking across.

"Good evening, Norrie," he said. "Enjoying a ramble over the hills?" Harry did not share his stepmother's opinion of her, and only smiled when he heard of her little escapades.

"Yes!" answered Norrie. "We've been out all day. We are soon going home now."

"Would you like to try and catch some trout before you go? There are plenty of them here."

Norrie's eyes fairly danced with delight. It was one of the things that she had always wished to do, but she never had a fishing rod.

"Oh, if you please, we would be so glad, I mean Lucy and me."

"And who is this little lady whom you call Lucy?" said Harry, as he crossed the river on a few large stepping stones.

"This is Doctor Hamilton's little girl, Mr. Brandford, Lucy." It was the first time Norrie had given an introduction, and she flattered herself she had got through it admirably.

"How do you do, Miss Hamilton?" said Harry, as he took her sunburned hand.

"Very well, thank you, Mr. Brandford."

"Now, who shall be the first to try?" as he freshly baited his hook.

"Oh, Lucy must try first," said generous Norrie, though she was impatient to be at it herself.

"Very well, then. Now, Lucy, this way," as he put the rod in her hands. "Throw out your line as far as you can and, when you see your float disappear under the water, throw in again, for you will then know there is a speckled beauty on your hook. Now, Norrie, move this way a little so that Lucy won't hook you instead of the trout." And he drew her a little distance off.

"How did you two find your way out here?"

"Find our way?" repeated Norrie, wonderingly. "Why, I could not lose my way if I tried on the hills, and there are ten of us—the rest of the girls are gone off picking berries. They will be back here soon, and then we are going home."

"Oh," said Harry, a sudden light breaking on him, and an amused smile coming over his face, "that just reminds me. Why, I think you raised quite a tempest in Tom Brown's field this morning. I happened to pass that way about dinner hour, when Tom came out of his house, and I walked with him as far as the field, where he said he was going to send the poor children to their dinner. He knew they must be hungry, and it was so good of them to wait 'til they were sent for. But when we got there, he found not a bit of hay made up and everything just as he had left it at nine o'clock. 'It's Norrie Moore,' he said. 'She must have come back again and enticed them away.' Then he told me all that happened and what you said to him. Don't you think that was a very naughty word for a little girl to use, Norrie, and then take eight more off from their work besides herself?"

"No, I do not, Mr. Brandford," she answered, saying to herself, he is as bad as the rest of them, "but I think it was real mean of Skipper Brown to keep them at his hay, when we had our picnic all arranged for today, and they all dying to come. But if he had not gone to tell on me, I would not have taken them from their work and, besides, I did not mean him to know what I said to him. I know it was rude of me. It's that nasty Tommy who told him."

"And what was the use of saying it at all if you did not mean him to hear you?"

"I don't know. I was mad with him and had to say something, and that was the first thing came to me."

"Well," said Harry, "I don't know what will be the end of it. There is going to be ructions[17] when you all get back," and he tried to look severe, though he was smiling inwardly.

"All the ructions there can be, Mr. Brandford, is that I will be locked in[18] for a week. The others won't be touched, because I'm going to say it's I who made them do it."

"Are you always as generous as this, Norrie?"

"I don't know, but I never let anyone else be punished for what's my fault."

Norrie had a vague idea that Harry Brandford did not approve of what she did, and was enjoying the uncomfortableness of her situation, and began to grow indignant. "I won't use his rod," she thought. "And when Lucy is ready, we will go."

"Oh, Mr. Brandford! The float has gone down."

"That's right, throw in now," said Harry, as he sprang to assist her. "That's a beauty," as a poor little trout came jumping and twisting on the bank, speckled with gold, crimson, purple, blue and pink. "Now throw out again," as he took off the trout and rearranged the bait.

"But, isn't Norrie going to try now?" said Lucy.

"We will wait 'til you catch three, then Norrie can try." And he went back to where she was sitting on the stump of an old tree.

"What a pity you don't try and be a good girl, Norrie."

"I didn't know I was so very bad," she answered, with a stronger determination not to use his rod.

"Not so very bad?" said Harry. "After all the dreadful things laid to your charge? Could you not try now and be a nice, gentle little girl like Lucy Hamilton?"

"I love Lucy better than anyone else in the world, and she's as good as an angel, but I don't want to be like her. I don't want to be like anyone but myself. Mr. Brandford, Lucy got her three trout now and we must go."

"Your turn now, Norrie," said Lucy, with much delight in her pretty face as she exhibited her catch.

"No, Lucy, I'm not going to catch any."

"Not going to try, Norrie? And you told me you were dying about it," said Harry wonderingly.

But Norrie was standing erect now, with bright defiant eyes and flaming cheeks.

"So I am," she answered, "but I would rather never trout in my life than use your rod, Mr. Brandford. You think I'm a dreadful girl, not fit to be with Lucy, just as Mrs. Brandford thinks, and you are glad I'm to be punished when I go home."

"Oh, Norrie," said Harry, with intense sorrow and concern in his face. "I had no idea you minded what I said in this way. Why, I was really only jesting. I beg a thousand pardons."

"It's no use then because I won't grant one."

"Oh, my child, you must really forgive me for my thoughtless words. Let me persuade you to use my rod."

"No, Mr. Brandford, I will not, not even if I could catch every trout in the river."

"Why, Norrie, you're so generous to everyone else, surely you won't refuse to be so to me, when I tell you I did not mean what I said, and that I will be positively unhappy if you do not oblige me by using my rod."

"Well, I will not be generous then, Mr. Brandford, and I won't like you anymore, because I don't believe you were in fun."

"Lucy, cannot you persuade her to accept the loan of my rod for a while?"

But Norrie was immovable. All the entreaties of Lucy and Harry together were of no avail. And, as the other children appeared in sight, she took Lucy's arm and, with the air of an injured little queen, bade Harry Brandford good evening and told the girls it was near sunset and time to go home.

"Who would ever think," mused Harry Brandford, as he slowly wended his way homeward, "that that little thing could be so sensitive and high-spirited? I am so sorry I spoke as I did. I shall never forgive myself for hurting the poor child's feelings. I must see her again and explain."

Harry Brandford was one of nature's gentlemen and felt more keen regret for hurting the feelings of this humble little fisher maiden than he would have felt were she a queen on her throne.

Poor Norrie's week of imprisonment came to an end at last and once more she and Lucy wandered forth into the bright sunshine. They were taking a ramble before breakfast. Norrie was always up with the sun, and today she had succeeded in arousing Lucy from her slumbers and bringing her along. They had unconsciously walked further than they intended and, on their return, Lucy's strength gave out, and she had to sit on the roadside to rest.

"Oh, Lucy, I had no right to bring you so far without your

breakfast. I forget sometimes that you are not strong like me. Your father will be vexed with me. I expect I'll have to leave you here and ask him to bring the carriage for you. Oh, here's one coming now," she said. "I wonder, if it's the magistrate's would he give you a lift home?"

But as it came in sight, whose should it prove to be but Mr. Brandford's, and he alone in it.

"Good morning, little girls," he said, raising his hat. "I am glad my business at Fir Cove was very urgent today as it resulted in my taking the carriage, and having the pleasure of giving you a drive home."

"Yes," said Norrie. "I'm glad, too, for Lucy could walk no further. But I'm all right. I could walk for miles yet without being tired."

"Oh, Norrie, you must come, too. I won't go if you don't."

"No, there is only room for two," said Norrie, "and, besides, I would rather not."

"You don't mean to say that you are not going to get into my carriage, Norrie? The seat holds three quite easily."

"Yes, I do, Mr. Brandford. I'd rather not."

"Oh, you must, Norrie," said Lucy. "I really won't get into the carriage if you don't," and Lucy could be determined when she chose, and this time she did choose.

"Well," said Norrie, "as Lucy won't go without me, I suppose I must."

"A very ungracious condescension, and a poor compliment to me," said Harry, as he helped them in. "I think you are generous to everyone but me, Norrie."

"I didn't know I was generous," said Norrie, with such simplicity that Harry was touched.

"The simplicity of the dove," he thought. "If she has the wisdom of the serpent combined,[19] this child will get through alright."

There were but few words spoken 'til Harry pulled up at Doctor Hamilton's door. He assisted Lucy out, but Norrie sprang to the ground with a bound.

"Won't you remain in 'til I drive round to your door?" asked Harry.

"Thanks, Mr. Brandford," said Lucy, "but Norrie has promised to spend the day with me."

"Oh, in that case I will wish you good morning." He took Lucy's hand and then reached for Norrie's, but she hesitated.

"What," he said, "am I not forgiven for those foolish unfortunate words of mine at the river yet?"

"I don't know," said Norrie, somewhat doubtfully. "I suppose though we must forgive our enemies,"[20] and she put her hand in his.

A softened expression stole over Harry Brandford's face. "Your enemy, my child? Surely you do not look upon me in that light? I trust, my dear little girl, that you will always find your enemies, if ever you have them, as staunch and true to you as I will ever be."

"What a strange, interesting child," thought Harry, "so noble, generous, self-sacrificing, and so obstinate in her likes and dislikes. She is one who will, I think, develop great strength of character. How much my mother wrongs her."

Doctor Hamilton's home was a bright, comfortable and pretty little cottage. There was a fair-sized garden in front filled with flowers of many varieties, and here Norrie and Lucy spent the evening. Norrie would have wished to ramble through the woods, climb trees and catch butterflies, but Lucy felt the fatigue of the morning walk and Norrie gladly gave up her own pleasures to suit those of her companion. They read, talked, did some fancy work 'til the doctor, thinking "twilight dampness too much for little girls in their thin dresses," as he laughingly told them, said they must come indoors, and Lucy should play something for them.

As it was the latter part of August, and the evening a little chilly, there was a cheerful fire burning in the drawing-room. It was a nice-sized cozy room, a richly coloured carpet covered the floor, the furniture was handsomely upholstered in crimson plush, some nice drawings hung on the walls, and a beautiful piano stood in a corner. The room looked the picture of comfort and refinement.

Mrs. Hamilton, with a smile of welcome and in her kind hospitable manner, drew chairs near the fire for the two girls. Norrie felt a sense of rest and contentment as she glanced round the room, and a longing that she could always live amongst such surroundings.

"Now, Lucy, play something nice for us," said Doctor Hamilton.

"Are you fond of music, Norrie?"

"Fond of it?" she answered. "I love it! Oh, I'd give almost anything in the world to be able to play like Lucy."

"Why do you not ask Mr. Moore to let you learn?"

Norrie laughed outright. "Ask Uncle John that?" she said. "Why, he would look at me and say I was gone mad altogether. He says I'm half mad."

Lucy played several pretty little pieces, during which Norrie held her breath and looked as if she would drink in every note. She seemed as if she forgot everything and everyone whilst listening to the music.

"Now, Lucy, play one of those little songs you all sing at school and make Norrie join in with you," said Mrs. Hamilton.

"Oh, yes, come, Norrie, and we will sing something together," said Lucy delightedly. "What shall it be?"

"Let us sing 'The Harp That Once,'"[21] said Norrie, and soon their fresh young voices floated through the room.

Lucy's voice was weak, but very sweet, whilst Norrie's was powerful and clear as a bell.

"What a magnificent voice she has!" said Mrs. Hamilton to her husband. "Just imagine what it would be, well trained!"

"Yes," he answered, "and how correctly she takes up the note from the piano, tho' not accustomed to it. Do you know, Agnes, I've half a mind to send her myself to learn music. What do you say?"

"You are certainly very generous, Lawrence, and I should not be the one to object, as we can well afford the small amount it would cost. But do you think giving her a taste of these things, when her life must be spent amongst far different occupations, a wise proceeding? Might it not, in a manner, unfit her for that life and give her more pain than pleasure?"

"Perhaps you may be right," he said, after a few moments thought, "but I don't see it. It has always been the saddest of sights to me to see an ardent young soul (like Norrie's here) longing with all its intensity for something which seems forever beyond its reach, and especially when the object desired is but a reasonable and natural one."

"You argue well, Lawrence," said his wife, with a smile, "and I shall leave it to your own judgment. You are generally right, and it is not often that your kindness has been misplaced."

"Yes," he said, half to himself, "little Norrie is that young ardent soul, longing with all her strength for what she cannot attain. I'll do it, Agnes. I'll settle with Miss Bryant this very evening and let her begin her lessons tomorrow." And shortly after, when he stood ready to accompany Norrie to her home, he told her of his plan.

The child was too dazed at first to comprehend it. She could scarcely believe her senses.

"Oh, Doctor Hamilton!" she exclaimed, clasping her hands, and looking at him with her large, brown eyes. "Do you really mean to say you are going to send me to learn music and be able to play like Lucy?"

"Yes, my child, that's just what I mean. Do you think you'll take long to learn?"

"Oh, no I'll do my best to learn as fast as I can, and I will try and be so good and not be giving trouble anymore. What makes you like me, Doctor Hamilton, and almost everyone else hate me, that is, the men and women, and say I'm not fit for nothing only swimming and rowing and idling?"

"I like you for your own bright, merry little self, and for your generosity and love for Lucy, and we will soon let all the people see that you can do more than row, swim and idle your time. Of course, Norrie, you must try and be less careless and wild, but that will come as you grow older."

Lucy's delight knew no bounds when she heard that her dear Norrie was going to learn to play.

"Oh, Norrie," she said, "we will have great fun, and we will learn to play duets and everything together, and oh, Papa, I almost forgot to ask you. I want to lend Norrie some of those books you have with the poetry in them. She is dying to read them."

But Norrie thought she was taking too much advantage of Doctor Hamilton's generosity already, and said, "Oh, no, I couldn't think of taking your papa's books, Lucy, and, besides, Uncle John and Aunt Bridget would not let me read them. They say they are only nonsense and not fit for me."

"To be sure, my child," said the kind-hearted doctor. "Take one and, when you read that, take another, and tell your uncle and aunt that I said they won't do you any harm, that is, as long as you don't neglect your duties, and read only during your recreation hours." And he put a small volume of some of Moore's simplest pieces[22] in her hand. "We will begin with your namesake, and anything you find hard to understand you can ask me just the same as Lucy would."

Doctor Hamilton and his wife never did things by halves and, as she was going, Mrs. Hamilton placed her hand on Norrie's brown curls, and said, "You must come every day for an hour's practice, Norrie, my dear. You know music lessons would be of little use without that."

Norrie was overwhelmed with such kindness, and felt as if she lived in quite another world. As she trotted along by Doctor Hamilton's side, her childish mind filled with an imaginary picture of herself seated at a piano, and her fingers actually ached to run over the beautiful white keys and send forth delicious sounds of harmony.

As Doctor Hamilton left her at her own door, he told her he would go then and arrange for the lessons to begin on the morrow, as school opened also. And that night, Norrie, kneeling by her own little bedside, prayed earnestly for Doctor and Mrs. Hamilton and Lucy and wondered, as she lay for some time awake, what she had done that they should be so good to her. All day and now tonight, some words kept haunting her, and oppressed her with an unusual sadness, which she could not resist. They were, "I trust, my dear little girl, that you will always find your enemies as staunch and true to you as I will ever be."

"How sorry he looked when he said it," she thought. "No, I don't believe he meant what he said that day by the river. He is too noble looking for anything mean like that. I must tell him I'm sorry for being so rude, when I see him again."

Norrie in her softened mood was ready to forgive everyone, even Tommy Brown. Soon she fell asleep and got poetry and music so mixed up she dreamed that she saw "The Immortal Tom Moore"[23] himself playing on Doctor Hamilton's piano.

Norrie was not at all as idle as some people imagined, young as she was. She could milk cows, skim cream, make butter, card and spin wool, work at hay in the field, and even at fish on the beach,[24] but that was when she felt like it. When she did not, it was just as good to put her translating Greek; for when her heart was not in her work, everything went wrong about it.

But next morning she was up before sunrise, helping her aunt about the house and dairy, for she determined to be real good today, as she said, to make a good beginning. So the morning work being done and breakfast over, she prepared for school. And when her brown curls were brushed out, her hands and nails carefully cleaned, and a neat print cotton put on, with white collar and apron, her eyes sparkling, and cheeks flushing with excitement, she looked like a little picture as she set forth in her wide leafed hat, almost dancing along the way, she felt so buoyant.

"Good morning, Jerry," she said, as he came shuffling towards her.

"Did dey let you out again? I tought ye war goin' to be locked in for a mont'. Ye desarves it anyhow, after makin' all de young wans lave Tom Brown's hay t'other day, and dat night it rained as I towled him 'twould, and din't stop for six days, so 'twas rotten before 'twas put in."[25]

"Oh, well, tattletales always get left, Jerry, and Tommy Brown and his da are of the worst kind." But she suddenly remembered she was relapsing into her slang ways again, and, fearing to trust herself lest she should be tempted to play some prank on Jerry or tease him, she ran off, leaving him grumbling to himself something about "sassy young ting."

Her next encounter was with Tommy Brown, who said, "Hallo, did ye get out after yer week? Dat was a dear[26] picnic, wasn't it, Nor?"

"Look here, Tom Brown," she said, standing erect before him. "I'm not going to have anything more to say to you. Nearly all the trouble I get into is your fault, so I'm not going to play with you anymore."

"No, not 'til ye wants me to help ye out wid a dory, an' find oars for ye."

"No, indeed. I won't be having much time for things like that now. I'm going to try and be good and read poetry. That's something you know nothing at all about. I didn't know much about it myself 'til yesterday, and I'm going to learn music, too." (This was emphasized by a vigorous nod of her head, and a defiant look from her mischievous brown eyes, as if she dared him to contradict her.)

"Whew," said Tommy, with a prolonged whistle. "S'pose we won't be able to touch ye wid a hay prong soon, yer gettin' so grand."

"I don't want you to touch me with a hay prong nor anything else, because you're too mean. To think of you telling your da what you heard me saying that day, and trying to keep us from having our picnic. But you see, you didn't stop us after all. We had it in spite of you. But I won't stay talking to you, for I know I'll get into trouble if I do. I only want to tell you that I have no more use for you." And with a toss of her little head, she tripped off and left him wondering what kind of a fit was on Norrie Moore now.

On the evening following the morning that Harry Brandford had taken Lucy and Norrie in his carriage, he was sitting in the drawing-room playing the violin, his favourite pastime. Besides having natural musical talent, he had received careful training, and the violin pleased him above all other instruments. It seemed to speak 'neath the magic of his touch; he was playing some sadly beautiful and pathetic[27] airs in which minor chords played a prominent part. Perhaps his thoughts were with the mother whom he remembered, and whose picture hung opposite him on the wall on which his eyes were fixed as he played. Beside it was his father's, who had been dead about six years; he loved this too, but he never gazed on it with the same love and sadness as he did on his mother's, whom he resembled very strongly.

Seated by the table was his stepmother, reading a popular novel. She glanced several times at her stepson as if she wished to say something, but wanted him to put down his violin first. But as he did not seem inclined to do this, she at last addressed him. "Harry, would you mind putting down your violin for a while? I've something to say to you."

"What it is, Mother?" as he rested the instrument against his arm.

"Why, I heard something today that I could scarcely believe about you."

"Oh, is that all?" And he was about to continue his playing when she said impatiently, "Can you not wait 'til I've finished, Harry? I called on the magistrate's wife today and she told me she saw you this morning passing in your carriage, and that saucy little Nora Moore beside you, and Doctor Hamilton's little girl, too, who is almost as bad as Nora now. I warned both the doctor and his wife when first they came of the danger they were allowing their child to incur by associating with her, and got no thanks for my pains. And now to think of my husband's son taking her in his carriage looks as if I am following their example."

"As if you are following their example?" said Harry, with his clear, steady gaze and determined air. "I fail to see where my doings can in any way affect yours."

Tho' living in the same house with him for years, Mrs. Brandford did not understand her stepson. She expected some excuse for his (in her eyes) unpardonable act, but his cool, self-possessed air and dark frown warned her for the first time that she had a difficult thing to accomplish in making Harry Brandford think as she did.

"Why, you should certainly have more respect for yourself and me than to take up a common little fisher girl in our carriage," she proudly retorted.

"I should certainly have no respect for myself," he haughtily answered, "did I do otherwise than I did this morning, and I shall do the same thing whenever the same occasion presents itself. And, what's more, Mrs. Brandford, I do not choose to have my actions criticized by the magistrate's wife nor even by you, or at least not in my hearing. You may talk away if it's any consolation to you outside of it."

As Mrs. Brandford looked at him, she felt it would be wiser to say but little on the subject. As for Harry, he certainly respected his father's widow as much as he could, but often her scornful words and behaviour to those whom she considered her inferiors annoyed him. And her allusion now to poor little Norrie in such an unkind manner disgusted him, and, when Harry Brandford was disgusted, he took good care to let those who caused it know.

"But, Harry, you should keep those kind of people in their own place," Mrs. Brandford ventured to say.

"I will have no buts in the matter," he said, holding up his hand with an imperative gesture. "And if you please, Mrs. Brandford, or whether you please or not, we will drop the subject." And he turned again to his violin.

While Mrs. Brandford was forced to acknowledge herself beaten.

CHAPTER FOUR

Nearly two years have passed away, bringing scarcely any changes to the quiet little village of St. Rose. Mrs. Brandford and Harry spent a part of each winter in town; this lady was connected with some very aristocratic families there and spent a few months out of every year with them, but Harry always put up at a hotel and enjoyed himself with his old college friends.

Doctor Hamilton, his wife and daughter spent but a few weeks in St. John's, as it did not agree with Lucy's health. But these two years have worked wonders with Norrie; she has grown taller, and prettier, and quite a marvel at music. She left Lucy far behind her, but her high spirits, gay light-hearted manner, and love of mischief did not leave her, but they had, of course, attained a milder form. She would not now tell anyone to "shut up" or "keep on their wool," and jigging squids and tomcods had somewhat lost their charm, but she could swim, manage a dory all alone, steer and scull[28] to perfection. Often after some hours of practice at her beloved music and study, she would run off and have one wild ramble over the beach or, perhaps, spring into a punt or dory, taking Lucy with her, and row across the harbour. Lucy had grown into a sweet, pretty girl and was now beginning to get a healthy bloom in her cheeks.

One evening early in May, the two girls were walking by the seashore, talking of Lucy's coming departure, for it was decided to send her away to a boarding school for some years. An excellent one had been selected, and she was to depart early in September. It was a trial for both of them, for their love had grown with the years. Norrie, whose feelings were deeper and affections stronger, felt the separation more keenly, tho' she spoke of it less. She tried to console Lucy whenever the subject was mentioned between them.

"I know I shall be ill again," said the latter. "I shall feel so lonely.

Oh, Norrie, if you were only coming with me."

"If I only were!" said Norrie. "But I could not allow myself to imagine such a thing; it would unfit me for anything else. I try at times to think what it will be like when you are gone, and I know I shall be desolate."

"You will write often to me, won't you, Norrie, all the time I'm away?"

"Yes," she replied, "for a time. But you know, Lucy (and she placed her arm round her), when we part next September you will, in a manner, go out of my life. You will make new friends at school and be quite a fashionable lady when you return, and will likely spend most of your time in St. John's. While I must remain here in my own sphere of life and try and live amongst my books and music, for which I shall ever bless your dear kind parents; these, together with my work, must make up my life." But Norrie never remained long in a mood of this kind, and presently she laughingly said, "But we've nearly four long months together yet. Why need we meet trouble half way? Would you like to go across the harbour, Lucy, and mount those hills on the other side? There's a splendid view from the top of the highest one."

"Oh, yes," said Lucy. "It would be delightful."

"There's a nice little dory here with oars and all," and Norrie began shoving it off from the shore. "You get in, Lucy, and fix yourself comfortably while I look for the row-locks."[29]

She got them in a short time and, as she was about to spring into the dory herself, she looked across the water with a critical eye.

"What are you looking so thoughtfully at the water for, Norrie?"

"I'm thinking we'd better not venture after all, Lucy."

"Oh! why, Norrie? I never was so much inclined for a row before."

"There's a strong breeze coming up from the northeast," said Norrie, who noticed every change in the elements, "and will be right against us coming back."

"But," said Lucy, in a disappointed tone, "can't we go and come back in a short time?"

"If there was only myself in question, I'd go," said Norrie. "But you know, Lucy, the dory is small and, if it blows hard, the water will be splashing in on us and you may catch cold, and then your father and mother would never forgive me."

But Lucy insisted on going. She did not understand the danger as Norrie did, and the latter, not wishing to seem disagreeable or cowardly, thought of a way to settle it.

"I'll tell you what I'll do, Lucy, if you will be satisfied. It's a chance."

"Well, a chance is better than not going at all. What is it?"

"I'll just run across the fields to your house and ask your father, and whatever he says we'll do."

"Very well," said Lucy, reluctantly. "I suppose we must be satisfied with his decision, tho' I know it will be no."

Norrie had not long disappeared when there came in sight, two girls and boys[30]—one was Tommy Brown, whose father happened to own the dory.

"Hello!" he said, as he saw Lucy alone in it. "Where's Norrie Moore?"

"We were thinking of going to the other side," said Lucy, "but just as we were about to shove off, Norrie seemed to get anxious about the point the wind is in, and said we should have a gale against us coming back."

"Oh, it's galin'[31] herself she is," said Tom, grinning, as he complimented himself on his wit. "It's as calm a day as ye'd ever see in May."

Tom knew the wind was coming up but would not give in to Norrie's judgment. They had not become better friends during these two years.

"It's hardly worth her while to turn cowardly now," he went on.

"She is not a bit afraid for herself," said Lucy, indignantly, "only she thinks Papa would be vexed if I got wet, and she is gone to ask his permission."

"Oh, well, we can't wait. Here's Kate Crane what lives on de udder side. She stayed at our house last night, and she just hard her mudder's took awful bad, and fadder sent me to put her across in dat dory an' be back again in a hurry coss we're all busy at de fish."

"Oh, I'm so sorry, Kate," said Lucy. "I hope your mother is not as bad as you think. I suppose I must get out and wait 'til Norrie comes."

"Why don't you stay in, Miss Hamilton, and enjoy the nice row over?" said Kate. "Tom won't be long going across. He'll just put me out at the nearest landing place. Norrie won't be back much before that. I would ask him to wait for her," she said, in an undertone, "only he is disagreeable, and they're busy, too. And, besides, I know he wouldn't wait for Norrie; they're not good friends."

Lucy thought to herself, "I know Papa won't let us go if Norrie says there's danger, and I really never felt such a longing in my life to be on the water. And if I don't take advantage of this opportunity, I'll lose it altogether."

She often, afterwards, wondered what made her so anxious that day to go across the harbour, even without Norrie's companionship. But what a small thing often changes the current of our lives. The simple fact of Lucy remaining in the dory that day changed the course of Norrie's life, and made her almost wish she had been left in the lonely sphere to which she belonged.

"Well," said Lucy, "if there was anyone here to tell Norrie should she come before we get back, I'd go."

"Oh, Bill here 'll do dat," said Tom, who was glad to have the triumph of taking Lucy off from Norrie. "He's not comin' over. He only came along wid us. Dere's only Kate and Polly Brien goin'. Polly's comin' back again, too."

"Very well," said Lucy. "I'll go. Billy, will you tell Norrie when she comes that we'll be back in less than half an hour?"

"All right, Miss," said Billy, as he seated himself on an old anchor.

Lucy would have enjoyed herself immensely but for a kind of uneasiness that seemed to come over her, such as we often feel when we're not doing exactly the right thing. She began to think she had acted very meanly by not waiting for Norrie, and she had allowed their enemy, Tom Brown, to bring her, too.

They were not long going over, for the wind, which was becoming stronger every minute, nearly blew them across, and Tom began to think they would have a tough time coming back.

Soon after, Norrie and Doctor Hamilton came, walking over the beach to the spot where the dory had been, and were surprised to find it gone, and no sign of Lucy.

Billy stood up, manfully delivered his message and ran off.

"That was very wrong of Lucy," said the doctor. "She should not have gone with anyone when you told her it was not safe. They'll have a stiff breeze coming back. We'll stand here, Norrie, 'til they come."

She could just make out the dory on the other side coming slowly—very slowly—towards them.

"Oh, they've landed Kate," said Norrie, "and are coming this way."

"What good eyes you must have, child," said the doctor. "How many are in the boat?"

"Only three," she answered. "Lucy, Polly Brien and Tom Brown." She felt pained that Lucy should go when she was not with her and, above all, with Tom Brown.

It took them some time to get to the middle of the harbour, for Tom found it hard to battle with two oars against the wind.

Suddenly, the little boat, in reality only large enough for two, seemed to lurch, then stand still. Norrie stood watching, with an anxious face. She could now see every movement of the occupants; then she saw Tom try to grasp his oar, which had fallen from his hand. Polly did the same, and he roared to her to keep quiet or she'd upset the dory.

Lucy, now thoroughly frightened, and wishing with all her heart that she had not come, sprang to her feet and, rushing to the side where Tom and Polly were trying to get the oar, the cranky little dory[32] went over, pitching them all in the water.

An agonized cry broke from the two watchers on shore, as the screams from the water reached them. Like a flash the men came running along the beach as the alarm was given, and boats were launched in an instant, while strong arms were rowing towards the drowning trio.

"Oh," cried Doctor Hamilton, "save my Lucy. I will give anything that's in my power." But the stout, brave hearts of the honest fishermen needed no bribe when a life was in danger. They were working with might and main to reach the spot in time.

The doctor himself was in one of the boats.

But where all this time was Norrie? Ah, it was not for nothing that she had almost lived in the open air, rowing, swimming, drinking in the fresh invigorating sea breeze. For now, it was to result in the saving of a human life.

The instant she had seen the boat capsize, she had plunged (unnoticed by the doctor) into the water, swimming with all her might to the spot where she saw Lucy floating.

"The doctor's little girl will be drowned," said one man, "before we can get to her. She's too much frightened to keep herself afloat."

"Try and cling to the boat, Lucy," cried Doctor Hamilton. "We are coming to you. Oh, my darling child, she will be drowned," he moaned, as he saw her almost disappear under the water.

Polly and Tom Brown were clinging to the dory and trying to get Lucy to do the same, but she was powerless with fright, and they could hold her no longer.

She had just sunk beneath the waters, only her long, golden hair was floating on the surface, when Doctor Hamilton saw a small, dark figure battling with the waves and making towards her.

"Who is that?" he said. "There were only three in the boat."

"Oh! that's Norrie Moore," said one of the men. "If she gets to her in time, she's saved."

Then, they saw her seize the hair floating on the water, and soon she had the half-drowning Lucy in one arm, whilst she kept herself afloat with the other.

Long of wind and strong of limb as she was, it proved nearly too much for her, and it was with almost superhuman strength that she kept herself and Lucy from sinking 'neath the cruel waves that seemed struggling to engulf them.

Lucy was perfectly unconscious, and Norrie nearly so, as strong arms lifted them into the boat. Tom and Polly were not much the worse except for the fright alone. They were taken into one of the other boats and brought home.

Doctor Hamilton told them to carry Norrie to his own home, where he could attend to her and Lucy at the one time. "She is truly a little heroine," he said, with tears of gratitude in his eyes as he looked down at the almost unconscious form.

Norrie's relatives and Lucy's mother were down to the seashore. Mrs. Hamilton was almost distracted with grief, and thought it was the dead form of her child she looked upon.

As quickly as possible the girls were borne to the house, where restoratives were applied, which soon revived them. Norrie, being the stronger, was nearly as well as ever next day, but Lucy had a severe illness, and it was several weeks before she could move about again. She could not bear Norrie to leave her at all, so during her illness the latter spent every day with her, only sleeping at home.

It was the topic of conversation in St. Rose, and even in St. John's, where the daily papers gave a glowing description of Norrie's brave deed. But she only looked surprised when anyone spoke of it and did not seem to think she had done anything wonderful. Doctor and Mrs. Hamilton felt for Norrie an affection next to that which they had for their own child, and tried in every way to express their gratitude.

One day during her convalescence, Lucy told Norrie how mean she had felt for going off with Tom Brown that day. "I don't know what made me do it," she said, as she held Norrie's hand in hers, "but I felt such a longing to be on the water that I could not resist it. And just think of all the trouble I caused, because I believe the dory would not have been upset but for me, and I nearly caused your death also. Oh, Norrie, how can I thank you for saving my life?"

"Simply by getting well and strong quickly," she answered.

"Norrie, I'm going to ask you a few questions, but I want you to promise me first that you won't be vexed, and excuse whatever may seem curious, because it's not through curiosity I'm asking you."

"Ask all the questions you wish, my dear," laughed Norrie, as she fondly put her arm around her, "and I'll answer all I can and will promise not to be vexed, not even if you ask if my teeth are false and if I wear a wig."

"Well, I'm not going to ask anything as commonplace as these but, as I've got your promise, I'll begin by asking if your guardian, Mr. Moore, is, well, what people call well off?" said Lucy, hesitatingly.

"That's more than I can tell, Lucy," said Norrie, looking quite serious. "He is comfortable enough and can get everything he wants, but I've an idea that there is some money belonging to me which my father and mother left me. I heard Uncle say something about it to Aunt a long time ago when he thought I was not near. I did not know then what he meant. It's only since I've grown up that I've thought about it, but whether it's a thousand dollars or one, I don't know."

"Well, now, for number two question, and it's a favour, too, that I want you to grant me. Norrie, will you accept your education from my father, and come with me to — Convent? He would gladly do it if you would only come."

Norrie looked for a moment as if she did not comprehend but, when the truth of Lucy's request flashed upon her, tears of gratitude filled her eyes, tho' she said, in a decided tone, and with a proud flush in her cheeks, "No, Lucy, no, I would not, under any condition, take any more advantage of your father's kindness. I've taken too much already, in allowing him to pay for my music, and I think it very mean of Uncle John to allow it, for I'm sure he could afford to send me. I thank you, Lucy, and your father and mother a thousand times for all their kindness, and I shall ever bless them, but, much as I crave education, I could not think of accepting any more from your father, and like a dear girl, Lucy, never speak of it again."

This was said in such a decided tone that Lucy knew it was useless to press the subject further.

"Well, then," she said, "it's settled. I'm not going unless you come with me."

"Oh, Lucy, you cannot refuse to go. You know your education must be attended to, as you will have to take your place in society bye and bye, and you know also that your father and mother must feel a great deal more at losing you for a few years than you can at going."

"Well, I don't care," said Lucy. "I positively won't go without you. I only felt like this since you saved me from drowning that day and I know it would break my heart to leave you," and the tears rolled down her cheeks.

Norrie remained in deep thought for some time, then said, "I'll tell you, Lucy, of something that has just occurred to me now," and she spoke almost in a whisper. "It's this. My uncle would not mind me talking, but if your father would tell him how much I long to be thoroughly educated and that, if there is any money belonging to me, I should prefer to spend it in this way."

Lucy's eyes brightened. "Oh, Norrie, it's an inspiration," she cried. "Yes, I'll tell Papa today. Who can tell but your uncle has money for you when you're grown up?"

"I'm sure he has some," said Norrie, "from what I heard, but it may be only a few dollars, for what I know, and we must not be too hopeful of success, because the disappointment would be terrible to bear afterwards."

"I tell you, Norrie, it's an inspiration," repeated the sanguine Lucy.

So it was settled between them before they parted that evening, that Lucy should tell her father of Norrie's plan, and ask him to go to John Moore and plead her cause.

Doctor Hamilton made no delay in complying with their request, for immediately after breakfast next day he set out for John Moore's residence. Norrie was busy this morning in the dairy making butter, but every now and then she would steal a march to the front door, to see if the doctor was coming.

"Whatever's the matter with the girl today?" said Mrs. Moore to herself, as she busied about the comfortable little kitchen. "She's made a dozen trips, if she's made one, to the door this morning."

At length Norrie was rewarded by seeing the well-known figure of the doctor coming up the walk towards the house. This time she remained at the door, smiling brightly, as she ushered him into the neat little parlour.

"Lucy has told you," she said to him in an undertone.

"She has, my dear," he answered, "and we hope I shall succeed with your uncle. And she has also told me what a proud, independent little girl you are, who would not accept from me the small recompense of giving you your education, when you've saved the life of my darling Lucy."

"Oh, Doctor Hamilton, please don't speak of such a thing when you are always doing something for me since the first happy day I've known you. If I had not saved Lucy that day, I should never see you nor dear Mrs. Hamilton again while I lived, which I know would not be long, because but for me she would not have been on the water that day."

"But if she had taken your wise counsel, Norrie, she would not have remained on it."

After placing a comfortable armchair for him, Norrie hastened to the garden at the back of the house and told John Moore that Doctor Hamilton had called and wished to see him.

"Who?" he asked. "Doctor Hamilton? What do he want me for?" as he glanced down at his clay-stained clothes and hands. The doctor was held in great respect by the people of St. Rose, and many often went to him for advice. John, after washing his hands in the porch and taking off his hat, went, with some curiosity, to the parlour.

"Good morning, Doctor," he said. "Glad to see you, sir."

"Thank you, Mr. Moore. I suppose I've disturbed you from your work, but I've called to see you on an important matter. Perhaps it may seem presumptuous of me to take the liberty of asking a few questions with regard to private family affairs, but, I assure you, I'm doing so with the best of intentions."

"Sartinly, Doctor, sartinly. I wouldn't think anything else of you, sir, whatever questions you ask."

"Well," said Doctor Hamilton, plunging at once into the subject. "I've heard it rumoured that your little cousin, Norrie, has some money left her by her parents. It may be only a small amount, but do you think I am presuming too far on friendly interest to ask if this is true?"

John Moore looked somewhat surprised; he was rather close over money,[33] and, for an instant, wondered what object the doctor could have in asking such a question. But, the next moment, remembering the goodness and generosity of the man, and being thoroughly honest himself, answered straightforwardly. "Yes, then, Doctor, there is a small amount of money left in our care for Norrie 'til she's of age, about four or five hundred dollars."

"Is this willed by Norrie's parents to come to her only when she's of age?"

John thought for a while, then said, "Well, no, her poor father, you know, taken from them as he was, had no time to settle anything, but when her mother was dying, she says to me and my wife, who were with her 'til the last, 'take care of whatever little money there is, for Norrie, 'til she's of age, but if you should see any important reason for allowing her to do as she likes with it before she's twenty-one, you can do so. I'll trust you and Bridget to do your duty to my child.' And we've always done it, Doctor, in every way. The money is safe and sound in the bank, together with whatever interest is on it. We would not think of paying ourselves for Norrie's expenses, tho' she's not come up to our expectations. She's not at all fond of work, sir, tho' she does it pretty well sometimes. But when she's inclined for roamin', or readin', or anything of that sort, it's just as good to let her at it. She's gettin' much more sense now, tho', I'll admit, and don't get into half the mischief she used to."

"Does Norrie know anything about the money?" asked the doctor.

"No, sir, we've never told her, on account of her idle habits, thinkin' 'twould, perhaps, give her notions not fit for her, for she's got enough of 'em already. She'd rather be readin' rhymes any day than milkin' cows or cardin' wool and since she's commenced larnin' the piana it's little time she gives to anything else. But we meant to tell her of it in a year or two."

Doctor Hamilton could not help smiling at John Moore's troubled face, as he summed up the account of Norrie's shortcomings.

"Well," he said, "that is just what I've come to talk to you about. Supposing, Mr. Moore, that you had in your garden a rare, beautiful plant, which you tried to train up to grow in a certain groove, and that, in spite of all your efforts, it refused to do so, and followed its own natural course, still retaining its goodness and beauty. Would you still try to force it to your own idea, or help it to grow and thrive in the way nature intended it?"

John seemed rather puzzled for a time, but soon answered, "I'd sartinly do all I could to help it along and let it grow its own way, to be sure, seein' 'twould only spoil it to bring it mine."

"Ah, that's just the thing I want to come at, Mr. Moore. It would certainly spoil it to bring it your way, and make it no good for anything. Now, Norrie is that rare, beautiful plant. You are trying (with the best of intentions, I know) to force her tastes and inclinations to your own ideas, which do not at all suit hers. She cannot help her own natural instincts, poor child, tho' she tries hard sometimes to do so. And, believe me, Mr. Moore, I am speaking from my conscience; if it continues much longer, it will spoil her life and make her unfit for anything. Norrie has rare, natural talents, and these talents need to be cultivated. She is very clever; she is good, true, and warm-hearted, truthful and honourable; and what you and your good wife call idleness is simply following her natural tastes and inclinations, which she cannot help, no more than you can studying what would be best for the success of your crops, for the better development of your cattle, and for the curing of your fish. Mr. Moore, that money which Norrie's mother left in charge of you for her child, and which, fortunately, she can have before she's of age, is required now to cultivate those talents which God has given her, and fit her for a different sphere of life from that which she would fill here. I have arranged to send my daughter, Lucy, to — Convent; it is a splendid establishment, where domestic economy, and a certain amount of house-keeping is taught besides a good, solid, English education, and other ornamental requisites, such as music, drawing, painting. The money you have in your care for Norrie would, at least, give her three years in this convent, where she will learn nothing but what is good, useful, and beautiful. Will you give it to her, and let her go with Lucy in September?"

John Moore listened, open-eyed and open-mouthed, with a look of real consternation on his face. At length he drew a long breath, and gasped, "Let her go and spend all her money on fine larnin' like your daughter? No, Doctor, I couldn't think of such a thing. It's all nonsense. Why should Norrie be intended for a different life than the rest of her kin?"

"A wiser hand than ours guides those things, Mr. Moore. It is not for us to ask why.[34] The fact remains, that she is not suited to the life here."

"Well, I can't think of doin' it, Doctor. Her mother never intended the money for such nonsense as sendin' her away to boardin' school. She can larn all she wants here, and I think she's got enough now. I'll fulfill her dying mother's wish, sir."

"Then, be careful, Mr. Moore, how you fulfill that mother's wish. It seems to me almost providential that she should use those words in dying: 'should you see any important reason for allowing her to do as she likes with it before she's twenty-one, you can do so.' That important reason has come, Mr. Moore, and take care how you carry out her last wishes."

But all the persuasions of the good doctor were of no avail. John remained obstinate. He could not be satisfied that he would be doing right in allowing Norrie's money to be squandered, as he called it, in this way.

"My dear man, you do not understand what you are saying. Far be it from me to do anything against the child's interest. It would not be as much squandered, as you call it, as if it were given her for a wedding dowry and spent to fit out her husband's banker[35] for a couple of years, or clear ground on his farm, or it may be all swallowed up in one year's bad fishery; whereas, if it's spent on her education, it may always turn in money to her. One as bright and clever as she is could quite easily earn a living by teaching. She could command a high salary anywhere. I would not wish to stand in your shoes, John Moore, and wrong a dead mother's child, as I believe you are doing, tho' it's a mistaken sense of duty, I know."

John began to look serious now. He did not like the idea of wronging Norrie, and would not wish to do so.

"If I thought I wasn't doin' right," he said, "I'd be very sorry to keep her money from her if she wants to get more larnin'. I'll talk it over with Bridget, Doctor, and I'll call at your house tomorrow and tell you our decision."

As Doctor Hamilton left the front door, Norrie left the back and, taking a short cut through a narrow wood-path which led from their grounds, met him a short distance from the house. She was breathless from running and pale from suspense; with her soul in her eyes and hands clasped tightly together, she stood before him. "Oh, what is it, Doctor? Is there any hope for me?" she said. "I could not wait 'til I go over this evening."

And Doctor Hamilton thought that if this ardent young soul was to be crushed with disappointment the words should come from other lips than his.

"Yes, Norrie, my dear," he said, "you may hope. Mr. Moore has promised to let me know his decision tomorrow, and you know when he hesitates, he means something."

"Oh, Doctor, what shall I ever do to thank you?"

"My dear child, there is nothing to thank me for. I am simply doing my duty to a little girl who has saved the life of my darling child, and whom I love almost as well."

As Norrie went back to her unfinished butter, one hope filled her heart, and it was that sometime she should be called upon to make a sacrifice for dear Doctor Hamilton, or his wife or child, so that she could prove to them her gratitude for the interest they had taken in her.

Next evening, according to his promises, John Moore wended his way to Doctor Hamilton's residence, who received him very kindly in his own private sitting-room.

"Well, Mr. Moore," he said, "what did Mrs. Moore think regarding our conversation of yesterday?"

"She didn't seem to take to it at all first, Doctor. She thought the same as I did, but, when we began to talk it over a bit, we both agreed that it must be the right thing when you said so. And we came to the conclusion to let her go on condition that we will keep a few dollars of her money 'til she's of age, and only pay for the sensible part of the schoolin'. We won't pay for any of the foll-dolls[36] like drawin' or paintin', and she ought to know enough about the piana, too; she's nearly two years at it now, thanks to you, Doctor."

"Very well, Mr. Moore," said the doctor, after a little consideration. "Then it's settled. Yes, I think you are wise to keep a little for her 'til she is of age; she may want it. And now, I'm going to ask you to keep a secret. Will you promise not even to tell your wife?"

"Yes, sir. I'll promise anything in rason you ask me."

"Well, then, don't you say anything to Norrie about what she's to learn or what she's not, and I'll see to the foll-dolls, as you call them. You must not, on any account, let her know this, because she is very proud, and would not accept it from me. So let it be a secret between us."

"You are very good to Norrie, Doctor, and I'm sure she ought to be grateful to you, sir, for all you've done for her."

"So she is, poor child, tho' what I have done for her is a mere nothing compared to what she has done for me."

John Moore felt a weight lifted from his shoulders as he went home to work. "Well, now," he said to his wife. "She's as good as done for. I know the doctor is right, and she'd never do for a fisherman's wife."

That evening when Norrie and Lucy met, they hugged and kissed each other. "Oh, Norrie," said Lucy, "to think you'll be coming with me after all!"

"I never dared to hope it, Lucy, 'til two days ago when you asked me if Uncle was well off. And ever since that, I've been full of the notion that somehow I would get to go."

"And so have I," Lucy replied. "I won't mind very much now saying goodbye to Mamma and Papa for a few years."

But, alas, it was destined that Lucy was to bid farewell to her father sooner than she thought.

One night, early in June, there came a hasty summons for him some miles distant, and he had to go by water. Four or five strong men were to row him to the place—a small island where only two or three families resided. A young man, one of the residents there, had accidentally shot himself, and was bleeding to death, unless something could be done to staunch[37] the blood. Doctor Hamilton had not been well for some days; he was suffering from the effect of a severe cold, and had just retired. But in a case of this kind he never had the heart to refuse and, tho' the night was cold and chilly (as they often are in Newfoundland at this season), and, in spite of the remonstrance of his wife, he arose and dressed for his journey. He felt the chill strike his heart as the skiff[38] glided over the calm, moonlit waters. They soon reached their destination, and the doctor's welcome form and cheery voice brought hope to the frightened inmates. The wound was not serious and, when it was dressed and a sleeping potion administered to the sufferer, the doctor took his departure, amid the thanks and blessings of the mother and sisters of the young man. And this was Doctor Hamilton's last mission of mercy.

Mrs. Hamilton was waiting up, and gave him a hot drink before going to bed, which he was never more to leave. Bronchitis set in, in its worst form, and the good, kindly man, who had helped and befriended so many, who had lived doing good for others, was snatched away in the prime of life, after a few days' illness.

Shortly before his death, he arranged all his worldly affairs with his heartbroken wife. He told her of his plan with regard to Norrie, with strict injunctions that they were to be carried out. "I would not have interfered some time ago," he said, "but since the day she saved my Lucy from drowning, I felt it my duty to do something for her. And the child will value this more than if I left her a fortune. You can let her remain as long as Lucy, and pay, if need be, whatever is required, as her people only consented to pay for three years. She has an idea that there is enough money to pay for all her education, and it's just as well to let her think so. I would wish you, Agnes," he said, "to keep this cottage as a summer resort. It is engaged for a term of years, as you know, and do not, on any account, delay the children's departure for school. Lucy's education has been neglected too long already, and perhaps you would like to spend the winters of Lucy's absence with Emily (this was her sister, Mrs. Dane, who was living in St. John's). I know you will feel hard to let her go, Agnes, but the child must be educated, and the years will soon slip by. I had hoped to see the happy day when she and Norrie would come home to brighten our lives once more with their sweet presence, but God has ordained it otherwise and we must be resigned."

"Oh, Lawrence, you break my heart," she cried. "What shall I have to live for when you are gone?"

"You must devote your life to Lucy, my dear. Do not let her remain long in town after her return from school, until she is thoroughly strong. Time softens all grief, Agnes, and you will learn to be happy after a little while. Now, send Lucy and Norrie to me. I want to speak to them while I can."

She left him and sent the girls in. Norrie threw herself on her knees by the bedside and, taking his hand in both of hers, covered it with tears and kisses. Lucy was almost weak from weeping.

"Do not cry, my children," he said. "I am only going to Heaven a little while before you, where I shall be always watching my two little girls, Lucy and Norrie, to see if they are growing up to be good virtuous women like Lucy's mother. And when you go to school, you must try and learn all that is possible and take every advantage that is offered you."

"Oh, Doctor Hamilton," sobbed Norrie. "I wish I could die instead of you. If I could do so now and let you live, I would do it gladly."

"I do not doubt it, Norrie, and when I am gone you can give the love you have for me to Lucy, together with what you've got for her now, and always take care of her and protect her whenever you can."

"I promise," said Norrie, in slow, solemn tones, "to love Lucy always, and to give up gladly, and freely, the dearest wish of my heart, my life's happiness, if need be, to save her any pain."

Ah, rash promise, made without fully understanding its meaning. How those words haunted her in the after years.

He then spoke a few words to Lucy, telling her always to be kind to Norrie, for she deserved it. And placing a hand on the head of each, said, "God bless you, my dears, may you always be fond, true, and devoted friends, loving each other as you do now."

Next day, Doctor Hamilton passed peacefully away to his reward in Heaven, and was laid to rest in the little cemetery of St. Rose.

Words could never describe the grief of Mrs. Hamilton. It was feared for a time that her mind would give way. Lucy, too, fell into a kind of quiet apathy. Mrs. Dane hurried to her sister as soon as possible after hearing the sad news; and she always said that it was Norrie's untiring ministration, and bright, cheerful disposition, which always seemed to infect the atmosphere which surrounded her, that saved them. She had taken a particular fancy to her the moment she had seen her; of course, she had heard of Norrie's brave act in saving Lucy's life, and felt some amount of curiosity regarding her. Mrs. Dane was younger than her sister, gayer and prettier, but very like her in goodness and generosity. She remained with her 'til the end of July, and insisted on them, Norrie included, going with her to St. John's and spending the month of August. It would take them 'til the first of September, she said, to make what preparations were needed for the girls' departure. And she had another plan which she did not yet unfold; she intended to persuade her sister to accompany her, with Lucy and Norrie, to the Convent. The travel and change of scene, she thought, would help to soften her grief more than anything else.

So Norrie said goodbye to the old home and the old life and, wishing to be on friendly terms with everyone, she sought Jerry Malone first and told him how sorry she had felt the day, four years ago, when she had let the bowl of water fall on his head, and that it had really been an accident. And she reached out her hand to say goodbye with such a winning smile that even Jerry, in spite of himself, had to relent. He shuffled, first on one foot, then on the other, and at last grumbled out as he shook hands with her, "Always said ye slapped it down on purpose. Spose ye didn't do, but yer gettin' a lot better den ye wur. 'Tis no sarvice keepin' in a bad feelin' for any wan. I hope ye'll like de new country yer goin' to. Goodbye!"

"Goodbye, Jerry. I'll be back again, you know, some day."

Tommy Brown and his father were the next. She saw them both in the hayfield, where she had, two years before, by the force of her eloquence, brought the children from their work and, as the memory of that day flashed upon her, it brought with it (for the first time since Doctor Hamilton's death) such a keen sense of humour that she could not, with truth, say she was sorry for what she had done. And Tom Brown went as far as to say he would miss her bright, pleasant face, and hoped she would be very happy where she was going. Then she shook hands with Tom the younger who told her he always felt mean since the dory accident, and liked her better than any girl in St. Rose, "for there's not another girl in the place id have the pluck to do what you done dat day."

Then her thoughts went to Harry Brandford. Since the day, two years ago, when she had called him her enemy, she had not spoken to him, tho' she had often resolved to do so, to tell him how sorry she felt for being so unreasonable. But somehow she never could summon up courage enough; and the few times they did meet, they passed with a smile and bow only. But she had Mrs. Brandford to see yet. This lady had called on Mrs. Hamilton after Mrs. Dane's arrival, with whom she was also acquainted; but Norrie, knowing the dislike she had always shown towards her, took care to keep out of her way during the visit. But before leaving St. Rose, Mrs. Dane intended returning her visit, and bringing Lucy also, to bid her goodbye. Mrs. Hamilton's bereavement, of course, exempted her from returning any calls, so, Norrie, being asked, resolved to beard the lioness in her den and go with them.

It was the evening before her departure, and they found Mrs. Brandford at home. She received them very ceremoniously in the drawing-room. She gave her hand to Mrs. Dane and Lucy, and inclined her head coldly towards Norrie, who returned the bow just as coldly and stately as she had received it. It was with the utmost disgust that she heard of Norrie being sent away to school. "It was nothing short of being sinful," she said, "the idea of taking that girl out of her proper place, and trying to fit her for one which she could never fill." She never once addressed her during the conversation, and the words which poor Norrie had been rehearsing for some time were never said, for the cold, haughty demeanour of the proud lady sent flying all her good resolutions and made her feel as if she would have liked to see another snowball fall in a shower over her head. But she did not succeed, as was her intention, in making Norrie feel awkward, for she and Lucy chatted away all the time, and Mrs. Dane took care to draw her into the conversation on every possible occasion, much to Mrs. Brandford's disgust. They shortened their visit as much as the rules of etiquette would allow; and after enquiring for Mr. Brandford, and being informed he was out, they took their leave.

"That woman is positively rude," Mrs. Dane afterwards remarked to her sister.

"Yes," answered Mrs. Hamilton, "it is simply ridiculous the prejudice she has always shown towards poor little Norrie."

"But the child holds her own perfectly, even with this proud woman," answered Mrs. Dane. "Do you know, Agnes, she will be very beautiful? She is that, even now, but when she gets the tan off her face and shows to more advantage the rich colour in her cheeks, she will be simply charming."

About seven o'clock Harry Brandford came to bid Mrs. Hamilton and Lucy goodbye. He told them he was sorry he had been absent when they called. He did not remain long, as he said he should go over and say farewell to little Norrie.

It was a beautiful evening. The sun had not quite disappeared behind the hills, but seemed to linger 'mid clouds of crimson and gold, which were clearly reflected in the calm water beneath; the scent of hay and clover filled the air.

Harry walked leisurely along, smoking a cigar, 'til he came within short distance of a stile[39] leading to a field near John Moore's house, and there he saw a picture that impressed him deeply.

Leaning against the stile was Norrie's tall, well-made figure. She wore a dark, plain dress, with a little bow of pink ribbon at her throat; her head was bare, and the brown curls hung in graceful disorder over her forehead and about her neck. Her chin was resting in her little brown hands, and she was gazing at the setting sun, with such an unaccountable expression in her large, brown eyes.

It never before struck Harry that she was really pretty. 'Twas the scent of the cigar that roused her and made her glance towards him.

"Oh, Mr. Brandford," she said. "Isn't it strange I was just thinking of you?"

Harry was not at all fond of paying fine compliments; he was of too candid and serious a disposition for that, so he only bowed and said, "Which is strange, Norrie? That you should be thinking of me, or that I'm here?"

"I mean, that you should come along just when I was thinking of you, and wishing to see you so much before I go. I wanted to ask you not to mind what I said that day long ago, about you being my enemy. I was very foolish then, and I often feel ashamed since, when I think of how unreasonable I was when you offered me the loan of your fishing rod. But I really believed you were glad I was going to be punished, and nothing could get the idea out of my head."

"But you do not think so meanly of me now, do you, Norrie?"

"Oh, no, Mr. Brandford, I do not, since the day you said you hoped all my enemies would be as true to me as you would ever be."

"And you waited two whole years to tell me so? Oh, Norrie."

"But you know I've not spoken to you since. I thought I should see you today when we called, but you were out."

"Yes," he said, "but I should have come over whether you had called or not, as I would like to bid God-speed to my little—what shall I say? Friend or enemy?"

"Oh, friend, please," said Norrie.

"What else were you thinking of when I came along, Norrie? I'm sure it could not be merely me that made you look so strangely."

"Was I looking strangely?" she asked, with a sigh. "Well, I was thinking of a great many things. I was wondering if dear Doctor Hamilton were looking at me and glad I am going tomorrow. And then I felt a bit sorry leaving this dear old place, and Uncle John and Aunt Bridget. I did not think I loved anything or anyone here so much, until now when I'm going away."

"I suppose you will be quite a stately, elegant young lady when we see you again, and I shall have to call you Miss Moore."

"Oh, no, please," she said, "I should not like that at all. I should like my friends to call me Norrie, always."

"Then I'm decidedly ranked amongst your friends?"

"Yes," she answered, looking steadily at him. "Didn't you say so?"

"Yes, my child, I did," and the habitual sad expression stole over his face, "and I hope you'll never doubt what I say, Norrie."

"I never would again," she said, "because I've learned to know a true face when I see it, since that time. I like truth always, and would rather have it, even when it is unpleasant, than an untruth."

"May you always be like this, Norrie. Never encourage those who come to you with high-flown compliments and soft, flattering words. Of course, where you are going, you'll not be likely to meet any of these. I am delighted you are getting the advantage of a good education, Norrie; it's just what you require to make you a perfect woman. I shall miss you a great deal, tho' I've so seldom seen or spoken to you. I've often thought of you, and wished you could get the opportunity you are now very wisely embracing."

"Thank you, Mr. Brandford. I like to hear someone say they will miss me. There are only few who are fond of me, you know."

A smile broke over Harry Brandford's face, making it simply sweet to look upon. How simple and innocent she is, he thought, tho' so wise in many ways. "I don't think that will be the case bye and bye," he said. "I daresay the trouble will be that you'll have too many fond of you."

Norrie laughed, not at all understanding what the words might mean. "Well, I must say goodbye now. Aunt and Uncle will be wondering where I am, that is, unless you come into the house, Mr. Brandford."

"Not now," he said. "I will wish you goodbye here. Give my kind regards to Mrs. and Mr. Moore." He held her hand while he said, "Goodbye, Norrie, always think kindly of me as you do now, and pray often for me. God bless you and send you safe home to us again."

Norrie watched the tall, straight figure as it walked down the narrow path and disappeared amongst the trees; then with a sigh she went into the house.

Next morning the four took passage for St. John's by the coastal steamer,[40] when Norrie had her first attack of seasickness, but only for a short time. She was on deck again in a few hours, and the mal-de-mer[41] troubled her no more. Lucy took a longer time to recover but, before they arrived in town, they were quite at home with every part of the ship, able to take their meals and do them full justice, too.

This was Norrie's first visit to town, and it was with some amount of curiosity that she watched the crowd on the wharf. As the steamer touched it, a tall, slight, young man of about twenty-one walked across the gangway and welcomed his mother, Mrs.

Dane, spoke a few words to his aunt and his cousin Lucy on their bereavement and, after being introduced to Norrie, led them a little distance from the wharf, where their own large, comfortable carriage was waiting, helped them in, and, as it could not conveniently hold more than four besides the coachman, remained standing, hat in hand, 'til they started off.

"How well Frank is looking!" said Mrs. Hamilton to her sister.

"Yes," she answered, with much pride, "and just as good as he is handsome."

As they drove through Water Street, Norrie looked with much interest at the prettily dressed windows of the stores. She had often longed to visit St. John's. Mrs. Dane's house was situated pretty well in the suburbs of the city and, as they drew up to the door, Norrie remarked to herself what a bright, elegant appearance it had. They were met at the door by May Dane, a pretty, intelligent-looking girl of about twenty, who greeted her mother, aunt and cousin affectionately, then turning to Norrie said, "And so this is the little heroine of St. Rose. Well you look just as mother described you in her letter. I should recognize you if no one told me your name. I'm sure you must be dying about her, Lucy."

"Yes," answered Lucy, "I never could tell you how much I love Norrie."

Mrs. Dane's was certainly the home of elegance and refinement, both in its inmates and surroundings. Everything was beautiful and costly, without being of too glaring a stamp, and free from all those frivolous little knick-knacks which make some homes so uncomfortable and which seem to say "touch me not or I fall."

Mr. Dane had been dead some years; he was an influential man in his day, a Member of Parliament besides being the owner of a large mercantile business, which he left in a flourishing condition to his son Frank.

May led the two girls upstairs to a neat little bedroom which was to be theirs during their stay and, when they had washed, and brushed, and made some alterations in their dress, felt just inclined to do justice to the tempting lunch awaiting them in the dining-room.

Norrie saw but little more of St. John's, as their time was pretty well taken up with preparations for their journey and Mrs. Hamilton's recent trouble kept them from visiting or receiving, with the exception of a few intimate friends, who looked first with curiosity and then admiration on Norrie. The only explanation Mrs. Hamilton gave regarding her was that she had promised her guardians to take charge of her as she was going to the same convent as Lucy to be educated.

Norrie grew very fond of May Dane and her mother, and also "Mr. Frank," who always looked at her with a pleasant smile, and prophesied wonderful things for herself and Lucy, whilst they were at school.

So, early in September the party left St. John's, Mrs. Dane carried her point and made her sister accompany them. The Convent was in a part of the United States. They saw the girls safely settled at school. Mrs. Hamilton, keeping strictly to her husband's wishes, had a private conversation with the Mother Superioress,[42] and arranged that the bills for Norrie's music, singing, drawing and French should be sent to her. She then, with Mrs. Dane, took an affectionate farewell of the girls, who shed bitter tears at parting, and returned to Newfoundland.

Mrs. Hamilton, much improved in health and spirits, tho' missing sadly her darling Lucy, spent the winter in St. John's with her sister.

CHAPTER FIVE

Four years have flown quickly by, and Norrie Moore has reached the height of her ambition. She is now a thoroughly educated and accomplished young lady. Those four years of school life and strict discipline have not been lost upon her. She carried off most all the prizes. Her voice had improved in strength and sweetness, besides being well trained, and she was a brilliant pianist, but her principal talent, and that which she loved most, was painting. She was far ahead of Lucy in almost every branch, not that the latter was dull; it was only that Norrie was extra bright. She was a favourite with all her companions. When recreation time came and she was free from study and restraint, the old, wild spirit would break forth, and then she was the life of the school. The Mother Superioress had felt an especial affection for her, and taken a more than ordinary interest in her future. She had had a short description of her life from Mrs. Hamilton.

The Convent was situated in a picturesque healthy country spot. Today there is quite a commotion in the largest classroom, as it is the day of exhibition and distribution of prizes, and the one before the summer vacation, when many young girls, who have spent years together and grown to love each other, must say goodbye and depart to their different homes. Some, perhaps, may never meet again, and the days of school life will, as the years go by, seem but a peaceful dream to them.

There are about a dozen young ladies who have graduated this year—Norrie and Lucy being of the number. They are all dressed in purest white. Norrie is certainly queen, and indeed she looks fair enough to grace any throne. She is taller than when last we saw her, her figure more developed, well formed and graceful in every movement; but the face is difficult to describe, not for its beauty alone but for its ever-changing expression, now bright, gay, the eyes sparkling, then pensive, thoughtful, even sad. As Mrs. Dane had prophesied, the coat of tan, which exposure to sun and wind had given her, had entirely disappeared, and her skin was soft and white, while her cheeks were of a rich, healthy bloom, a little paler than usual today from excitement and hard study during the past few months; her lips had a sweet, beautiful curve and were of a deep crimson; finely penciled dark eyebrows; the forehead broad and intellectual looking; the face not quite round, but full and dimpled. But the eyes, those wonderful, dark, brown eyes, were its chief charm; they were large, deep and mystic looking, with a beautiful soul shining through them, and often, when the old love of mischief was upon her, they would gleam and brighten with fun and merriment. The brown curls had, after long training, become straight enough to allow them to be dressed after the fashion of the day; but a young growth of soft curls was peeping out over her forehead.

A stage had been erected at the head of the large classroom, and some of the most influential ladies and gentlemen of the place were present. The exhibition was to open with an instrumental solo by Miss Moore. She came gracefully forward and made her bow to the audience; sweet and charming she looked in her simple dress of white art muslin, with the air of unconscious grace in her bearing. She gave an exquisite rendering of one of Chopin's most difficult pieces. When she had finished, subdued murmurs of approval went through the audience:—

"Who is she?" several asked.

"A young lady from Newfoundland," was the answer.

"Then, Newfoundland might well feel proud of such a daughter," said a famous statesman. "Such beauty, grace and talent are rarely met with."

Then Lucy came forward. Those four years have changed her somewhat also. She is much healthier, and has a dainty bloom in her cheeks; her eyes brighter, and of heaven's own blue; her hair was a deeper shade of gold. She is not quite as tall as Norrie, much slighter, and just what one would call a very pretty girl. Her manner is more timid than Norrie's but, tho' slightly nervous, she played Thalberg's "Home Sweet Home"[43] with much taste and expression.

Then came the recitations and vocal music, in which Norrie excelled. She chose for her song, "Ye Banks and Braes o' Bonnie Doon";[44] it just suited her rich, sweet voice, and she sang it with such pathos that she drew tears from many eyes.

Her greatest charm was her perfect freedom from anything

approaching affection. It was her unconsciousness alone that kept away all nervousness and timidity. She seemed to forget herself and her audience in her song.

Lucy sang in exquisite style, "The Last Rose of Summer."[45] Then there were some duets, quartets and full choruses, and the exhibition concluded with the distribution of prizes.

The Superioress sought Norrie before she retired that night to have, as she said, a farewell chat with her. Norrie was always pleased with these little confidential conversations for, next to Mrs. Hamilton and Lucy, she loved this kind Superioress.

"Norrie, my dear," she began, "what do you intend doing with your future?"

"I've thought a great deal of it lately, dear Mother," she answered, as a serious air took the place of the bright smile. "I must teach, of course. I am thinking that after spending a short time at home, I will go to St. John's and open a music, singing, and painting school. I've got to support myself, you know."

"Yes, dear, that would be nice," answered the Superioress, "and Mrs. Hamilton, I am sure, would help you to secure some pupils."

"I am sure she will," said Norrie. "What is it she has not done for me? I often wonder what I shall ever do to repay her. But for her and dear Doctor Hamilton, Uncle John would never have consented to my coming."

"Well, who knows, my child, but it may yet lie in your power to do for Mrs. Hamilton or Lucy what no one else can?"

"I hope and pray that day may come," the girl replied.

When that day did come, with its bitter sorrow and desolation, Norrie remembered those words.

"Well, dear," went on the Superioress, "I want to give you a little advice. You know no one is perfect; everyone in this world has his or her own particular failing. You, Norrie, are very impulsive. You act sometimes the instant a thought strikes you, without waiting to think if it is the proper thing to do or not, and often in important matters, too. Now, child, you must avoid this habit; always consult those older and wiser than yourself before any serious undertaking. You may make grave mistakes by not doing so and, if this fault is not corrected, Norrie, it may lead to yet graver ones. Be sure and let me know when you begin to teach, and how you are getting on with your school. And always remember, Norrie, that wherever you are, your interest and welfare shall be ever dear to me and, if in any way I can assist you, be sure and call upon me."

"Oh, thank you, dear Mother," she said, "a thousand times. I shall remember your kind advice, and try to correct those faults you speak of."

Next morning, with tears and farewells they parted.

Lucy and Norrie were the only ones bound for Newfoundland. When they arrived in New York City, they were met by a gentleman friend of Mrs. Hamilton's, who happened to be returning to Newfoundland and was to take charge of them during the voyage. And soon they found themselves on the deck of the steamer *Portia*[46] bound for "home, sweet home."

The journey proved to be a smooth and pleasant one, and it was with fast beating hearts and tears of gladness shining in their eyes that the two girls stood on deck, as the good ship entered the narrows of St. John's.[47]

None but those who have returned after some years' absence can understand the joy that fills the heart, as their native shores appear in sight. As the steamer neared the wharf, not a few were attracted by the two pretty girls. They were such a contrast to each other: one small, dainty, rather delicate-looking; the other, tall, finely made, queenly looking. They were both dressed in dark travelling suits. And now they began to scan eagerly the faces of those on shore. Ah! soon they see them: the dear familiar ones for whom they are watching.

"Look, Lucy!" said Norrie. "There is your mother! How slowly the steamer moves!"

"Oh! how I wish we were near her!" murmured Lucy, clasping her hands.

"She sees us! She is smiling!" said Norrie.

"And there are Aunt Emily, May, and Frank, too," said Lucy.

It was not long before the steamer was moored, and Mrs. Hamilton clasped once more in her arms the darling of her heart, and then Norrie, whom she loved almost as dearly.

"Well," said May, "to think of how you've grown, and how you've both improved in every way. My! I'll be altogether in the shade with your pretty faces near me."

Frank Dane gazed in silent admiration at Norrie. May, looking at him, thought, as she smiled a little: "What if it were to happen? Well! I should be glad. She has no fortune, I suppose, nor aristocratic connections, but she is sweet, brave, good, and beautiful and would grace the home of any man."

They soon arrived at Mrs. Dane's home and the day passed pleasantly, in questions, answers and explanations.

In a few days Mrs. Hamilton intended leaving with the two girls for St. Rose. It was the middle of July, and the heat was so intense, that, remembering her husband's injunctions, she feared it might tell[48] on Lucy's health. She had spent part of each summer there during the girls' absence, Mrs. Dane or May generally going with her, and now she intended remaining 'til near Christmas. "It would just build Lucy up," she said, "after hard study, and make her strong for the winter."

This was Monday and they intended leaving on Thursday.

Mrs. Dane took them driving a few times, and Norrie saw more of the town than she had during her previous visit. She never lost her old love for early morning rambles and, on the second day after her arrival, she arose at six and, not wishing to disturb anyone else, she stole noiselessly out into the bright, glorious sunshine. She went some distance out into the country and, thinking at last she remained too long and might keep them waiting breakfast for her, began to return more hurriedly than she had gone, and took a few short turns, which brought her into a small, narrow lane. It was not of the cleanest sort either and, Norrie, always accustomed to pure country air, felt sickened at the nauseous odour of the place, and turned to leave it, when a little boy came running out of a house, crying bitterly.

"Oh, miss," he said, on catching sight of Norrie, "will you come in? Jenny is dying, I know she is. I can't hold her in the cradle and Mother is gone to the well for water and told me to mind her 'til she got back."

Norrie, ever ready to help those in distress, went into the house. There was a little girl about three or four years of age, lying in a cradle and working into convulsions. Norrie tried to hold the child in her arms and soothe her somewhat, but it was impossible. The little fellow had called some of the neighbours, and soon the mother came, almost distracted with grief. She had sat up with her all night and thought, as the child was sleeping, she could safely leave her with Johnnie while she went for water. It was scarletina,[49] she told them, the little one had. And, "now," wailed the poor mother, "that convulsions have set in, I fear I shall lose her." The child grew quieter after a time, and Norrie, when she had helped the woman a little from her slender purse, retraced her steps homewards.

That night she felt far from well and on Wednesday was so ill that, in spite of her remonstrance, Mrs. Dane sent for the doctor. What was their consternation when, after feeling her pulse and looking serious for a time, he pronounced her to be suffering from scarletina. Norrie's first thought was for Lucy. Mrs. Hamilton, in her usual kindness of heart, wanted to delay her departure 'til Norrie was well enough to accompany them, but the latter would not listen to it. "You must go tomorrow, dear Mrs. Hamilton," she said, "and take Lucy away out of danger. You know I'm strong and healthy, and the doctor says it's only a mild form, but she is so delicate it would not be well for her to run the risk of taking it."

"But, Norrie, my child, it seems heartless for us both to go away and leave you ill; and Lucy vows she won't."

"Well, you must insist on her going, Mrs. Hamilton. Please do not add this to my trouble. It's bad enough to know that I've been the means of bringing the disease to Mrs. Dane's house, and it will prolong my illness if you don't take Lucy home. When I know she is out of danger, I will get well much quicker and, as soon as ever the doctor will allow me, I'll go home."

"Goodbye, now, Mrs. Hamilton, don't come near me again, not even to say goodbye, and let me hear in the morning that you've both left for home."

So Norrie, as usual, won the day, for Mrs. Hamilton insisted, despite Lucy's tears, that they should leave next morning.

"Mamma, I think it's the most unkind thing I've ever heard of. If things were reversed, Norrie would not leave us."

"But, my dear, I tell you that Norrie would worry herself to death if we did not go. She is so anxious about you. Of course, if we were amongst strangers, I would send you home and remain myself; but she is with kind friends who will do just as much for her as we could and even if you did remain, Lucy, you would not be allowed to go near her, and that would be just as hard on you. I would fain[50] remain with the dear child, but she positively will not allow me."

So Lucy had to be satisfied, but they could not prevent her from looking into Norrie's room as they were leaving next morning. She would have gone to the bedside only that Norrie raised a warning finger, saying, "Not another step now, Lucy, unless you want to vex me, and make me worse. It won't take me long to get well, and I'll be home in a few weeks after you."

"I'm really mad with you, Norrie, for turning mother and me home. May told me you asked three times today if we were gone yet."

"Run off, dear," she answered smilingly, as she threw her a kiss.

Lucy returned the salute, but, when she had closed the door and passed down the stairs, Norrie allowed the tears, which she had been bravely trying to keep back, to come freely, for she felt a great sense of loneliness without Lucy. It was years since they had been separated, even for a day. But she was not one to give way to melancholy for any length of time, and soon brightened up with the thought that her chief care now was to get well in a hurry.

May then came in and sat by the bedside. "Well, dear, how are you feeling now?" she asked.

"I do not feel very sick at all, May," she answered. "What is hardest on me is the thought of the trouble I've brought on you all."

"Now, Norrie," said May. "Have I not asked you a dozen times to cease tormenting yourself and hurting mother and me by saying such things? We've all had the scarletina so there's no danger of that kind, and your illness is so light that there is no necessity for anyone remaining up at night with you. Then where in the name of common sense is the trouble you speak of? Now, really, Norrie, if I hear you say anything more about it, I won't forgive you. You have simply done an act of charity, which any Christian girl in your place would have done (for, of course, they had heard from Norrie of her adventure, which was the means of her taking the disease)."

As the doctor said, Norrie's illness was light. A good, healthy constitution and a cheerful disposition helped to make her recovery speedy and in little over a week she was able to be downstairs.

Frank Dane never forgot the first time he had seen her after her illness. Her wardrobe was not an extensive one, but what dresses she had were pretty and becoming. May insisted on dressing her, and she chose a wrapper of a very delicate pink, which showed to advantage her dark brown curls, and her cheeks had lost just a little of their bloom. May, after seeing her downstairs and settled comfortably in an armchair, went to look for Frank. She and her mother often wondered why he was so indifferent to the charms of the fair sex in general; he was twenty-five now and had not been the smallest bit in love yet. "Well," thought May, as she led him into the sitting-room, "if he does not fall in love now, he never will. That's my opinion." It never occurred to her that, if Frank did fall in love, it might not be returned. But he was in love with sweet Norrie Moore, as he secretly called her, since the day he had seen her on the deck of the *Portia* and now, when he saw her looking so fair and lovely, he determined, if possible, to win her for his wife. His disposition was something like Norrie's own—bright and cheery. His blue eyes had a kindly expression, and they lighted up with a glad smile as he advanced and took both Norrie's hands in his.

"This is, indeed, a happy day, Miss Moore. I'm so glad to see you are able to be about again and looking none the worse, either, after your illness."

"Thank you, Mr. Dane. Indeed, I don't know how I am ever going to thank you all and make up for the trouble I've given. The idea of my taking[51] scarletina like any child!"

"What you call trouble is only pleasure to us, Miss Moore," as he seated himself beside her.

"Would it be a pleasure to you if I were always ill?" said Norrie, with some of the old mischief peeping from her eyes. "Oh, Mr. Dane!"

"A pleasure to see you ill? You certainly know better than to think this of me," he answered (putting on a more serious look than was necessary), "and you could not give trouble if you tried."

"I would not advise you to try me too far, then. Ask some of the folks from St. Rose and they'll tell you of what trouble I can give." And Norrie laughed merrily as some recollections of her madcap days flashed back upon her.

"You know, Mr. Dane, I was a terrible girl when I was young."

"Are you so old now?" he smiled.

"I'm nearly nineteen, and I daresay that's too old to do anything very terrible."

"I cannot agree with you there. I think it's just the age for young ladies to do terrible things, and only laugh when they do them."

"Well, when I did terrible things long ago, I always laughed; but I paid the penalty, too, for I was generally punished for what I did."

"Yes, that's where the difference lies. Now you cannot be punished, tho' you may do mischief of a more serious nature."

"I don't know what could be more serious than putting a lump on one man's head that he will carry to the grave with him; and spoiling another's field of hay; and striking a lady on the new bonnet with a snowball, for which I'm not forgiven yet, I suppose."

"I know what's worse; for instance, if you had broken that man's heart instead of his head, the damage would be far greater, and—"

But here Frank stopped short, for Norrie was off into fits of laughter. He tried to laugh, too, for company, and kept it up for a considerable length of time but, not having the remotest idea of what he was laughing at, and was, in fact, just a little taken back at Norrie's merriment, just when he was turning the conversation into a sentimental channel, said, "What in the world are you laughing at? I'm quite at a loss to know."

"Well (when she managed to get breath), if ever you see Jerry Malone, you'll know. The idea of anyone speaking of breaking poor Jerry's heart, if he has one at all." And she broke into another peal of laughter.

"It would certainly be worth seeing him if it would make me laugh like that."

When Norrie's merriment had subsided somewhat, she gave him a more accurate account of Jerry. And then Mrs. Dane and May entering, the conversation became general.

A few days after, Frank took the two girls for a drive around Quidi Vidi Lake.

Norrie had received two letters from Lucy, who was pining for her presence; but still, from the tone of her communication, it seemed that she was not quite as lonely as she said she would be. In one letter she made a slight allusion to Harry Brandford. Norrie had often thought of him as she had seen him that last evening before leaving home.

It was only now she would answer Lucy's letters, for she feared that even the paper might bring danger to her. Of course, Mrs. Dane had written and told her sister how her protégé was progressing. And now Norrie thought she might safely venture home. She had trespassed long enough on Mrs. Dane's kindness, as she told her.

"My dear child, your presence here has only been a source of pleasure to us all," said that lady, "and I think you should remain a little longer to make sure that you are thoroughly recovered."

"A thousand thanks, dear Mrs. Dane, for all your kindness, but I am really as strong as I ever was, and what will Uncle and Aunt think of me if I remain longer than is necessary?"

Frank and May then added their persuasions, and at last she consented to remain a little longer. She had made a few acquaintances during the past week; one was a Mr. Philip Weston, who, she soon learned, was to take May for his own, on a day not far distant. He was a tall, dignified-looking man with black hair and moustache.

Frank Dane had determined to tell Norrie of his love before her departure for home. He fondly hoped she would try and return his affection sometime, for something told him she did not do so now nor had she the faintest idea of his feelings towards her.

How perfectly innocent she is, he thought, and how bright and merry she always seems. He, often in his mind, appropriated to her the words of Caroline Norton:[52]

Too innocent for coquetry—too fond for idle scorning,
Oh! friend, I fear the lightest heart makes sometimes
    heaviest mourning.[53]

"I trust my sweet Norrie's heart shall never wear heavy mourning," he thought.

On the evening before Norrie was to leave for St. Rose, there were a few friends invited to the house: Mr. Weston, and Lena, his sister, tall and dignified like her brother. Lilian Roy, a friend of May's, a pretty, merry little thing, of about eighteen, whom Norrie liked much better than Miss Weston; then there were her two brothers, Jack and Will, aged twenty and twenty-two. They were handsome, manly looking fellows, and both seemed to be enraptured with Norrie and hung around her, much to Frank's disgust.

At last, unable to bear it any longer, he asked her to come and play an accompaniment to his song. She arose eagerly and went to the piano. He had a fine voice and sang well. Then there was a general request for a song from Norrie. She always played her own accompaniments, but Frank lingered near her on pretence of turning the music. She sang one of her favourite songs, "Ever of Thee I'm Fondly Dreaming."[54] All present were charmed at the sweetness and power of her voice. When she had finished, Frank led her out on the verandah, as she complained of feeling warm.

"One would think, Miss Moore, that there was really someone of whom you were fondly dreaming; you put such expression in your song."

"There is not, then," answered Norrie, as she rested both elbows on the rail, "at least, not in the sense that is meant by the song."

"Then, you are heart-whole, and fancy-free still?" said Frank.

"Yes," she answered. "I'm heart-whole and fancy-free still and am likely to be for some time to come. I cannot afford to think of love or lovers yet; I've got my work before me."

"Your work?" he echoed. "What work?"

"I've got to teach, and make a living for myself."

"But, Miss Moore, if you found one who loved you very much and would devote his whole life to your happiness, take you from the tiresome task of teaching to be his wife and live in a home of luxury, would you not abandon this idea of making a living for yourself?"

"No," she answered, shaking her head with slow determination. "Nothing should tempt me from it. It has been a fixed idea in my head for years."

Then Frank changed his mind. He would not run the risk of losing his chance of winning her by speaking of his love now. It was hard, he thought, but he must have patience, and surely she was well worth spending years to win.

She had no idea of the deep love he felt for her. She thought so little about herself that she never dreamed of the power she possessed in the charm of her face, voice and manner, and Frank

Dane, with a firm will, kept back the words he meant to have spoken.

Next morning Norrie bade farewell to the friends who had shown her such kindness.

"I wonder will you ever dream of me, Norrie?" said Frank, calling her for the first time by her Christian name.

"Indeed I shall often, Mr. Dane, and of May and your dear kind mother, too. I think of you as a dear brother; I wish I had a brother like you."

Frank winced a little at those words. It was not a brother's love he wished to claim from her, but he must bide his time. She loved no one else, and that was a consolation.

Frank's was the last face she saw as the ship steamed slowly out the harbour.

CHAPTER SIX

Back among the old folks once again.[55]

Mrs. Hamilton and Lucy were warmly welcomed by the good people of St. Rose. Many called to see them, and eager questions were asked concerning Norrie, to which they answered that she was with Mrs. Dane, being detained by a slight illness, and would be home in a few weeks.

John and Bridget Moore were disappointed very much, for they felt a longing to see Norrie, whom, of course, they loved in their own way. Harry and Mrs. Brandford were amongst the callers, and they were simply charmed with Lucy. Her gentle, lady-like, unassuming manner, and her pretty face and fairy-like figure attracted attention wherever she went. Harry never mixed much in the society of ladies—young ones especially. He had peculiar notions with regard to them and, once they overstepped the boundary of what he termed womanly dignity, they lost their charm for him. In his eyes Lucy possessed all that was sweet and good. He spent most every evening in her company. He sometimes brought his violin, and together they played and sang. Harry often wished he had had a sister to brighten his home, and he felt for Lucy the same affection which he would have borne one. But was it to be wondered at, if she felt day by day growing stronger, an affection of a different nature for him?

Harry had developed considerably during the past four years. He was fully six feet, broad shouldered, and somewhat bronzed, for he took a great deal of outdoor exercise, fishing, shooting and rowing. The deep, grey eyes were still the same, earnest, true, and often melancholy. There was something more than beauty in his face, a charm which one can feel and understand but cannot explain. Mrs. Brandford noticed his frequent visits to Lucy and thought, "Well if he does think of marrying, it's time. He is twenty-five now, and Lucy Hamilton has a large fortune and good connections. She is pretty and accomplished. Still, I would rather he had chosen from some of my own young lady friends in town." While Mrs. Hamilton looked on with pleasure for, of all the young men she had met, there was not one to whom she would as safely entrust the happiness of her darling, as Harry Brandford. And he, quite unconscious of their ideas, spent nearly all his evenings at Mrs. Hamilton's.

Mrs. Hamilton and Lucy had been invited to spend an evening at Mrs. Brandford's. That lady had never spoken one word to them concerning Norrie, but Lucy had given Harry a full history of all their school days, of Norrie's beauty, talent and goodness.

"I'm not surprised," said Harry. "I always said she had genius and that she would develop into a good and beautiful woman."

It was the evening before Norrie was expected home that they went to Mrs. Brandford's. She received them very courteously, and Mrs. Brandford could be very entertaining when she chose, and today she exerted herself to be more so than usual. Harry and Lucy amused each other; they wandered through the grounds, gathering wild roses and pretty ferns. The two ladies smiled inwardly as, on coming into the garden at dusk, they found them sitting together on one of the seats. But a keen observer would have noticed that Harry, never by word nor look, gave Lucy any reason to think he had any more than a brotherly affection for her: he was kind, thoughtful, solicitous for her comfort, and courteous, but that was all; nor did he ever dream of being more. He never gave much thought to marriage; when he did think a little about it, it seemed something afar off in the distance, when he should meet an ideal he had in a misty sort of manner pictured to himself. He could not tell, nor did he think much, whether she should be dark or light, tall or short, beautiful or not; but still his ideal often rose before him in imagination—a woman strong and tender, good and true. He felt she should possess these qualities, but he never went beyond them.

They all entered the house and did full justice to a dainty supper. Then Harry and Lucy played and sang; and soon after, as they arose to go, Mrs. Hamilton remarked that they would have Norrie home on the morrow.

In an instant Mrs. Brandford's face changed.

"Oh!" she said. "Did they succeed in making anything of her at the Convent?"

"Making anything of her?" repeated Lucy. "Why, Norrie was the cleverest girl at the Convent. She took prizes for everything, and she has perfect genius for painting and music."

"Yes," said Mrs. Hamilton, "Norrie has great talent. Her voice is magnificent, too, and she is a thorough lady in every way."

"I cannot understand it," said the unreasonable woman. "The ill-breeding of her early life will come out at some time or another."

"I think, Mrs. Brandford, that you are unreasonably prejudiced against Norrie," said Mrs. Hamilton. "She did not require the training and education she's received to refine her. She possessed innate refinement and, tho' according to the ideas of high-toned[56] society she may not be a born one, she is as thorough a lady as one would meet in any part of the world."

Lucy's face brightened, and she looked lovingly at her mother as she spoke so nobly in defence of her favourite.

"I thought so always, and I think so still," answered Mrs. Brandford, "that it was entirely a mistake, taking Nora Moore from the humble life to which she belonged, and forcing her society upon people, who, for politeness' sake, I suppose, try to tolerate her. I, for one, shall never receive her as an equal."

"Happily for the world, Mrs. Brandford, that everyone does not think as you do," said Harry, who had been standing near the door, waiting to escort the ladies home. He always called her Mrs. Brandford when she tried his patience too much.

Lucy's face flushed indignantly. "The idea," she thought, "of our proud Norrie forcing her society upon anyone." "There's not the slightest danger," she could not help replying, "of Norrie forcing herself upon society. It is quite the other way; society's forcing itself upon her."

This little argument resulted in a rather cool adieu from each party.

It was a delightful evening, balmy and sweet; the air laden with the scent of hay and clover, while the murmuring of the sea, lowing of cattle and, now and again, the distant tinkle of the cowbells were the only sounds to break the stillness. The distance to Mrs. Hamilton's house was short; she entered immediately upon arriving, leaving the young people lingering in the flower garden.

Harry felt as if he should make some apology for his stepmother's words.

"My mother has some peculiar notions about caste and society, and all that sort of nonsense," he said. "She makes many mistakes, and it is impossible to get an idea or a prejudice out of her head once it takes possession of her."

"Mrs. Brandford must be very hard, indeed, if, after seeing

Norrie, she still retains the prejudice she has always shown towards her," answered Lucy. "One could not help being fond of her if one tried."

"I wonder does Norrie know the strong champion she has in you, Miss Hamilton?" said Harry, looking admiringly at her.

"Oh, yes," she answered. "Norrie and I know we would die for each other."

"That is certainly a strong way of putting it," he smilingly replied, "and it's easier said than done. Still, there are things we value more than our lives, and which we would feel harder to part with."

Lucy opened her large, blue eyes in wonder. "Mr. Brandford, what would you feel harder to give up than your life?"

"Why, one's happiness, peace of mind, the life of one dear to us; of course, I'm leaving myself out of the question, as I've never reached that goal of earthly happiness that I would feel harder to part with than my life, and I've no one in this wide world very dear to me; neither am I very dear to anyone."

His words fell with a chill on Lucy's heart. Why? She could hardly tell for an instant, for as yet she had never analyzed her feelings with regard to Harry Brandford. She was but an innocent, dreaming maiden, whose thoughts 'til lately had never gone beyond her studies and school duties. But now, like a flash, the truth dawned upon her; and instinctively with this humiliating knowledge came the determination to guard her secret from him at any cost. Harry was not looking attentively at her or he would have noticed the sudden pallor and then flushing of her fair face. She recovered herself very quickly, as every girl will under similar circumstances and replied, "Of course, these things would be harder than life for a very brave person to give up; but I think I should be a veritable coward where my life is concerned. Norrie would not; she has the stuff heroines are made of."

"I trust, my child, you shall never be put to the test. None of us know what we can or cannot do 'til we've had the trial; and it has often turned out that the apparently weakest persons have shown the greatest courage."

"I should certainly not hesitate to give my life for those I love were it to be a natural death; but, think of being beheaded like Mary Queen of Scots, guillotined like Marie Antoinette, or burned at the stake like Joan of Arc! I don't think I should trust myself," and Lucy shuddered.

"Well, you're brave enough to admit it, and there's a certain amount of courage, even in that," laughed Harry. "But we've got quite tragic in our conversation."

"Perhaps if ever I reach that goal of happiness, which you say you've not yet attained, I may become braver," said Lucy.

"You shall certainly reach it some day, very soon I'll prophesy. Wait 'til you make your debut in town next winter; you'll have half the men in it making love to you."

It was not often Harry talked as lightly as this; but he fancied Lucy was not looking as bright as she did all day, and he wished to arouse her.

"Why is it that you have not reached it before now, and you spend part of every winter in town?"

"I? Oh!" he said, very slowly, while a sweet, grave expression stole over his face. "I may never reach it. I don't expect to do so soon, however."

"But why, Mr. Brandford? Are you so fastidious that it is impossible to please you, or are you above such weakness as loving anyone?"

"I scarcely know, perhaps 'tis hard to please me. Perhaps I do not please others, but I don't, by any means, consider loving a weakness. True love is the most sacred feeling of which the human heart is capable: it is a blessing from Heaven; the crowning of a good man's or woman's life; the acme of earthly happiness; and the nearest approach to heavenly bliss, which we mortals are permitted to know."

"How earnestly he thinks and speaks, sometimes," thought Lucy. She could have listened to him for hours, and it was with an effort she aroused herself. The beauty of the night, together with the unspeakable charm of the face and voice of the man near her, seemed to cast a spell over her senses.

"I trust," she said, "that you will soon find someone to whom you will be inexpressibly dear, and whose love will be the crowning of your life, Mr. Brandford. I must wish you good night, or Mamma will accuse me of going in danger of taking cold."

"Good night, Miss Hamilton, and thank you for your kind wishes. I suppose we shall have your heroine, Norrie, home tomorrow!"

"Oh, yes!" and Lucy's face brightened at the thought. "I wish it was tomorrow now."

"Well, good night, and pleasant dreams," as he lifted his hat and strode down the garden path.

Tomorrow came, bright, golden, and beautiful. Lucy was up at sunrise, singing like a lark; even her disappointment of last night was for a time forgotten. The back of the house faced the sea, and here she took her position of watching for the first sight of the steamer. It seemed to her the birds never sang so sweetly; and she fancied their song was "Norrie's coming, Norrie's coming." Presently she caught sight of a little curl of smoke, rising over the top of the highest hill. Ah, that was surely it! No other steamer was expected at St. Rose; and, bounding into the house, ran with the news to her mother. When they had breakfasted, the good ship was steaming into the harbour. Soon, Lucy and her mother were standing on the pier; the former waving her handkerchief in response to Norrie's signal, and brown eyes and blue beamed with love, as the girls were clasped in each other's arms.

John and Bridget Moore almost lost their breath as they gazed at Norrie.

"Child, how tall you've grown," said Bridget, "and how pretty!"

"I'll expect ye'll soon get tired of St. Rose," said John, "after so much travilin' and sightseein'."

"No, indeed, Uncle, there's no place in the world like it. I felt more gladness of heart coming in just now than I've known since I left home."

Lucy, of course, went home with Norrie for the remainder of the day. It was late in the evening when a lull came in their conversation; they had so much to talk of, all their little adventures during their few weeks of separation. They had just gone in now from the garden, and were sitting in the humble but clean and pretty little parlour.

"Lucy," said Norrie, "what about the Brandfords? You never told me whether they are living or dead."

"Oh, they are well," answered Lucy, trying in vain to keep back the flush that would rise. "Mamma and I were there yesterday evening. I don't like Mrs. Brandford at all; she is just as proud and nonsensical as ever."

"That means, I suppose," said Norrie, with her bright smile, "that she has not forgiven me for breaking the fetters that bound me to the life of my ancestors."

"Yes, Norrie," she said after a moment's hesitation. "I can't deceive you. It is so, but don't let that trouble you, dear," as she twined both arms around her.

"Not at all, Lucy," Norrie said, returning the caress. "It does not make an iota of difference to me what Mrs. Brandford thinks. But what about Mr. Harry, Lucy?"

"Mr. Brandford is very nice, as he always was. He has been to our house very often, and he plays and sings beautifully. We were talking of you last night."

"I think you are a great rogue, Lucy," Norrie said, with one of her old mischievous smiles. "I'm sure it's not to play and sing, merely, that he goes often to your house. Now Lucy, honour bright, are you not keeping something back?"

"No, Norrie, I understand what you mean, but it's not so; I would tell you if it were. We are real good friends, fond of each other as such, and that is all." And Lucy smiled brightly, for not even to Norrie would she admit that she had loved unasked. A light tap came on the door. Norrie opened it and looked, first surprised, and then glad, for there stood the tall, manly form of her one time enemy, Harry Brandford.

Norrie wore a dress of creamy mull muslin,[57] her only ornament being a bunch of pansies fastened at her neck; her dark brown hair, gathered in a large coil at the back of her head; her eyes soft and dreamy; the rich, bright colour on cheeks and lips which, when they parted in a glad smile, showed to advantage her pearly white teeth.

Harry had been thinking of "little Norrie," as he had always called her, as she was when last he had seen her: in a short dress, with tangled brown curls hanging about her head; of her quaint sayings with often a touch of the bad accent of the fisherfolk, and her wild harum-scarum ways; and so was totally unprepared for the vision that now stood before him. He would not dare call this tall, dignified young lady, Norrie. In silence, with his usual calm, serious look, he took her outstretched hand, once brown and somewhat hardened, now soft and white.

"Oh, Mr. Brandford, I'm so glad to see you. You look just the same except (with a critical glance), yes, you have got a little taller."

"And you, Miss Moore, have got a great deal taller and do not look the same."

"Have I changed?" said Norrie. "I hope it is for the better?"

"As far as appearance goes you've decidedly changed for the better," answered Harry.

"Only as far as appearance, Mr. Brandford?"

"I trust so, Miss Moore, for your heart and mind, I hope, are still unchanged. They required none, except what knowledge and wisdom years of study and discipline have given them."

"And what do you think of Lucy, Mr. Brandford? She has improved a great deal in appearance, has she not? See, what a healthy colour she has in her once pale little cheeks!"

"Yes, Miss Hamilton has improved even more so than yourself

in appearance. Still, strange to say, the change is not so marked."

"Then I must have been quite a fright before I went away," laughed Norrie.

"I think you are making a mistake, Mr. Brandford," said Lucy. "Norrie always appeared (to me anyway) just as nice as she does now."

"Oh! well, you know you were looking with the eyes of love," said Harry.

"I don't know how that can correspond with the theory of the person who says love is blind," said Lucy, intentionally ignoring the true meaning of the phrase, which Harry explained by saying, "But you must remember, love is only blind to the faults of the loved one."

"And I can tell you I always had, and I daresay always shall have, a fair share of these," said Norrie.

"You could not be human and be faultless, Miss Moore, tho' Miss Hamilton here thinks you nothing short of a saint."

"Oh! Lucy, my dear, how small your idea of a saint must be!" replied Norrie, laughing merrily. "The fact is, Mr. Brandford, it's Lucy herself who's the saint and, if ever in time to come there may be a particle of the angelic about me, I shall have gotten it from her."

"I was not aware," smiled Harry, "that young ladies used to flatter each other so much."

"Truth is not flattery, Mr. Brandford," said Norrie.

They talked on as young people will 'til the moon rose round and full above the hills and its soft light seemed to linger caressingly on meadow, wood and stream, on Norrie's dark head and Lucy's golden one as they walked with Harry in the little flower garden. At length Lucy said, "Mamma will think I've run away."

"Yes," answered Harry, "that reminds me. I called at your mother's as I was passing and she told me she had not seen you since morning."

"The day seemed too short for us," laughed Norrie. "We had so much to talk about."

"Oh! yes, we have not done yet," said Lucy, "but do you know, Norrie, I think we are very thoughtless. I am sure you need some rest, dear, after your journey, and we should not remain so long."

"Rest?" repeated Norrie. "Who could go to bed on such a glorious night? I shall sit up for hours yet, watching the man in the moon."

"If you'll allow me, Miss Moore, I'd advise you to use your eyes on something more substantial," said Harry, with a smile.

"Oh, I've firm faith in the man in the moon," said Norrie. "That is the man I wish to see there."

"Norrie has a theory of her own, that she will sometime see the face of her ideal in the moon," said Lucy. "She has seen one often, but she says he is not her ideal."

"Might I inquire what he is like?" asked Harry.

"Oh, no, you might not," said Lucy, before Norrie had time to answer. "She will not even tell me that, tho' she has promised to do so some day."

Norrie seemed a trifle uneasy, and felt inclined to change the subject.

Shortly after, Harry and Lucy bade her good night, and took their departure; and so ended Norrie's first day at home.

The house seemed lonely to her as she entered. Mr. and Mrs. Moore always retired at sunset in the summer days, for they should be up before sunrise; and on this night they made no difference. Just for an instant the thought crossed Norrie's mind that her aunt might have remained up for a little, on this the first night of her homecoming, to speak a few words to her before retiring. But the next she called herself selfish, for she thought of course they must be tired after their hard day's work; but her heart yearned for affection. She sat at the window for some time, thinking sadly of the mother whose face she distinctly remembered. She thought how glad she would be now were she alive to have her home, how she would love and care for her. "I wonder does she see me now," she thought, "and is she glad the money she left for me is spent on my education?" Then she thought of Dr. Hamilton: was he watching her now as he said he always would be, and was she fulfilling the promise she had made him, of always taking care of and being kind to Lucy?

She soon chased away the sad thoughts. They were deep and true while they lasted, but she never allowed them to remain long.

"Now," she said, "I will look at the moon 'til I see my ideal." After gazing for some time, lost in thought, she turned away with an impatient gesture. "There it is again," she said. "I positively won't try it any more. Why will no other face but his ever come there? He is not my ideal either. It was so thoughtless of me to say anything about watching the man in the moon. How glad I am now that I never even told Lucy whose face I see there. I must laugh it off from henceforth and say it is all nonsense, which, of course, it is."

CHAPTER SEVEN

The remainder of the month of August passed pleasantly away. Norrie spent almost every evening with Lucy, where Harry Brandford generally joined them. She took up the favourite amusements of her childhood days. She often rowed Lucy across the harbour in a dory, and took her for long rambles over the hills; but Harry now was sometimes their escort.

The month of September was looked forward to with much pleasure, for it promised to be one of unusual enjoyment to them. May and Frank Dane were coming on a visit to Lucy; also Lilian Roy, whose brothers, Jack and Will, together with Philip Weston, May's betrothed, were to stay a few weeks with Harry Brandford. Norrie and Lucy were busy preparing and planning all sorts of amusements for their friends—picnics, excursions, boating, etc. Norrie had, a few days after her arrival home, taken up her old-time duties; she made the butter, skimmed the cream, and spent a few hours every day at the spinning-wheel.[58] She was a little out of practice at first, but soon got into it again. She intended opening a music and painting school in St. John's after the Christmas holidays. She felt she could never spend her days in St. Rose at the old occupations; it was only yielding to the entreaties of Mrs. Hamilton and Lucy that she did not begin immediately. Both Mrs. Hamilton and Mrs. Brandford still believed that Lucy was the attraction for Harry. He never missed an evening now without seeing her, and always accompanied Norrie to her own home; this, of course, was only an act of courtesy which any gentleman should do. Some evenings he and Lucy would visit Norrie. She had met Mrs. Brandford once since her arrival, at Mrs. Hamilton's, and that lady still maintained her cold, haughty demeanour towards her. She was inwardly surprised and mortified at Norrie's rare beauty, perfect manners and intellectual conversation. She was much pleased at (what she considered) Harry's interest in Lucy. She thought her one of those gentle girls who could quite easily be moulded to her own way of thinking, and so foresaw herself mistress of Harry Brandford's house for the rest of her life.

On the third of September the coastal steamer arrived at St. Rose, bringing the visitors. Norrie, Lucy and Harry met them on the pier. Frank Dane had eyes for no one but Norrie; she seemed to him sweeter and brighter than ever. She and May welcomed each other warmly. After some merry jest and happy laughter, the party divided; Lucy bearing off May, Lilian, Frank and Norrie, too, for the remainder of the day, while Jack, Will, and Philip Weston went with Harry.

"Well," said Lucy, as they separated, "we are better off than you are, Mr. Brandford; we have, at least, one gentleman, but you've no lady."

"I hope they won't spoil you, Frank," said Will Roy.

"Spoil him?" echoed May. "There's no chance of that. We'll make him mind his p's and q's, and dance attendance on us all day."

"Mind, Frank," said Harry, raising his voice as they were getting further apart, "if you are persecuted too much, remember, my doors are open to you, and you've only to come along."

"We won't allow him a smoke for a week," laughed Lilian. But Frank thought himself blest to be where Norrie was, provided[59] he never got a smoke.

About seven o'clock the same evening, the four gentlemen arrived at Mrs. Hamilton's to make arrangements for next day's programme. The weather was clear and beautiful, and gave every promise of next day being the same. They held a consultation in the flower garden.

"Who is to be our pilot?" asked May. "We shall want one."

"Yes," said Lilian. "I for one don't feel like getting lost in the woods and being food for the bears."

"We could not find a better one than Norrie," said Lucy. "There's not a hill, pond, river or marsh that she's not familiar with."

"But, Miss Hamilton," said Jack Roy, "do you forget the discredit it would reflect on us for the rest of our lives if we allowed a lady to pilot a party of picnickers, and five gentlemen being some of the number; just fancy if it reached town and the *Telegram*[60] got hold of it." At which they all laughed heartily.

"Well," said Lucy, "jesting aside, we all know who'll be our pilot. Mr. Brandford, of course, considering he is the only one who can be."

"I'll propose," said Harry, with a steady look at Norrie, "that as you've unanimously proclaimed us the most competent, Miss Moore and myself will lead the party, and pilot you all through."

"Yes," assented Lucy, "but Norrie must choose where our excursion is to be. She is the best judge of that," to which they all agreed, except Frank Dane, who had counted on being Norrie's escort, and now Harry Brandford had appropriated the pleasure to himself.

Before they separated, it was arranged to start off immediately after an early breakfast for a place called Beach Bay. They were to go by water in a large skiff. Harry was to engage four men to row them out, and from there to proceed on foot over hills and through narrow wood-paths, which led to a place famed for its beauty called Rocky Falls.

As there were five gentlemen and but four ladies, they invited Miss Eva Fenton, the magistrate's daughter (whom, in days gone by, Norrie had chased with a dead muskrat), to join them. She was a quiet, gentle little thing of seventeen.

They all agreed to retire early in order to have themselves strong and fresh for their journey on the morrow.

Harry was very silent and grave-looking on the way home, so much so that they all noticed it.

"Aren't you pleased at the prospect of our excursion tomorrow?" asked Philip Weston.

"Pleased with it?" said Harry. "Why, certainly! It's a long time since I've looked forward to anything with such pleasure."

"He has a strange way of showing when he is pleased," thought Philip.

The cause of Harry's grave appearance was that Norrie had accepted Frank Dane's escort to her home that evening and with such apparent pleasure that he fell to thinking deeply. He remembered how in consequence of her illness she had remained with the Danes a few weeks after Lucy and her mother had left, and what could be more natural than for Frank to fall in love with her. In fact, how could he help it, with her sweet presence before him every day; and would it not also be very natural for Norrie to return that love?

Frank was good, handsome, always gay and light-hearted like herself, and, if so, why should he be sorry? He lay awake for some hours after retiring, and the truth stared him in the face, that unconsciously to himself he had learned to love sweet, bright, mischief-loving Norrie Moore. But had he learned it too late? Had another won the prize? How tenderly he thought of her! What would he not give to win her: to claim for himself the priceless treasure of her true, womanly heart, with her beauty, her genius, her youth and innocence, and, better than all these, the beauty and goodness of soul, which shone forth from her dark, brown eyes.

In his grand simplicity he deemed himself unworthy of her. "My disposition is too dull, and serious," he told himself, "to attract one as gay and mirth-loving as the queen of my heart, Norrie Moore. And, besides, if Dane has the prior claim, what right have I to try?" He entertained too humble an opinion of himself to remember his own personal attractions: the manly beauty of his face, together with the irresistible charm of voice and manner, while a true, brave and noble soul looked out from his dark, grey eyes. It was just the face to win the heart of a girl like Norrie. But did he win? She was fighting desperately now for the mastery over her own heart, for Norrie was quick of perception. She loved Lucy so well that she soon read her heart and, when one week home, had understood how things were between her and Harry. Up 'til now she had not dreamed of his growing affection for herself; and the thought that he was becoming in the smallest degree dear to her, made her angry with herself. How she wished that he would learn to love Lucy. It went to her heart to see Lucy bravely trying to hide her pain, and she resolved to do all in her power to secure her happiness.

Next morning they all assembled at Lucy's with very doubtful faces, for the day was not at all as fine as they wished. It was dull, with heavy hanging clouds, but no rain as yet. They assembled in the sitting-room, where a consultation was held, Mrs. Hamilton presiding. She advised them to consult Jerry Malone, who was at work in the garden. Jerry grinned as he looked north, south, east and east; he generally enjoyed spoiling sport.[61]

"Dere's goin' to be lashins a rain[62] afore twelve," he said.

"Oh, Jerry!" they all said in chorus. "And we with our baskets packed, all ready to go!"

"I'm not bringin' de rain," he said, shuffling on one foot and then on the other. "I'm only tellin' ye it's comin'. I don't care wedder ye goes or stays, an' I don't care if ye gets wet or not," he muttered to himself, as he hobbled off to his work.

Philip Weston, with a grave face after studying the elements for some time, was of opinion that there might be a few light showers, but that's all. "And could we not provide against these," May said, "by bringing rain coats, umbrellas and rubber shoes?"

"We've got the rubber shoes all right," said Norrie. "We want them and heavy leather shoes, too, if it never rained; for I can tell you it's none of your fine St. John's travelling we are going to do today."

"Norrie, you are a fair judge of the weather," said Mrs. Hamilton. "What do you think of it?"

"Norrie refuses to give an opinion," said May Dane.

"Ah, wise Norrie!" said Lilian Roy. "She's afraid she might be mistaken and so lose her reputation as a weather prophet."

"Well," laughed Norrie, "it took eighteen years to gain that reputation, and I don't feel inclined to run the risk of losing it." She was near the window, her face all radiant with smiles, and her eyes—well, what was in them? something of the old mischief of her earlier days.

Lucy was the only one who thoroughly understood that look and, when she got a chance of speaking to her, unheard by the others, said, "Norrie, what is it? You're up to something, I know."

"Oh! Lucy," as she grasped her hand, "I can hardly keep from laughing outright. Just imagine the tall, dignified Mr. Weston standing under the showering rain, after he saying we will have none, an umbrella in one hand, and a basket or something in the other. What will he look like? I'm dying to see it, but I'm afraid for you, Lucy. You must put on some extra clothing and bring two rain cloaks."

"Why, are you so sure of the rain, Norrie?"

"As sure as I am that Philip Weston does not know the first thing about the weather, and pretends he does."

At length the sun came out in a sickly, uncertain way, and they all agreed to go as Mrs. Hamilton did not oppose them.

"Ah! did I not tell you 'twould be fine?" said Philip. "See the sun now. I'm a fair judge always at this time of the morning," and looked so self-complaisant as he gave his opinion that it added to Norrie's secret enjoyment.

Soon they were all settled comfortably in the skiff, with a plentiful and substantial lunch, armed with no end of rain coats, both ladies' and gentlemen's, also umbrellas; Harry, being the only gentleman who disdained such a womanly weapon, wore a mackintosh and rain cap. "The only man here," thought Norrie, as she looked admiringly at his grave, handsome face.

There was an umbrella put in the skiff for her use, but she had her doubts about using it. She always considered them encumbrances, unless it was to save a good hat from spoiling; but today they all wore hats to suit the weather. They laughed and sang as the skiff, aided by the strong arms of the fishermen, bore them swiftly over the water. Now there was some fun: the skiff-men had to go back to their work, as it was a busy time, and would return for them about sunset, and all the luggage, with the unexpected weapons for rain, had to be carried by the gentlemen.

Norrie was nearly bursting with merriment as she put into Philip Weston's hand a large tin kettle; he looked so out of place with it. She was the life and soul of that party; her spirits knew no bounds.

Years afterwards they often spoke of that day, and laughed as they recalled some of her quaint sayings, her bright, sparkling, infectious laughter. She was simply irresistible: the rich, glowing colour on cheeks and lips; the merry mischievous brown eyes, which were playing havoc with some hearts. The grave expression deepened on Harry Brandford's face as he realized more than ever how unsuitable one of his disposition was for such a bright, merry creature. They walked along in groups 'til the road ended and several narrow wood-paths branched off.

Harry and Norrie, being the only two familiar with the one leading to Rocky Falls, took the lead. The path was only wide enough for two, and so they paired off.

Norrie gave Lucy in charge of Will Roy, with strict injunctions that he was to lift her over all the fences, which were low and built of longers.[63]

May and her stiff lover (as Norrie termed him), of course, went together. Jack Roy took charge of Eva Fenton, and Frank Dane and Lilian Roy brought up the rear. Poor Frank did not care who fell to his lot, when Norrie was taken from him. "Confound the fellow," he thought. "He had a right to let Miss Moore remain at the end of this procession. How nice it will be should they go on some distance in advance, and some of us take the wrong path?" But Harry was too thoughtful for anything like this to happen. Whenever they came to a spot where another path branched off from the right, they halted 'til the whole party came in sight. There was much laughter when they came to the fences; Norrie sprang over so gracefully and quickly that Harry hardly knew when she went.

"How thoroughly you enjoy yourself, Miss Moore!"

"Yes, Mr. Brandford, anything I love I enjoy to its fullest extent; do you not?"

"Anything I love? Yes."

"That is said as tho' you don't love many things. Perhaps you don't love this?"

"You wrong me there. It is one of the few things I do love. Who would not? The pure country air, the babbling of brooks, the song of the birds, with nothing but Heaven's canopy above us, the scent of trees and wild flowers, and—shall I complete the picture, Miss Moore?"

"Certainly, Mr. Brandford. I did not know you were so romantic."

"And, by my side, one of the fairest, brightest, and truest of women."

"Mr. Brandford, you're the last person from whom I would expect to hear such a speech."

"And why?" asked Harry.

"Well, I thought you too much of a business man to be romantic, and too honest for flattery."

"I'll answer you in the words you used yourself, some time ago, Miss Moore, 'truth is not flattery.'"

"How do you know it is true, that I am one of the truest of women?"

"That is more than I can explain. Instinct, I suppose."

"Instinct may be mistaken in some cases."

"So it may, but not with me in this. Imagination, I should say, is more likely to be mistaken (and Harry looked at her with a strange smile); for instance, a young lady imagining she could see the face of her ideal in the moon."

Norrie blushed deeply, and did not look at all pleased.

"I know you mean me, Mr. Brandford, but my imagination does not work there. I've not seen my ideal yet." And she tried to persuade herself she was telling the truth.

"Do you mean in the moon, or in the flesh?" said Harry.

"In neither. Of course, it's only nonsense. I read some time ago that if one gazed for a considerable length of time at the moon, one would see the face of his or her ideal there; and (she continued, in a hesitating manner), I acknowledge that it took such a strong hold of my imagination that I began trying the experiment."

"And failed?" put in Harry.

"And failed completely," she assented, looking anywhere but at him.

"Did you ever see a face at all there?"

"How closely you do question one, Mr. Brandford?"

"Now that is an evasion, I am sure. You do not say you saw no face there."

"Why, do you believe I could really see a face in the moon, except the one that's always there?"

"Of course, that's understood. There is no one who would be foolish enough to believe they could see a face in reality there. It is only what their imagination would conjure up, and surely your imagination must have some time conjured up a face before your vision."

"Yes, but not my ideal," said Norrie, in an unguarded moment.

"Oh, then, you have seen someone? And how do you know he is not your ideal?"

"Because I don't want him to be (rather crossly)."

"I think you are mistaken. If it is the face of someone you've known, he must be very much in your thoughts, as it is thinking of the person makes you fancy you see him. You would not require gazing at the moon at all to do so."

"But I gaze at the moon to see a face I've never seen. A type of face which I fancy would be my idea, and, while I look, I seem to forget what I'm looking for, and this other face rises before me," she concluded, driven to desperation, as she felt herself being cornered.

"That shows that he, whoever the fortunate fellow may be, will certainly be your ideal some day, as he most undoubtedly occupies a large share of your thoughts. Will you tell me what he is like?"

"I could not do that," said Norrie. "Did not Lucy tell you I would not even tell her?"

"Then, if Lucy is left out in the cold, what can I expect?"

"Did you ever form an ideal in your imagination, Mr. Brandford (anxious to escape more questioning)?"

"No (and suddenly his face and voice changed from light bantering to grave, almost sad seriousness), except in a far off uncertain kind of manner."

"Ah! then you have not seen her yet?"

"Yes, I have seen her!"

"And what is she like?"

"Is it fair to ask me that, when you would not satisfy my curiosity?"

"Well, perhaps I know her."

"You do, undoubtedly."

A sudden light sprang into Norrie's eyes. "What if he should care for Lucy after all?" She would try to know, anyway.

"Do I know her well?" she asked.

"Very well."

"Shall I describe her?"

"If you can do so, certainly."

"Then, she is a sweet, angelic creature, not quite as tall as I am, pretty and graceful, beautiful golden hair, and dark blue eyes."

Harry seemed startled. "Why, surely," he thought, "she is describing Lucy Hamilton." "And her home?" he asked.

"Is here in St. Rose, at present. Am I not right, Mr. Brandford?" and she looked at him with an anxious face.

"No, you're wrong, entirely wrong. Have not even gone near her in appearance."

Norrie's face clouded with disappointment; but, she thought, with sudden resolution, "since he, perhaps, guesses whom I mean, I'll go further." "Then, Mr. Brandford, I'm very much surprised and disappointed."

"Indeed! Why?"

"Why? Because I thought, and I'm sure a great many think the same, that you—well, that you admire Lucy a great deal."

"You and a great many are right there. I do admire Miss Hamilton very much. She is sweet and pretty and as true-hearted a girl as, perhaps, one seldom meets with. I've often longed for a sister, and, if I were told I was about to meet one whom I had never known, I would wish her to be just like Lucy Hamilton."

"And yet she is not your ideal?"

"Of all that is good, noble and womanly, yes, but she could never be the one bright star of my existence, the queen of my heart, the one being in this world who could fill my home with sunshine, my life with happiness, the one whose place in my heart shall never be supplied by another; tho' for aught I know, she may be as far from me as one of Heaven's bright planets."

Norrie began to grow interested. "I wonder who it is?" she thought. "He says I know her well." "I should like to hear you describe her, Mr. Brandford," and she looked at him with eyes full of sympathy. "Please do not mind my not telling you what you asked, and oblige me."

"Very well, then. Mind it's your own wish. But I'll do better than describing her. I'll tell you where you'll see her." And, looking at her with a calm, even cold, expression, said, "When you return home this evening, go to your mirror, and there you will see reflected the face of my ideal."

A bright wave of colour rose to her brow; then her eyes fell, her manner changed; she became cold and dignified, and he felt sorry he had spoken so plainly. But, he told himself, "It was better to know the truth."

"I trust, Miss Moore," he said, "that I have not offended you, and that you will not allow what I've said to trouble you in the least. And, now, prove your forgiveness by telling me what your ideal is like. Perhaps I know him?"

She looked at him now with wide frightened eyes. Tell him whose face often came to her imagination, while gazing at the moon in search of her ideal? No—not for worlds: Lucy's happiness was in danger enough now, but, if he only knew that. "No, Mr. Brandford, I can never tell you that, but I am not displeased at what you've said. I'm only sorry. But please do not speak of it again, and we will try to forget it, and be friends, as we've always been."

The sound of voices and laughter from behind greeted them now, and the others came in sight.

"How quickly you must have walked!" said Lucy. "We've hurried so much to keep up with you that I'm quite out of breath."

"Oh, my, that's too bad," said Norrie, full of concern. "Will Roy, is this the care you've taken of the charge given you?"

"It's very easy to ask that question, Miss Moore, but when a young lady takes the notion into her head, that her cavalier is incapable of the charge allotted to him. Oh yes (as Lucy made a protest), don't deny it. I've noticed that you did not want me at all, and set my authority at defiance on every occasion, and proved it by taking charge of me instead. She actually laughed, when I tried to show her the best way to climb a fence, and said, 'why, Norrie and I have served our time at climbing fences,' which, of course, meant, you don't suppose I need a greenhorn from St. John's to show me that. Then she started to walk fast, fearing you would get too far ahead, and we should take the wrong path. Of course, there was no use in my saying, take your time, young lady, I'm not such a chicken as to get lost in the woods. She simply looked at me with a contemptuous smile which seemed to say, 'what do you know about it, anyway?'"

They all laughed heartily, especially when they saw Will's flushed face, whilst he carried a couple of umbrellas under one arm and a mackintosh on the other.

Norrie's merriment increased as she looked at Philip Weston, bearing in his arms a large tin kettle, two umbrellas and two mackintoshes.

"Say, boys, this is a confounded nuisance!"

"What, Mr. Weston?" asked Norrie, innocently.

"Why, all this rubbish that I'm bringing along with me."

"Philip Weston (and May Dane looked a few inches taller for a time), please to remember that you are bringing me with you, and mark the distinction this minute, sir, between what is rubbish and what is not."

"There is no one here, I'm sure," said Philip, with a glance at each face, and a more serious air than was necessary, "who would for a moment think I'd apply such a term to you, and I only call these rubbish (with a glance at his luggage) because I know they are unnecessary."

"Well, you know, Phil," said Harry, "it's better to bring them, even if we had no rain, than leave them behind and get a wetting."

"We are near the Falls now," said Norrie. "I hear the noise of the water. We can rest then and the sight that will meet our eyes will repay us for our tiresome walk."

And, indeed it did. They soon came to it; first, a level run of water, with trees on each side for some distance, then an immense fall, where the noise of the water drowned their voices. They began to descend, which was no easy matter, as the shelving stones on each side of the falls were jagged and far apart, and in some places slippery, where the water often washed them. There was some trouble, and some fun, getting down; clinging to branches of trees, which would sometimes slip from the hand of the one in advance, and come with a bang into the face of the unfortunate one behind; now, picking their steps over stones, which the water slightly covered.

"Talk of roughing it," roared Philip Weston, trying to make himself heard. "But this is it with a vengeance," as the top of a var[64] bough slapped him in the face and caused him to drop one umbrella. While trying to scramble for it, he got one foot in the water and then came sitting down on the kettle, flattening the handle on the cover. Norrie was trying to subdue her laughter.

"Just wait 'til the rain comes," she said to Lucy. "That will be the cream of it all."

A little distance on, they came to another fall of water, and the scene that met their gaze was like a dream of fairyland; the fall was about fifty feet, and down below, the water seemed suddenly to cease its deafening roar, and flow peacefully and tranquilly along: it ran some hundred yards like this. It was not deep, for the large, flat stones underneath could be seen, and a sure-footed person could cross without much difficulty from one side to the other. Wild flowers grew in abundance on either side, where there were several shady little nooks. They selected the most comfortable of these, and began to prepare their luncheon. The gentlemen made the fire and filled the kettle from the river. None but those who've enjoyed it can imagine what tea in the woods is like, when one's appetite is sharpened by the country air and a long walk, and, all confessed, they were so hungry that they thought it would never be ready.

One cut and buttered the bread, another the cake, someone else sliced the meat, another spread the cloth on the smooth grass, while the gentlemen were busy, opening bottles of pickles, nectar and lemonade.

"I tell you what," said Will Roy, "'twould be a grand life if a fellow could live always like this. I don't wonder at the gypsies loving their life. What do you all say if we form a little company and call ourselves gypsies?"

"Oh! I should love it!" said Lilian Roy, clapping her hands.

"Who would be our queen?" asked Eva Fenton.

Instinctively, all eyes turned towards Norrie.

"I should say, without a doubt," said Frank Dane, "that Miss Moore should be unanimously elected queen of this gypsy band."

"Yes," said Lucy, "Norrie was certainly born to be queen of something."

"Then that settles it," roared Will Roy. "We are gypsies for this day, and Miss Norrie Moore is our queen." And, rising to his feet, cap in hand, he bowed low before her, saying, "Allow me, the humblest of thy subjects, to be the first to salute thee, O queen, and to know the wishes of thy majesty."

"Well," answered Norrie, "her wishes for the present are simple, but very exacting: that you will cease spilling your tea into the cream, take your foot off the cloth, and stop speaking while your mouth is full."

"I call this a right jolly day," said Jack Roy to Eva Fenton, whose quiet, gentle manners charmed him not a little.

"Yes," she answered, "and such a glorious one. Jerry Malone will lose caste[65] in our eyes after today."

"I did not mind what Jerry said," spoke Philip Weston, who had overheard their remarks. "I knew we'd have no rain today; and Brandford would insist on us bringing a pile of unnecessary clothing when an umbrella each would have been sufficient."

Norrie and Harry glanced at the sky, then at each other, and smiled. They had their doubts.

The meal over, the ladies began amusing themselves crossing and re-crossing the river on the stones, which resulted in some slips and wet feet. They then gathered wild flowers, while the gentlemen smoked cigars and Philip Weston, much to May's disgust, began talking politics with Harry Brandford.

Things went on like this for some time. At last the ladies got tired out and, after exploring everything in and around Rocky Falls, the whole party sat down to rest.

"Three o'clock," said Philip, "and no rain yet. I shall certainly have reason to pride myself on my judgment of today."

"Oh, Phil," said Will Roy. "Do give us a rest about your judgment, and don't holler 'til you're out of the woods or you'll jink[66] the fine day."

"Will, I'm shocked at your using such slang," said Lilian.

But, suddenly, as if in response to Will's warning, a large, dark cloud began to spread itself in the heavens, sending down a gloomy aspect on the face of nature, and causing a shade of anxiety to overcast each countenance, and soon, slowly but surely, large heavy drops began to fall.

"A slight sunshower," muttered Phil.

"I hope so," said Frank Dane, in a weak voice.

"Surely 'twould have better manners than to rain on us," said Jack.

"Ha, ha, ha," roared Will. "Make up your mind to it, Johnny. We're in for it. I knew Weston's bragging would jink it."

"I'm afraid we are in for an evening of it," said Harry. "You had better put on all the clothes and rain cloaks you've brought with you, ladies."

"Oh my, it really can't rain," pouted May.

"It will soon let us know whether it can or not," laughed Norrie, enjoying immensely Philip Weston's grim face as he leaned against a tree in silence. They began donning their rain apparel with mingled mirth and grief.

"I think you gentlemen had better set to work and build a bough house,"[67] said Lucy.

"A very wise plan," assented Harry.

They selected a large tree, whose branches spread out some distance and, with the aid of a few more, which they took from other trees, they soon had a temporary though frail protection from the rain. And now it came in heavy showers. Philip Weston stood, as Norrie had predicted, with an umbrella over his head, not deigning to sit under the protection of the friendly tree. Harry walked about outside, trying in vain to kindle into life the few remaining sparks of the fire, as he feared the ladies would take cold. Soon the rain began to penetrate the boughs, so the gentlemen left it to the ladies, selecting the dry spots for them. Will Roy perched himself on top of a large boulder opposite, where he said he would get the full benefit of the shower, and challenged it to come and do its worst.

"How about the gypsy life now?" asked Norrie. "It was all very well while the sun shone and you were eating bread and cake, cream and jam, drinking tea and nectar."

"I gubbs it up," said Will, "as the niggers say to Massa Johnson.

The life doesn't become me, even with such a queen as Miss Moore."

"O coward!" said Norrie. "All the rain in the heavens would not scare me and, I can tell you, I am not going to remain in this cramped position much longer. I'm actually half paralyzed. I must get out and have a run up the rocks and across the river."

Not a word from Philip.

"Oh, Lucy, do look at him," said Norrie. "It's a long time since I've enjoyed anything like this. He holds on to the umbrella as a drowning man to an oar." "Mr. Weston," she said, trying to smother her laughter, "don't you think you ought to take a diploma for being such a judge of the weather?"

"The lay of the land and the play of the winds here confused me a bit," he answered. "I should know better next time."

"How about the rain costumes being a rubbish and nuisance now, Weston?" roared Will. "Oh, you do take the bun for a judge!"[68]

Norrie could stand it no longer; she longed to be out on the rocks where she could laugh and pretend she was not laughing at Philip Weston.

Harry and Lucy alone knew the cause of her mirth, so muffling the latter up well to protect her from the dampness, she issued forth from the shelter, springing lightly and gracefully from rock to rock, now up, now down, now across the river, laughing and enjoying herself to her heart's content, 'til the rain had drenched her brown curls, deepened the bloom on her cheeks, and the sparkle in her eyes. At length their shelter was vacated by all, the rain beginning to come through in every part. Umbrellas were seen pacing briskly to and fro. Philip Weston never left his post near the tree where he first took up his position, nor Will his perch on the boulder. He sang song after song 'til he grew hoarse. At last all the gentlemen except Philip assembled round Harry to hold a consultation.

"Come on!" roared Will, addressing the rain. "Come on as hard as you can! You've done your worst, rain away; bring thunder and lightning, too, for company." Then he saw Harry, together with Frank and Jack, coming up to him. "Say, men, this is beastly to make the best of it."

"Well," laughed Harry, "it seemed as if you thought you would never get enough; you could not remain down below where you might have got a little shelter."

"The girls will get their deaths," said Frank.

"I trust not," said Harry. "The exercise, you know, will keep them from catching cold."

"But what's to be done?" asked Will.

"That's just what we have come up to you about. As far as we are concerned, it's only a laughing matter, but the ladies must run no risk. I am sorry we came today. I was almost sure that it would not hold fine 'til we got into the skiff again. What we propose is this: by taking a short cut across the woods, the distance is not quite a mile to Cape — where Mr. Murphy, with his wife and family live, and the distance to where we meet the skiff is over two, and, besides, they cannot come to meet us 'til sunset. So we must all go to Mr. Murphy's. It's rough travelling, certainly, but it's better than standing here and catching cold. Then, when the ladies have dried their clothing, we can get the loan of a punt or skiff from Mr. Murphy, as we can go by water to the very spot where we are to meet our own."

"Good," roared Will. "Three cheers, hip, hip, hooray!" and he flourished his cap in the air. "Say, Brandford," he went on in a lower voice, "what ails Weston? Is he petrified or glued to that tree?"

"He is put out at the unpleasantness of the weather, I daresay," smiled Harry, "and sorry he said so often we'd have no rain."

Soon their plan was unfolded to the rest of the party, and they were on their journey, with merry jests and laughter, for they all, with the exception of Philip Weston, keenly enjoyed the ludicrousness of their situation.

It was no easy matter for ladies to travel a roughly cut wood-path; some places it was so narrow that they had to go in single file, making, as Norrie said, a sorry-looking band of gypsies. But all things have an ending, and so had their journey. They were thankful to reach the friendly shelter of Mr. Murphy's home, where his good wife and daughter did all in their power for the forlorn picnickers. And after they had rested, taken tea, and dried their clothing somewhat, felt very much refreshed.

The rain had now ceased, and a sweet, refreshing breeze come up, which, Mr. Murphy said, would give them a delightful run with a sail. Soon they were settled comfortably in his large skiff, the sail spread, and on their way to Beach Bay.

"I've heard a great deal of the beauty of Rocky Falls," said Phil Weston, in an undertone to May as he sat near her, "but it shall always have unpleasant recollections for me."

"Phil, I'm really ashamed of you," she said. "You've behaved most foolishly all day. Why, we girls were not afraid of the rain."

"It's not a case of being afraid of the rain, May, but do you think I did not know Miss Moore was laughing at me all day, and delighted when she saw the rain to prove my judgment at fault? And as for that Will Roy, I should like to cut a piece off his tongue."

"That's because you were so serious over it. Why could you not laugh it off and acknowledge you had made a mistake? Norrie is always full of mischief, and cannot help laughing when she sees anyone act as ridiculously as you have today."

"It's bad enough for a fellow to be laughed at and gibed[69] by the whole company all day," said Phil, putting on an injured air, "but to have the one who is dearest in all the world to him tell him it serves him right, is too much."

"Oh, Phil, I did not mean that," said May, with a softened look, slipping her hand into his. "You know you are more to me than Norrie and Will and all of them together and, if I did not care so much about you, I would tell you they were all horrid and you perfection. It is because I do care that I speak plainly so that you won't do the same on a similar occasion."

"Protect me from a similar occasion," smiled Phil, quite pacified now that his lady love, at least, was not laughing at him.

Arriving at Beach Bay, the gentlemen drew the boat upon the shore and assisted the ladies to land. Their own had not yet arrived, for which they were not sorry, for the beauty of the place entranced them.

The beach was long and wide, and covered with soft, fine sand, which seemed like a carpet to the feet but not soft enough to make the walking tiresome. The sand was compressed from being continually washed by the sea, for at times it was covered completely. It was now strewn with pretty shells of various colours. The bay was very wide and the sea rolled in, in big white waves, murmuring to itself in its own deep, mysterious language.

The sun had just set and the moon was rising. Large crimson and gold clouds hung in the heavens, towards where the sun was sinking, and melted into purple, violet and numerous shades 'til they faded into the palest blue, where the moon was rising.

"What a beautiful scene to paint!" said Norrie, as she stood gazing in rapt admiration at sea and sky.

Harry came up to her, saying, "What a pity you have not your drawing materials with you, Miss Moore. You might sketch the outlines and fill in your colours afterwards."

"A sunset painting never satisfies me, Mr. Brandford," she answered. "It falls too far short of the reality."

"Have you ever tried to paint the face of your ideal?" he asked, with (Norrie imagined) a trifle of irony in his voice.

"No," she answered. ("I seldom paint anything from imagination, and never a face.")

"Not even the one you imagine you see in the moon? Surely you could remember that well enough to paint it."

"But I tell you, he is not my ideal."

"And I tell you, Miss Moore, he must be. The face that appears to your imagination, whenever you get thinking of what you would wish your ideal to be like, must surely be the one dearest to you, but then you do not require to call imagination to your aid to paint him, as you have the reality near enough to you at present." Ah! how near he was to the truth without knowing it. He was determined to find out if his suspicions were correct with regard to Frank Dane, to whom he was now alluding.

Norrie started and looked quickly at him.

"What does he mean?" she thought. "Surely he cannot read my thoughts?" "Since you seem to know so much, Mr. Brandford," she answered, with a rather dignified air, "perhaps you will tell me whether it is Mr. Weston or one of the Roys?"

"How carefully she avoids Dane's name," he thought, then said, "There are two you did not name, Frank Dane and my humble self; the latter, of course, is out of the question, as you've given me to understand this morning."

"Then you take it for granted that it is Mr. Dane?"

"Without a doubt," he answered, his suspicions being confirmed as he noticed, even in the twilight, a deep blush o'erspread her face.

"You're the quickest I've ever known for jumping to conclusions, Mr. Brandford. Ah, here is our skiff!" she said, in a relieved tone, as she caught sight of a white sail in the distance.

"I may have jumped quickly," he said, "but not in the wrong direction," and, as she made no reply, thought, "That ends it; silence I suppose gives consent."

The sail home was equally enjoyable, the rippling waves sparkling in the moonlight, the soft varied hues of the sky above, and the rich autumnal tinted verdure of the hills around them, with youth, health and freedom from worldly cares, the dearest possessions of mankind, their portion. And all agreed, even Philip Weston, that taking rain and all into consideration, it was a jolly day.

Will Roy's loud tenor rang out clearly over the moonlit waters in "White wings they never grow weary."[70]

Then Norrie was begged to favour them. She was sitting with Frank Dane in the bow of the boat, and had relapsed into perfect silence.

"What has made you so quiet, Norrie?" asked May.

"I expect her fun for one day is quite exhausted," said Lucy.

"You should be more economical over it, Miss Moore," said Will.

"I shall know better next time," said Norrie, smiling good-naturedly. "There's nothing like making mistakes, you know, for teaching one."

"But that's not the song, Miss Moore," said Frank.

Finding she would not be let off, she sang, in her rich, pathetic voice, "The last rose of summer."[71]

Then Harry was persuaded to give them one more 'ere they reached shore. And his deep musical voice seemed to float over the waters with lingering tenderness in that sweet old love song—

Genevieve, sweet Genevieve,
    The days may come, the days may go,
But still the hands of memory weave,
    The blissful dreams of long ago.[72]

It was with some regret that the boat at last touched land, and the company wended their way to Mrs. Hamilton's, who was not a little anxious since the heavy rain had come. But none of them suffered any bad effects from their wetting. Norrie again accepted Frank Dane's escort to her home, while Jack Roy did the honours for Eva Fenton.

CHAPTER EIGHT

That night, when all else were sleeping, Harry Brandford paced to and fro 'neath the verandah of his dwelling. "And so 'tis over and done with," he thought, "the sweet hope that I've allowed to fill my heart for the past few weeks—beautiful Norrie Moore, with her bright, merry, winsome ways, her pure and candid soul, her loving, faithful heart, can never be mine. I might have known it. I'm too quiet and serious to attract such a gay, light-hearted creature, even if Dane were not before me. Well, may he make you happy, dearest, if he is fortunate enough to win you. Life will be more dreary than ever to me now, for I feel I can never learn to forget. Well, dear one, I will never pain you by speaking of my bitter disappointment. Let us be friends, as we've always been, you said, and I will try to be, no matter how hard the task, for your sweet sake."

At the open window of her bedroom, her chin resting in both hands, her usual attitude when in deep thought, sits Norrie, gazing with large, solemn eyes at the stars. All the buoyancy, sparkle and mischief have left her now; her face wears a pained, thoughtful expression, a look of resolve has settled in the lines of her mouth. "Yes," she thought, "that is what I must do. Lucy and her mother will oppose me, I know, as I promised to wait 'til we'd go together, but I must be firm. I will go with May and Lilian. But, oh, how happy I might be if there was no obstacle—if I could only allow myself. But I will be brave and fight down my own feelings. He thinks Frank Dane and I care for each other, and I let him do so. It is best for a time whatever. How sad he looked when I asked him to let us be friends. I am acting falsely, to him and to myself, but, for Lucy's sweet sake, I will bear it. I wonder, does she think I do not see the pain in her dear face, and how bravely she tries to hide it? She must never suspect my feelings towards him. I don't know whether she is aware that he cares for me or not. I hope she won't know it."

"No, Dr. Hamilton," she went on, an expression more solemn and resolute stealing over her face. "On your death-bed I promised to ever love and care for your Lucy, and did I not wish for something to prove my gratitude for all your kindness? Yes, and I even promised to give up my own happiness if need be to save her pain, and could I accept it now while she suffered? No, a thousand times no. They may think what they will of me, but I will go to St. John's at the end of the month and begin my work. And, then, who knows? Perhaps his heart may turn to her when I am not here, and I shall be glad tho' I may suffer a little."

The next day was a fishing excursion; the gentleman managed to supply the ladies with rods. Frank Dane was Norrie's attendant on this occasion; he kept her flies in order and baited her hook when necessary, whilst Harry saw to Lucy's requirements. They had caught several dozen fine trout, when there seemed to be a great commotion at one part of the pond. Will Roy had secured a very large eel. Of course, all gathered round to inspect it. Norrie did not seem as curious as the others for, she said, eels were no strangers to her, and moved off some distance to attend to her fishing. They must not have been strangers to Harry Brandford either, for he, too, moved off in her direction. He had scarcely spoken a word to her during the day.

"Do you find that rod too heavy for you, Miss Moore?" he asked, in a cold tone of voice.

"Not at all, Mr. Brandford. I like a heavy rod. It just strikes me I have not thanked you for the loan of it."

"There are no thanks necessary," he answered. "I had a fancy to give you that rod, as it is the one you refused to accept the loan of some years ago."

"Yes," said Norrie. "I knew it the moment I had seen it. I remembered the curious carving on this ferrule[73] (pointing to one of them). Is it your name?"

"Not exactly. It is the name in shorthand of the person who gave me the rod, together with the date of the month and year."

The line became tangled on the reel now, and he took the rod to arrange it, resting it against his body as he did so, and the pressure caused a small locket to become detached from his watch chain and fall at Norrie's feet, opening as it touched the ground.

She stooped to pick it up, and handed it to him, saying, "Do you always wear your own picture, Mr. Brandford?"

He looked at her with a curious smile. "My own picture?" he

repeated. "I certainly would not do anything so foolish. You do not know me as well as you do my rod. Take another look (as he handed it back to her) and tell me if you think it's me."

She took it, glancing from him to the picture several times.

"Oh, no," she said slowly. "I see now it's not you, tho' very like. The features are the same but the expression is entirely different."

"In what way?" he asked.

"Well," she said, hesitatingly, "the eyes have not such a deep, thoughtful expression, and the face is brighter looking. You know, Mr. Brandford, you often, when your features are in repose, have a rather grave expression. I should say it was your brother, if you had one, or yours when you were"—and she stopped suddenly, looking rather confused.

"Mine when I was what, or where?" he asked.

"I was going to say, yours when you were perfectly happy."

"That time never was," he said, "unless when I was a very young child, nor do I think it ever will be."

"But you surely cannot be very unhappy, Mr. Brandford?"

"I do not say that I am. I say that I've never been, nor never expect to be, perfectly happy. In fact, it's not to be found in this world."

"But don't you expect to have as much as there is allotted in this world?"

"No! I don't even expect that."

"But, why?" she persisted.

For answer, he looked at her without speaking, a steady, reproachful gaze, which made her tender heart go out to him more yearningly than ever.

"You had better take your rod now," he said, handing it to her. "I've just seen some fine trout jumping. October is the best month for this pond. May I have the pleasure of escorting you and Miss Hamilton here then?"

"I am sorry to say I cannot come then, as I hope to open school in St. John's by the first of next month."

"Oh!" and Norrie thought his voice grew colder as he spoke. "I thought you did not intend opening 'til the first of next year."

"Nor did I 'til a few days ago."

"Does not care to remain long after Dane goes," he thought. Aloud he said, "I suppose you've taken advantage of the woman's privilege of changing your mind?"

"It's not a mere matter of changing my mind," she said, "but I cannot bear my life here, so dull and inactive, when I've work before me."

"Of course, it's only quite natural you should feel so, especially when the present company leaves." It was said so coldly, and matter of fact, that Norrie thought, "Perhaps after all he does not care as much as I think."

"Dane is coming over, and I must attend to Miss Hamilton," he said. "Goodbye!"

"But you have not told me whose picture you wear yet, Mr. Brandford."

"Only a cousin and namesake of mine, who has been in the United States for the past ten years," as he moved off in the direction of Lucy.

A few days later, Norrie entertained the visitors in her own home. Mrs. Brandford was quite indignant when she found Harry and the other gentlemen were going. "That girl does not know how to keep her own place," she thought.

Soon after this came the first open breach between her and her stepson. At Harry's suggestion, she had decided to give an evening party to his young friends. She entered into the thing with unusual zest, and determined to have, as she said, a ball on a small scale.

There were several other gentlemen besides Harry's visitors staying at St. Rose for the shooting season,[74] with whom she was acquainted, so that she could count on ten.

Now, to secure an equal number of young ladies was more difficult. Harry named several nice girls of the place, but she would not hear of them.

At last she decided to invite a few of her aristocratic friends from town. The coastal steamer would not be coming at the time appointed for the ball, and the nearest railway station to St. Rose was some miles distant, so it was arranged to meet the guests with their own new and pretty little schooner.

Before sending out the invitations to those in St. Rose, Mrs. Brandford handed them to Harry to read. As he finished the last one, he seemed rather puzzled.

"Why, Mother! You've forgotten Miss Moore," he said (looking much displeased).

Mrs. Brandford only stared, in haughty surprise, at her stepson.

"Forgotten whom?" she asked.

"I think I've spoken very plainly, Mother, and your hearing is not at fault." It was the last time he ever addressed her by that name.

"Harry Brandford, surely you do not for a moment imagine that because Mrs. Hamilton and Mrs. Dane are foolish enough to overlook Nora Moore's inferiority of birth, that I'm going to do the same. I did not forget her, because I never, for an instant, entertained the smallest idea of inviting her."

"Then you will have to entertain it now, Mrs. Brandford, for if this evening party, or whatever you choose to call it, takes place here, Miss Moore is to be invited."

He spoke with calm determination, and Mrs. Brandford felt that this was to be the hardest fought battle between them yet; but, she told herself, she would win. He had, on several occasions, given way to her, simply to save trouble between them; for as she was his father's widow, he always respected her and wished to do so still, tho' he was determined now at any cost that Norrie should not be slighted.

"You choose to be very dictatorial, Harry, but it makes no difference with my decision."

"I repeat, Mrs. Brandford, that Miss Moore is to be invited."

She thought it wiser to curb her indignation somewhat, and try to reason with him, but it was all to no avail, for it only seemed to anger him.

At last her pent-up passion burst forth in all its fury; she rose to her feet, saying, as she moved towards the door, "Since it is useless wasting words on you, and you forget yourself so far as to dare to ask me to invite a low-born fisher girl (because she managed to scrape up an education through the mistaken charity of fools, whose favour she was clever enough to win), amongst refined ladies and gentlemen, I shall leave you to cool off the heat of your temper somewhat."

Harry moved quickly to the door, placing his hand on it. "When you have written out Miss Moore's invitation, you may leave the room, but not 'til then."

"Do you intend to make me a prisoner, sir?"

"'Til you've done as I tell you," he answered.

"That I shall never do, Harry Brandford. Nora Moore," she sneered, "may be well enough to go on excursions through the woods—it's what she's best used to, and very well for you or Frank Dane to flirt with, since you chose to forget yourselves so far—but I do not think her good enough to associate with my friends." Harry grew very white.

"Mrs. Brandford," he said, "were you a man, I should strike you for these words. As you are a woman, and my father's widow, I am ashamed of and despise you. You are right in one thing: Miss Moore is not your equal, for she is as far above you as the angels are above Satan. Now, Mrs. Brandford, since you've put me to it, I must remind you that this house is mine, and, but for the courtesy due my guests, and the unpleasant remarks it might create, I would forbid the whole thing taking place. But should you persist in refusing to write out the invitation in question, at any cost, I shall put a stop to it. Remember, I say at any cost."

Mrs. Brandford fairly held her breath. She knew what he said was true, and that he would keep his word.

"You do not mean to say you will be ungentlemanly enough to stop it when the invitations have been sent to St. John's, and perhaps the party on their way?"

"I mean to say I'll be ungentlemanly enough for that, if you choose to think so. I will leave you now for an hour, and when I return I shall expect to be shown the invitation, written out," and with a white, sad face, and a deep sigh, as he glanced at his dead mother's picture over the mantel, he left her.

At first she decided not to do it. "Let him do his worst," she thought, but then the humiliation of having to inform her high-toned friends that the ball on a small scale, to which they were invited, was not to take place, she could not bear. "If I could only write it out so coldly that she would not accept it," she thought, "but I cannot, for he will be sure to read it." So with no small amount of repugnance, it was at last completed. She would not remain in the room until he returned, but left the note open, on the desk near the others. When Harry entered an hour afterwards, he read it, sealed and addressed them all, and sent a messenger with them immediately.

"You've gained your point, Master Harry," thought Mrs. Brandford, as she watched the boy go, from her bedroom window. "But I shall be even with you by making Nora Moore sorry she ever got that invitation. At first, I wished I could word the note in a curt manner, thinking it might prevent her accepting; now I am glad I could not do so, for I will snub her unmercifully." The thought seemed to please her immensely, for she went downstairs with a triumphant smile. "He shall see what asserting that iron will of his will cost him when he finds the rustic beauty slighted by my friends."

CHAPTER NINE

Two days after, Mrs. Brandford was seated in her private room, with her housekeeper—a woman nearly as old as her mistress, and who had lived with the latter since she was married to Mr. Brandford. The woman always tried to please her employer and was attached to her after a fashion, for, of course, it was to her interest to cater to all the proud lady's whims and pretend she thought her incapable of wrongdoing. Mrs. Brandford sometimes became very confidential with her, and often alluded to the mesalliance[75] she had made when she married Mr. Brandford, and to some of the doings of her high-toned ancestors: of the good blood which flowed in her veins. The housekeeper often did the work of secretary, too, for she was educated to a certain degree. Her occupation now was reading to her mistress the answers to her invitations. She had finished all but one, when she made the remark, "not one refusal unless this is."

"Refusal," repeated Mrs. Brandford, indignantly. "That is what I've never yet received to any invitation I have ever given. This must be Nora Moore's. There's not the slightest chance of her refusing; she is only too glad to come and exhibit her so-called talents. It's hardly worthwhile reading it. I suppose, tho', we may as well hear what she says."

"Please excuse my presumption, dear Mrs. Brandford, but I'm really surprised at your inviting that girl here."

"My inviting her is not more surprising to you than being almost forced to do so was to me, tho' certainly, I could have withheld the invitation on condition (she did not name it). But since Mr. Harry became so stubborn over it, I decided to ask her; in fact, I'm glad she's coming, as I intend to make her realize her position socially, and keep her in her proper place for the future. Read it,

Jane; quickly, I'm in a hurry."

The woman opened Norrie's little note. Written, in a firm, clear hand, were the words:

Miss Moore declines the honour of Mrs. Brandford's invitation for the 15th inst.

Mrs. Brandford looked up with a dazed expression. "She has actually dared to refuse my invitation," she managed to say at last.

"I don't know what it is that Norrie Moore would not dare do," murmured Jane.

"Go and ask Mr. Brandford to come here immediately," she ordered. "Quick, tell him it's on important business," and she paced the room as if it was not half large enough for her.

In a few minutes Harry appeared in the doorway. "What is it?" he asked, icily.

"Look at that," she said, pointing to the open note on the table.

He advanced, glanced at it and smiled.

"You laugh," she said. "Is it on purpose to humiliate me that you insisted on me inviting that girl here? Did you have it planned with her to refuse, and in such a curt manner, too?"

"Planning and scheming belong to such natures as yours, Mrs. Brandford. Ladies and gentlemen always deal openly. I will reply to your first question by saying that I insisted on Miss Moore being invited because I would not allow her to be slighted, but I'm not at all surprised at her refusing; in fact, I half expected it."

"And yet you allowed the invitation to be sent?"

"Certainly," he said, quite coolly. "I can understand her motive. Hers is such a sensitive disposition that she could not go where she knows she's not welcome. She is aware of your aversion towards her, and has, perhaps, made a shrewd guess as to how reluctantly the invitation was sent."

"It's what I've always said," went on the indignant woman. "Ill-breeding is sure to come to the surface some time."

"Since when is it counted ill-breeding for a lady to refuse an invitation which is distasteful to her?" asked Harry. "And another question, Mrs. Brandford (as she seemed at a loss for an answer). Why does Miss Moore's refusal seem to affect you so much, since her presence is so annoying to you?" He gazed at her so sternly and searchingly that her eyes fell. "I see," he said, turning disgustedly away, for he seemed to read her thoughts with those calm, grey eyes of his. "No doubt instinct has warned the poor girl of what would have been in store for her."

So the ball came off and was a success. The visitors from town were charmed. Norrie's refusal of Mrs. Brandford's invitation excited some curiosity amongst their own little party. Lucy and her mother knew the real cause, for, as Harry had suspected, she felt sure he must have interfered or it would not have been sent. Lucy did not care to go but, of course, could not refuse on account of her guests.

Two days afterwards, the gentlemen visitors returned to town, as their business places required them, together with the six young ladies Mrs. Brandford had invited from there. May and Lilian were to remain 'til the end of September, and Norrie had decided to go with them. Next day she told Mrs. Hamilton and Lucy of her intention. They remonstrated and coaxed, but all to no purpose. And at last they seemed displeased altogether, which hurt Norrie very much, but, remembering her object, was determined to carry out her resolution, and immediately sent her card to be published in the leading papers.

"I always thought you loved me as much as I do you, Norrie," said Lucy, a few days before her departure.

"And what makes you think differently now, dear?" asked Norrie, throwing her arms round her.

"Because you know how dull and lonely I shall be when you are gone, and, besides, you promised to remain and go with Mamma and me before Christmas."

"Lucy, you ought to know I would do more than that for you, but I cannot stay on idling here 'til then, and living on Uncle John. I feel as if I must be at something, and you know I never had much taste for the work here. Besides, it will be but a few weeks 'til you and your mother come on."

"Then, spend the remainder of the year with us, Norrie dear," said kind-hearted Mrs. Hamilton.

"Thank you a thousand times, dear Mrs. Hamilton," she said, with tears of gratitude. "It makes me feel very unhappy not to accept your generosity on this occasion, but I really cannot. It would only hurt my uncle and aunt, for they've never complained in the least of having me, and perhaps cause a great many unkind things to be said of them. So you and Lucy will forgive me, I know, for having my own way this time." And there was nothing for them but to be resigned.

So the day of departure dawned at last. Harry and Lucy stood on the pier watching the steamer as she slowly moved off. Harry had spoken but few words to Norrie during the past few weeks.

She gave him but little opportunity for doing so.

"Do not work too hard," he said as he held her hand when saying goodbye, gazing at her with his habitual half-sad expression. "Remember 'tis easier to lose strength than to gain it, and teaching is a very trying occupation."

"I only hope I shall get plenty of work," she answered. "I do not think it will injure my health. I am very strong, you know," and she smiled that sweet, sunny smile of hers.

"I shall be in town myself about the New Year," he said. "It is only then we get our business settled up here."

"I shall be glad to see you, Mr. Brandford. I am very, very sorry leaving dear Lucy. Take good care of her and keep up her spirits 'til she gets over her loneliness." "If he would only take care of her always, and love her as she does him, how happy it would make me," she thought, as the distance widened between them, and they faded from view.

There were a great number of passengers on board, and Norrie, May and Lilian occupied the same stateroom as it contained three berths. Lilian and May were very poor sailors but Norrie was only seasick one day; after that she could remain on deck all the time. On the day before their arrival in town, she was sitting in the stern of the ship on a coil of rope, her arms leaning on the rail, thinking deeply on what lay before her. She had counted out the contents of her purse, and the sum was small indeed. She should have to find some quiet, cheap lodgings 'til she could afford better. Then there was a classroom to be rented and a piano to be hired. She felt she had to face many difficulties, but she was brave and hopeful. She would do her best and trust the rest to providence.

"I must go below," she said at last, "and see how they are getting on."

She entered the stateroom, bright and smiling, singing, "A life on the ocean wave."[76]

"Oh, girls, what a pity you cannot come on deck. It's glorious. I really believe 'twould cure you. Do let me help you up."

"Oh, Norrie, I could not stir for worlds," moaned May, as she lay on her pillow with closed eyes and a white face.

"Could you try, Lilian?" she asked.

"I hardly know, Norrie," she answered. "I don't think I'm as bad as May tho'. Perhaps it would revive me a little if I could get on deck."

"Certainly, dear, it would. Let me help you." And soon she had her settled comfortably on deck, and then went below to try and induce May to come. She found her sitting up in her berth.

"I felt well enough to go with Lilian," she said, "but I wanted to see you alone, and this, I know, is the only chance before we reach town." And taking Norrie's hand, she said, "I want you to do me a great favour, tho' I know it is something you will not like, but it would give Mother and me great pleasure if you will only grant it."

"If there is anything in my power that would give you and your mother pleasure," Norrie replied, "you've but to name it, May dear, and it shall be done."

"It will demand a little sacrifice on your part, that is all, dear," said May.

"I should not think anything a sacrifice that would add to your and your mother's pleasure, May, for next to Lucy and her mother, I love you both, better than anyone else in the world."

"Well, now for the favour," said May. "Give up your idea of opening school for the present and come and stay with me 'til my marriage, which takes place about the last of November."

"Oh, May (reproachfully), how can you ask me to do this?"

"And I say, oh Norrie, how can you refuse? Remember, you've given your promise beforehand."

"But, May, you'll not keep me to it, for I gave it, never dreaming it was this. I could not do it really. Don't ask me any more, dear."

"Well, Norrie Moore, this is the first favour I've ever asked of you, and you refuse to grant it. And just fancy me, with so much to be done, and no sister. Lucy would get ill in town at this time of the year, and Mother will have her hands full of lots of things, and I shall have no one to go shopping with me, nor to tell me how anything becomes me."

"But, May, I could go to you every day when school is over," said Norrie eagerly.

"Why, what do you think you're made of?" said May. "I would not dream of taking up your time. Once you open school, that will be quite enough for you to attend to."

"Could not Lilian go?" pleaded Norrie. "Or Miss Weston?"

"But I don't want Lilian or Miss Weston," pouted May.

"I want you. They have no taste in harmonizing colours as you have."

"Oh May, if it were only something else."

"Oh, of course, the sacrifice is too great, I suppose," said May, appearing to be vexed, or she knew this was the surest way of gaining her point.

"It's not that, May. You know," said Norrie, "refusing your kind request would be the greater sacrifice."

"Well, then, what is it?"

"What will Mrs. Hamilton and Lucy think of me? And they wanted me to remain with them 'til they were coming."

"I told them both," said May, "when bidding them goodbye, that I would use every means to induce you to stay with me, and they said they hoped I would succeed. I also wrote Mother to the same effect last mail."

Norrie remained in deep thought for some time, her companion watching her anxiously. "I'll tell you what, May," she said at last, "let us make a compromise. I'll give up opening the regular classes which I intended for a while longer, but you know your mother has been kind enough to secure some pupils for me, and I could go out to these with a few others if I get them, and just give a certain number of lessons weekly."

"Very well," said May, delightedly. "Mother and I shall limit the number tho'."

So all the economical planning was set aside for the present, and Norrie once more took up her residence with the Danes.

CHAPTER TEN

Frank's delight knew no bounds when he found that Norrie was to be once more an inmate of his home. He seemed to be always looking for some little service to render her or some attention to show her. The music and painting lessons were limited to six in the week, two every second day, and she was paid well for them. Frank determined, if he could do it, that she should never take any more, for he intended, after May's marriage, to speak of his love to her and ask her to be his wife.

The days seemed to fly past, and soon there were but a few left before May's wedding. Philip Weston and Norrie became better friends and grew so confidential that he told her he knew she was laughing at him that day at Rocky Falls and delighted at all the mishaps he had made.

"Yes," she laughingly acknowledged, "and more delighted at the mistake you made about the rain than I was at anything else."

Norrie was to be first bridesmaid, and Frank Dane best man. The wedding day came at last, soft and sunny for that time of the year. They were married in the morning and started a few hours after on their wedding tour, which was to last about six months, as they were to visit parts of Ireland, England, and return by way of America. May Weston, when bidding goodbye to Norrie, extracted from her a promise that she would not leave her mother 'til after the Christmas holidays. Mrs. Dane grew very fond of her and said one day that she should insist on her making her home with them after she had opened school.

December set in, clear and frosty. About one week before Christmas, Lucy and her mother arrived in town. Norrie told herself all along that her first glance at Lucy's face would tell her if her wishes were fulfilled, and her darling made happy. But, no,

Lucy looked well, happy too, everyone would say, but Norrie, who knew every expression of that dear face, noticed the oft-times sad and pained expression there. On Christmas Eve, both girls busied themselves decorating the house with evergreen, pretty ferns, and bright holly, for they knew at this season Mrs. Dane would miss more than ever her dear, absent daughter, and, so, did all in their power to make up for her absence. Lucy retired early, as she was tired and did not feel well, but Norrie remained to hear the joy-bells ring in the Christmas morn. She and Frank stood in the open doorway. It was a clear, beautiful night, with just a few snowflakes gently falling, shrouding the earth in a soft, white mantle, and seeming to obey the voice of the deep-toned bells by giving to nature the aspect of their tidings, "Peace on earth, good will to men."[77]

"I wonder," said Norrie, "what changes will there be when the bells again ring in the Christmas morn?"

"Perhaps none, perhaps many," said Frank. "What changes would you wish?"

"I did not say I'd wish any," she answered, "but I should like a great many all the same."

"I should wish one only," said Frank.

"You are very moderate, indeed, Mr. Dane. Have you any objections to telling me what that one change is?"

"No, Norrie," he said, taking her hand. "It is the very thing for which I've followed you out here."

Norrie felt a trifle uneasy, tho' she could scarcely tell why, and wished she had remained in her own room to listen to the bells.

"I should like," went on Frank, "to be standing just where I am, this night twelve months, with you by my side, not as Norrie Moore, but as Norrie Dane, my dear and cherished wife. You cannot help knowing, dear, that I've cared for you for a long time now. Even before you went to St. Rose last August, I intended to speak to you, but, one night, if you remember, you told me you were still heart-whole and fancy-free, and, knowing the candour of your disposition, my hopes were crushed, but I did not give up. I concluded to wait 'til I should have another opportunity of winning even a small share of your affections, and I'm not sure yet if I've won even a thought of yours. But I ask you to try and care a little for me, and my own love and devotion will make up for whatever is wanting in yours. Promise, Norrie, that you will give up this tiresome task of teaching and become my wife soon."

A great temptation came to her to consent; it would be the surest way of not interfering with her friend's happiness. Knowing that she was the wife of another, Harry would perhaps think more of Lucy, and, being constantly in her company, surely could not help learning to love her. But it only lasted for a moment. She was too true a woman to marry a man to whom she could not give the love which is his due, and also to wrong that man, by marrying him, merely to secure the happiness of another. She answered him calmly, kindly, but firmly.

"No, Frank, you have not won that place in my heart which you say you've hoped to, but you wrong me by saying you are not sure of ever winning a thought of mine, for I've often thought of you, as I do your mother and sister, with gratitude and affection. But, Frank, I'm sorry if it pains you to say it. I could never care for you as I would wish to care for the man I should marry."

"Oh, Norrie, don't you think you might learn to care even a little for me in time? You have no idea, nor can I tell you in words how dear you are to me, tho' you've never given me reason to hope. Still, I feel bitterly disappointed. Think well, Norrie, and take time to answer me, for I hardly dare think what effect this disappointment may have on me."

"No, Frank, it's kinder to you and to myself, when I know that nothing could ever change my feelings towards you, to tell you so now, and it shall be my final answer. And, Frank, you would be no true man if you let such a small thing affect you. The world is full of women, and, believe me, you'll find one far better and more worthy of you in every way than I am."

"Then, Norrie, you are decided that I'm to expect no other answer?"

"Yes, Frank, I'm decided, without the smallest doubt. It may seem unkind to you now that I speak so plainly, but in time to come you'll know it's for the best."

"In time to come," he repeated bitterly. "It's quite easy for you to moralize. Goodness only knows where I'll be in time to come. Well, good night, or morning rather," and he left her.

Norrie would have given anything that Frank Dane had not spoken to her as he had. She could judge from her own experience that he must be suffering, and she felt deeply sorry for him. It prevented her from being her usually bright self on Christmas Day, much to everyone's astonishment. Before a week had passed, all noticed the restraint and coolness between her and Frank, and guessed the cause. And if Mrs. Dane did seem a trifle cooler to Norrie, we must make some allowance. He was her only son, good and handsome, and, like every mother, she wondered how any girl could resist him. Norrie had advertised her classes to open the first Monday after the New Year. Of course, she could not think of remaining longer in Frank Dane's home, and she wished also to be where she would not meet Harry often. She had engaged two rooms only, a classroom and bedroom, from an old lady with whom she was also to board. Mrs. Dane, of course, knew 'twould be both useless and unwise to ask Norrie to remain longer.

"It seems as if we are continually separating now, Norrie," said Lucy, on the day of her departure from them.

"Yes," she answered sadly. "I shall miss you and your mother so much, but you'll come and see me often, won't you, dear?"

"Certainly, whenever you are at leisure. But you'll come to us often also?"

"Not often, Lucy. It would not be quite right, I suppose, after what has happened. Your aunt is a little cool with me ever since, too, and it hurts me to see it."

"I know, Norrie, and I think it's a downright shame. I'm sure you could not help Frank falling in love with you."

So, that night Norrie slept in her new home for which her labours were to pay, and next day Harry Brandford arrived in town. He expected to find her still at Mrs. Dane's and was disappointed when he called. To Lucy he said, "It would have been kinder for them to have made Miss Moore remain here. It must be dull for her living almost alone. I suppose tho' she will spend all her leisure hours here."

"No, she will spend very little time here, but I know Aunt would have insisted on her remaining, only for what happened."

"Why? What happened?" said Harry, looking surprised.

"I suppose I ought not to tell you," said Lucy, hesitatingly. "It's a breach of confidence, but I cannot explain her non-appearance here unless I do. She refused to marry Frank, that's all."

Harry simply nodded and asked no further questions.

"Has your mother come with you?" asked Lucy.

"Mrs. Brandford came," he answered.

"She does not stay with you, I suppose?"

"No, she is staying with some friends of hers, and I am at the Atlantic."[78]

After arranging with Lucy to call on Norrie that same evening, he took his leave.

"What a fool I've been," he thought, "to take so much for granted. She must not have cared for Dane after all; she is free still, and I'm at liberty to win her if I can."

CHAPTER ELEVEN

Norrie was sitting by a cozy little fire in the classroom, looking over some drawings of her pupils, when Harry and Lucy arrived.

She was just feeling a little bit lonely, she told them, and it looked like old times to see them coming together.

"So you've got your heart's desire, and are into work hard and fast," said Harry, looking gravely at her. "You will have to be careful tho'; I fancy you're not looking quite so well as when you left home."

"If I'm not," said Norrie, smiling, "it must be that idling does not agree with me, for that's what I've been doing since I came. It's only today that I've really begun work."

"And now, you are living in a little home of your own," said Harry, glancing around the room.

"Yes," answered Norrie, proudly, "and this has to be sitting-room and classroom, too. I cannot afford more at present."

"What an economical little lady you are!" laughed Harry. "What hour is work over every day?"

"At four," she answered.

"Well, we must make you take some open-air exercise, such as walking, sleighing and skating. Miss Hamilton and myself will call for you every evening at four."

"Oh, that will be delightful," said Lucy.

How glad Norrie felt that he included Lucy with them.

The month of January passed pleasantly away. Norrie went a little oftener now to see Mrs. Dane, and the coolness was wearing away somewhat, but Frank was always cold and polite almost to freezing point. They spent several evenings at Lilian Roy's, an evening at Miss Weston's, several at Mrs. Dane's; they attended concerts, theatres, and had plenty of sleighing and skating. But

Norrie's hopes with regard to Lucy and Harry were shattered. She was growing nervous and morbid from the constant restraint she had placed upon herself. She knew now that he would never care for Lucy, and her own heart was going out to him more and more every day. He was her attendant on every possible occasion. If only she could get away somewhere, for, be happy with him while Lucy was miserable, she never would. Sometimes, when sitting near him, she would fancy Lucy was looking at her with pained, reproachful eyes, then she would make some excuse and leave him.

Lucy Hamilton was well aware now of Harry's love for Norrie, and was trying to bear up bravely, but she could not understand her, for she had not the least idea that her own secret was suspected, nor of the sacrifice Norrie was making all these months for her sake; but there was not the smallest atom of envy in her gentle nature towards her friend.

Harry, too, was puzzled beyond measure; he felt sure now that Norrie cared something for him, but what her motive was for always avoiding him, he could not understand. He wondered if it was pride, because she thought herself not his equal in position; he made up his mind to find out soon.

Norrie now had another trouble. Frank Dane, who had hitherto been a model young man, had of late taken to bad habits, staying out late at night, taking more wine than was good for him. He felt that Harry's deep, quiet but everlasting love for Norrie would win her yet, and he was weak-minded enough to let this knowledge make him desperate, and careless of his duties.

"I think I must have been born to give trouble to those who are always kind to me," she often thought.

One evening, the whole party set out for a few hours' skating on Quidi Vidi Lake. It was just the day for it, calm, frosty and bright. There had been rain for some days, which had melted the snow, and the surface of the lake, from the King's Bridge down past Pleasantville (the name of the principal hotel[79] situated near), was one immense sheet of smooth ice. The scene which met their view was something to be remembered. The glittering surface, filled with skaters; the bright steel of their skates flashing in the sunlight as they glided gracefully over the ice; the gay-coloured dresses and wraps of the ladies, varying in hues. The sloping snow-clad hills on either side made the lake appear as a valley. The sky was soft and blue as a summer's sky, with big, white, fleecy clouds rolling lazily thro' it.

Lucy was a little timid on the ice and not sorry for the support of Will Roy's arm. But Norrie was perfectly at home, and flew away with lightning-like rapidity, disdaining any support. Harry started off in pursuit. She saw him several times making up to her, and skated on more swiftly, making a number of unnecessary turns to avoid him. Her strength as a skater could not long hold out against his, and at last she stopped, like a stag brought to bay. Her cheeks glowing, her eyes sparkling, she turned and faced him with the words, "Why do you follow me, Mr. Brandford?"

She did not say them angrily, but in a distressed tone of voice, which seemed to imply, "It's no use. Why do you not cease?"

"Why do you fly from me, Miss Moore?" was Harry's response. "Answer my questions and I shall immediately answer yours."

Ah, why did she? She wished with all her heart she could tell him, but Lucy's secret must not be betrayed. She took his offered arm and in silence they skated on at a somewhat slower pace.

"Are you going to answer my question, Norrie?" He often called her that now.

"No, Mr. Brandford, I cannot, except to say what you already know, that it is to avoid you."

"But why do you wish to avoid me? Is my presence distasteful to you?"

"No!"

"Are you afraid of me?"

"No."

"Then what is it?"

"Oh, don't ask me," she said, with a heavy sigh. "I only know I'm in everybody's way, and I wish everybody, men in particular, would let me alone."

"That is the penalty which every fair woman has to pay. The men will not let them alone, and there are few who would wish them to, either. You, I think, are about the only one I've heard express the wish. You do not wish to lead the life of a recluse, do you, Norrie?"

"No, far from it. I enjoy life too much for that. I like pleasure and happiness, but I do not like bringing trouble to people as I always seem to be."

"That is only your own idea. I don't know anyone to whom you've brought trouble. You cannot help the sins of others, and I think Frank Dane cowardly to hold you responsible for his."

"I did not say anything about him," said Norrie.

"No, but you think about him and allow the way he is behaving to trouble you more than is necessary. Believe me, my child, there is no fault on your side. You acted as any true woman should have done under the circumstances."

"How do you know that I think about him?"

He looked at her silently for some time, then said, "Do you think anything could trouble you and I not find out what it is? Do you think there is one pleasure of yours that I do not enjoy for your sake, or a thought I do not understand?"

"You cannot know all my thoughts," she answered, looking quickly at him.

"You need not look so frightened," he smiled. "I do not know the cause of your avoidance of me, but I trust I shall know it soon. I would rather die, Norrie, than force my companionship upon you, did I not know that you cared something for me. Forgive me if in my presumption I made a mistake, but I don't think I do. I did make a very stupid one last summer at St. Rose, and you, mischievous little lady, would not undeceive me. But I won't trouble you for an answer now, child. I see you are pained and troubled about something, and not prepared to give one. Neither do I intend to pry into this secret of yours, but should it continue much longer to be an impediment to our happiness, I shall feel myself in duty-bound to insist on your confiding to me the nature of it, and allowing me to judge. Will you promise to do this some day, dear?" He looked at her so earnestly and with such a winning, pleasing expression in his eyes that she had to battle with herself, to keep from saying, "The impediment is of my own making. I can break it when I please, and will do so now if you tell me to."

The remembrance of her promise to Doctor Hamilton alone restrained her. "No!" she answered at last. "I can never tell you what it is, Harry, and it must always remain a secret. I would rather you did not ask me to do so now nor at any other time."

"Then it must not be the means of making us unhappy. I shall insist on this some time very soon, Norrie."

After that day she loved and admired him more than ever. His manner was so gentle, so full of consideration, so deferential, and yet so masterful. She felt that she should never hold out against him, if he once set his mind on winning from her the confession he spoke of, and, day after day, it became harder to resist him.

'Ere they left the lake, the moon had risen round, soft and full; it appeared between two snow-clad hills which form the background of what is called Quidi Vidi Gut, and shed its soft, mellow light over all, making the beauty of the scene entrancing.

"How glorious for a winter's evening!" remarked Norrie.

"Yes," assented Harry. "I shall never forget this evening, not merely for its beauty tho'. Bye the bye," speaking in a lighter tone, "how about your ideal? Do you ever see him now?"

"I've given up looking," she said evasively.

"Norrie, will you tell me whose face always appeared to you when you tried to find your ideal in the moon?" he asked.

"I'll promise to do so some day, if you'll only not tease me about it now," she answered, blushingly.

"Very well, then, it's a bargain. I won't tease you now, but I think I can guess whose it was."

From that evening, Harry seemed to take more complete charge of her, and, strange to say, with all a woman's clear insight and perception of things, it was only now that Mrs. Hamilton began to notice that Norrie, and not her idolized daughter, was the attraction for Harry Brandford. Then she noticed Lucy at times looking sad and depressed, and with all a mother's anxiety, questioned her on the subject. Lucy assured her mother that Harry never gave her any reason to think that he regarded her in any other light than that of a dear friend. And also, that she had known he cared for Norrie for some time.

"And does she return his affection?" asked Mrs. Hamilton.

"That is what I cannot find out," answered Lucy.

"I should think you and Norrie ought to have no secrets between you. Have you never asked her?"

"No, Mamma," she answered, wearily, the fact being that his name was seldom mentioned between them, for neither would trust herself.

"And," continued Mrs. Hamilton, looking anxiously at her daughter, "have you nothing more than a friendly affection for him?"

"Oh, Mamma! Do not ask me those questions," but she was no longer deceived. With a passionate burst of tears, which she could not overcome, Lucy threw herself in her mother's arms and sobbed out her grief.

"How contrary things go in this world," mused Mrs. Hamilton. "Now, if Norrie would only marry Frank, then I know Harry would learn to love Lucy in time." It had piqued her somewhat to know that Norrie had won the affections which she once thought were her daughter's, for even in the heart of the most perfect, and Mrs. Hamilton was one of these, little atoms of resentment, unreasonableness and partiality for one's own will sometimes find a resting place.

CHAPTER TWELVE

Lucy was not without admirers; she and Norrie attracted much attention wherever they went. Many questions were asked regarding Norrie. When they entered a concert room or a theatre, murmurs such as "Who is that tall, graceful girl with Miss Hamilton? Who is that pretty, bright-looking girl with the stately carriage?" The answers were generally, "A Miss Moore from St. Rose, a friend of the Danes."

Many young gentlemen took no small amount of trouble to procure an introduction but, as her home was not with Mrs. Dane, she did not receive as many invitations as Lucy. And besides, her duties prevented her accompanying them many places, for she had met with great success, and had now many private lessons to give, after the regular classes for the day were ended.

Thus the winter passed speedily and, almost before they were aware of it, spring was upon them. Easter was early this year, and great preparations were being made for the annual Irish Ball,[80] to take place at that season. Lucy and Mrs. Hamilton insisted on Norrie going with them. All her friends were to attend: the Roys, Miss Weston, Harry and Frank, and a number of other acquaintances. Soon after, Harry was to depart for St. Rose, as his duties awaited him with the spring business.

The night of the Ball arrived at last. Norrie was to dress at Mrs. Dane's. She and Lucy had looked forward to it with much pleasure: they wore pure white, and their dresses, cut square at the neck, were a mixture of satin, lace and flowers. Both girls looked beautiful, but Norrie was simply radiant, and, as she entered the ballroom, her queenly figure became the centre of attraction. Her programme was soon filled. Harry was not a dancing man and probably only attended the Ball for Norrie's sake, but he managed to secure from her the first and last dance, with a few between. Harry was well known in town; he was decidedly the finest man present. Norrie was a stranger to a great many, and soon it was whispered about that they were really engaged, much to the disappointment of many a fair damsel. Lucy, also, had plenty of partners; Harry danced with her twice, after one of which he congratulated her on fulfilling the prophecy he had made regarding her some time ago, of having half the young men in St. John's in love with her.

"Yes, ballroom love," said Lucy, with a quiet smile. "It's not worth much; it generally ends with the ball, does it not?"

"That all depends on the lady. If you were a flirt now, you would have each one thinking himself the favoured individual, and so keep it up as long as you choose. But then you're not that. You are a good, true and wise little woman, who does not trouble her head about love or lovers, 'til the right one comes along: I suppose he has not appeared yet, has he, Lucy?"

This was a trying question for her to answer, so she adopted the Irish style of replying to one question by asking another, and said, "What do you mean by the right one?"

"Why, the one to whom all other men appear to you as shadow—the one you will marry."

"No," she answered, slowly. "The one I shall marry has not yet appeared. But, what about you, Harry? I think you have at last reached that goal of earthly happiness from which you would feel harder to part than your life. You see my memory is as good as yours."

"Yes, Lucy," he answered, in a more serious tone. "I have reached it, but I cannot tell if it shall ever really be mine. I will not keep my secret from you, Lucy, tho' I daresay it's no secret to you."

"No!" she answered. "It's Norrie."

"Yes, it's Norrie," he said, "whom you love also, but for some reason she continually avoids me on every possible occasion, and sometimes will not remain in my company, unless I make merely commonplace remarks and, what's more, tells me I'm never to expect anything else from her, and the strangest part of it all is, that I believe in spite of all, she cares something for me."

"That is very unlike Norrie," answered Lucy, after a little thought. "She is always candid and outspoken with those she loves, but she has never mentioned the matter to me."

Harry never knew what it cost Lucy to stand and talk to him of his love for another. She was glad when the first few bars of the lancers[81] fell on their ears, and her partner came to claim her. This was one of Harry's dances with Norrie. When it ended, he led her to a refreshment room. "Are you really enjoying yourself, Norrie?" he asked.

She looked at him, with her ever-bright smile. "I suppose I must be," she said. "'Twould be treason to say no, would it not? Every girl enjoys her first ball."

"What strange answers you always give!" he laughed. "To my mind it's never treason to say what is true."

"Then you want to hear the exact truth from me on the matter?"

"Certainly!"

"Well, the ball is a dead failure, as far as real, thorough enjoyment is concerned, and don't half come up to my expectations. Now, are you not surprised?"

"No! Not hearing such a verdict from you: your ideas of enjoyment lead to something higher than the empty flattery and unreality of the ballroom."

"But I don't mean," said Norrie, "to give you the impression that I've not enjoyed it at all. It is certainly very pleasurable to a certain extent; the music is delightful, the decorations most artistic, the dresses rich and beautiful, and everyone so polite and agreeable, but, for whole-souled enjoyment give me a little dory with two oars, and put me out on the dear, delightful sea, or the running river, with the blue sky above, and the green hills around me, and the most alluring ballroom would never tempt me from it. The call of the blood, I suppose, coming to me through a long line of ancestors."

"Worthy daughter of a noble race!" laughed Harry. "Norrie," he went on, speaking in a more serious tone, "in three days from now I must return to St. Rose. Will you not even give me hope that when we meet again, you will confide to me the secret which keeps us apart?"

She was silent for some time. The only thing, she thought, would be, if she saw Lucy could find, amongst the many good and true admirers which she had, one who would fill his place in her heart. Unless this happened, her answer must ever be the same. She looked up at last and said, "Harry, it pains me to say it, but I think it is best for you and me not to meet again. I am satisfied to meet you as a friend, but you are not, and it is not fair to expect it of you; that which stands between us, I fear, shall always remain so."

"You fear?" he said. "Then it is not impossible for it to be removed?"

"No, not impossible, but I think very improbable."

"Then," he added, with a sigh, "I shall try to be patient for a while longer."

They entered the ballroom together, and Lucy looking up saw the distressed look on Norrie's face.

"I wish they could be happy," she thought. "I wonder what notion has Norrie got into her head. She generally gets different ones from other people."

Next day the topic of conversation was, of course, "the ball," and "Miss Moore" was, without doubt, proclaimed "the belle," tho' a few more admired "sweet Miss Hamilton." Harry and his stepmother rarely met in town, as they moved in a different circle. She and Norrie met once, in the street, and the latter returned her condescending nod with a graceful and coldly polite bow.

"What a beautiful face that girl has!" remarked a lady who accompanied Mrs. Brandford. "Who is she?"

"She belongs to St. Rose," answered her companion. "One of the fishermen's daughters."

"I've never seen such a sweet face," said the lady. "Whoever she belongs to might well be proud of her; she seems a perfect lady, too."

"You would not say that if you knew her as well as I do. She is the girl whom Doctor Hamilton and his wife seemed to take under their wing since she saved their daughter from drowning some years ago, and they got her educated somehow or other. I believe the girl is a bit clever; her name is Moore," and the tone of Mrs. Brandford's voice implied that she wished the subject dropped, and it was with some amount of annoyance that, a short time afterwards, she heard her spoken of as "The Belle of the Irish Ball."

CHAPTER THIRTEEN

On the day before Harry Brandford's departure for St. Rose, he went to bid Norrie goodbye. It was a nice, mild evening, and he succeeded in tempting her out for a walk. She was looking pale, he said, from being so much indoors. They talked of a great many things, but since the night of the ball Harry had never alluded to the subject dearest to him. Tonight, however, he made up his mind to make another appeal, but it was only with the same result.

"You must forgive me, dear," he said, "for annoying you so often, but I really believe that if you confided this trouble to me, I could set it right for you, for I know it is only imaginary."

"No, indeed, Harry, it is not. It is painfully real."

"And do you think there might be any chance of this trouble being less when you return to St. Rose for your vacation?"

"I am not decided about going home at all during vacation time," said Norrie, hesitatingly. "It is scarcely worthwhile for a few weeks."

"You do not mean to tell me that you are dreaming of remaining in town instead of going home, and taking the benefit of the pure country air, which you need so much after your months of hard work?"

"I think it's best for me to remain," she faltered.

"Now, Norrie, this is on my account and, child, listen to me. I shall insist on getting from you tonight a solemn promise that you will come to St. Rose as soon as you possibly can. Why, what do you think I am, Norrie? A tyrant that you should fear, instead of one who would gladly give his life to spare you trouble? If you won't promise to come, I shall leave St. Rose during your visit rather than have you lose the benefit of it."

"Oh, Harry," she said, with much concern, "please do not think of doing anything of the sort. I do not wish to be the means of making you leave your home when your business requires you in it."

"Well, unless you promise to come, if I remain, I shall certainly do so."

"Then I must abandon the idea of remaining in town and go, I suppose."

"But, do you give me your solemn promise to do so?"

"Yes, I give you my solemn promise."

They paid a short visit to Lucy, and then he saw her to the door of her home.

"Goodbye, Norrie," he said, holding her hand. "Take care of yourself, and I pray that this miserable, so-called trouble will have vanished into thin air when you come home."

"From my heart I echo that prayer," she answered.

How lonely and desolate everything seemed after he had gone. "What shall I do?" she often thought. "If this goes on much longer 'twill break me down, for I cannot stand it."

A few weeks later, Mrs. Hamilton and Lucy went to St. Rose. The latter's health, as usual, required the bracing country air. Before her departure, she had spoken to Norrie for the first time with regard to Harry.

"Why do you always try to avoid him," she asked, "and he loves you so much? Don't you think you could be happy with him?"

Norrie could not bear this. The thought of Lucy, the one barrier to their happiness, pleading Harry's cause affected her deeply.

"Do not ask me to tell you why, Lucy," she answered, "for I must continue to avoid him for a longer time than he thinks, perhaps."

"Is it on account of Mrs. Brandford?" asked Lucy.

"No, dear, it is not. I've too much contempt for women of her stamp to allow them to interfere with me."

Mrs. Brandford returned to St. Rose at the same time as Mrs. Hamilton and Lucy. Norrie sadly missed the company of Lucy and her mother. Lilian Roy, who said she should try and fill Lucy's place, called often to see her, and sometimes took her off after school hours to spend the evening with her.

At the end of May, Mr. and Mrs. Weston returned from their wedding tour, looking well and happy, and took up residence, just for the present, with Mrs. Dane, as she pleaded them so earnestly to do so.

On this account, Norrie's visits there became a little more frequent, and she very rarely met Frank. The summer proved to be unusually hot; and by the time July came in, Norrie felt so much the need of freedom from her duties and a longing for home that she was heartily glad she had given her promise to Harry.

The day before she was to start for St. Rose, she went to call upon a lady whose little girl was taking lessons from her. It was just dusk when she reached the house, and the maid who answered the door showed her into a large drawing-room, while she went to inform her mistress who wished to see her. This room was separated from another by folding doors, which were slightly ajar.

Soon after the girl disappeared, the front door opened, and four or five gentlemen entered. One was the young man of the house; they passed through the hall and entered the room on the other side of the one which Norrie occupied. There was much talking and laughing for some time, and Norrie felt she ought in some way make known her presence there, 'til one sentence attracted her attention: it was this (from the young man who seemed to be proprietor, as he switched on the light, revealing to Norrie the faces of all the occupants). "Well, boys, Frank Dane is the greatest fool I've ever met. He is useful to us tho', very generous in the money line."

"Awfully cut up about that little beauty from St. Rose," laughed one of his companions.

"What did she do? Throw him over?" asked another.

"Something of the sort, I believe," he was answered.

"Very glad she did," sneered the first speaker. "I'm really obliged to her."

"Is he there for the racket[82] tomorrow night?" asked another.

"Oh! He is all right. There was only a little bit of coaxing necessary, and anyone can do that with Dane if he is only handled the right way."

The lady of the house entered now, and with a slight frown, as she caught sight of the occupants of the other room, hastily closed the folding doors and gave her attention to Norrie, who, when her business was concluded, slowly and thoughtfully wended her way to Mrs. Dane's, where, at May's earnest request, she had been spending the day, and was to remain for the night.

"Yes," she thought. "I feel certain I would be justified in making use of the conversation I've just heard, for a good purpose. I believe it would cure him."

That night, May Weston, her mother, and Norrie sat talking 'til midnight. Mrs. Dane glanced uneasily several times at the clock. Norrie noticed a few silver threads among her dark hair, and, acting on a sudden impulse, she threw herself on her knees by her side, and taking her hand said, as she gently touched the white threads,

"Dear Mrs. Dane, I am the cause of these. I who have received nothing but kindness from you, and, oh! I would give anything to be able to lessen your trouble."

"Do not reproach yourself, my dear child," said Mrs. Dane, laying her hand on Norrie's brown curls. "I was unreasonable enough to blame you at first, but I do not now. He must have been weak, or he would not allow a disappointment to make him forget himself. Perhaps it may be for the best; he is still young and may see his errors as he grows older and wiser, better than if he commenced this sort of thing later in life."

"I do hope and pray that he may," said Norrie, fervently.

Mrs. Dane then arose and went to the window.

"I wonder, Norrie, if you would speak to him, and give him a good scolding for the way he is acting. Would it have any effect on him?" said May.

"I will try," she answered.

"Do you know?" went on May. "I think Lilian Roy cares a little for Frank."

"I have thought so, too," answered Norrie, "and I think she is just the kind of girl to make a man happy."

Shortly after, May prevailed on her mother to go to bed, and she and Norrie would wait up for Frank.

They talked on 'til the small hours, when suddenly May said, "My, how selfish I am, keeping you up when you should be in bed hours ago, getting the rest you need for your journey tomorrow, or rather today."

"No, May, you are not keeping me. I am determined to see Frank before I go, and the only chance I have is to wait 'til he comes."

Soon they heard the latch key grate in the lock, and Frank came, flushed and a trifle unsteadily, into the room.

"Frank, is this the way you intend to spend the rest of your life?" asked his sister.

"I don't see why my life should trouble you so much." Then, seeing Norrie, he seemed a little ashamed and sat quietly in a corner.

"I must go and tell mother you are come," said May. "I know she is not asleep," and she left the room.

He looked up and seeing Norrie's eyes fixed sorrowfully on him, said, "Did they bring you here specially to see me in this condition, and are you satisfied at what you've made of me?"

"Hush! Frank Dane," she said, holding up her finger authoritatively, "I'll not listen to another word of this kind. No one has made anything of you, only what you've made of yourself. I'm ashamed of you, Frank. Do you think for a moment that you ever had the love you professed to have for me? No! Love only ennobles a man; it does not make him forget he has a soul, and that his life is not his own to wreck and ruin as his selfish nature dictates. Have you no manhood? No will? Are you weaker than the weakest of women, that you allow a slight disappointment to whirl you off into all kinds of dissipation?"

Frank looked surprised. He had never seen Norrie indignant before. "It's very easy to preach," he said, sulkily, "but not so to practice."

"It is not," went on Norrie, "nor don't you deceive yourself into thinking that it is, trying to forget me that is making you forget yourself. You've got over that long ago. I know I'm no more to you now than any other girl. It's simply following the bent of your own selfish inclination and, if you do not break off immediately with those pretended friends of yours, who laugh at you behind your back, your life will soon pay the forfeit."

"Who dares to laugh at me behind my back?" he asked.

And here, Norrie related every word of the conversation she had accidentally overheard.

"Can you name the men who said these words?"

"I can and will, if you'll promise to break off with them right away, and have no more intercourse with them."

"Yes," he answered, after a moment's thought. "I can faithfully promise to have no more intercourse with the men who have said these things of me."

Norrie mentioned the name of each one.

"Well! I'm glad," he said at last. "I see now they've made a tool of me. If I only had the strength to resist them!"

"The first effort will be the hardest, Frank," she said, in a gentle tone. "Make that firmly and the rest will come easier. Will you promise me here, now, solemnly, that when those friends, or enemies they really are, call for you tomorrow night you will refuse to see them? It would make me so happy, not to speak of the joy it would give your dear mother, whose heart is breaking on your account, and yet who will not say a hard word against you."

He sat down again and buried his face in his hands for some time, then seemed to rouse himself.

"Yes, he said. "I'm a different man from this hour. I know I've been a brute to mother, May and you, to everyone. It was mean and cowardly of me to continually make you an excuse for my conduct. I don't know how I could have forgotten myself so far. Thank you, Norrie, a thousand times, for what you've told me tonight. Pray for me to be firm. I did not think I was such a weak man."

"Nor are you really weak, Frank, when you acknowledge your errors like this. And indeed I will pray for you, and I firmly believe you will succeed."

"Well, good morning," he said. "You are going home today, are you not?"

"Yes, and I go happy, now that I know you are going to be a good man again."

He smiled as he left her, saying, "I will go directly now, and ask mother's pardon for the trouble I've given her, and tell her of my promise to you."

And Norrie's few hours of sleep did her more good than if she had been in bed before midnight.

When Mrs. Dane kissed her goodbye next morning, she said, "God bless you, Norrie. You are a good and noble girl and deserve a better man than Frank. All things happen for the best, I think, and perhaps it is better for my eyes to be opened to his failings, for I thought him perfection. But I find he is only human after all."

May, her husband, her brother, and Lilian Roy saw Norrie on board the steamer, and the latter was glad to see a look of firm resolve in Frank's eyes. She called Lilian aside when the shrill sound of the first whistle had died away, and said, "Lilian, I am going to ask you to take charge of someone, and save him from the hands of his enemies."

"Oh! it's a he, is it? Is his life in danger, and, if so, how am I to save him?"

"No, Lilian," she answered, "and I'm really serious. It's something more precious than his life. It's his soul, and his mother's happiness. It is Frank Dane I mean."

"Oh," and Lilian grew quite serious also. "But, Norrie, I would not interfere for the world."

"Not if you thought you could keep him up to the resolutions he made this morning—of mending his ways? Could you not make an effort?"

"Yes, but I've no influence over him. Now it's different with you; you know he worships you."

"Not at all," said Norrie. "That is all a mistake. He thought he did at one time, and I'm sure he thinks me quite a virago[83] after this morning, for I gave him a strong lecture, and he does not like that. He prefers quiet, gentle girls, as he thought I was before he knew better."

"But what do you want me to do?"

"Go to the house often. You can easily do so without creating talk while May lives there. Invite him to your house sometimes with her and Mr. Weston, and make Will and Jack have an eye after him. Once he gets fully free from those fast companions he has made, he will come out all right."

"I'll promise to do my best, Norrie," as she kissed her goodbye. But on the way home she thought to herself, "I wonder now if Miss Norrie Moore isn't aiming at trying to make me heal the wound that she has made." And Lilian never made a shrewder guess in her life.

"Well," thought Norrie, "here I am, bound for home once more." Then she smiled to herself as a curious thought struck her. "I fear I'm turning out quite a matchmaker," she thought. "But I only hope it will be a better success than my first attempt," and she sighed, as she thought of the two most dear in the world to her.

CHAPTER FOURTEEN

Norrie was delighted to find upon her arrival that Lucy was looking well and in good spirits. She and Harry met her at the pier. Then followed some of the happiest days of Norrie's life, days she often afterwards loved to look back upon and dream over, for, seeing that Lucy was looking bright and happy, she came to the conclusion that she must be learning to forget her love for Harry, and so, gave herself up to the sweet influence of "Love's young dream."[84] There was one drawback, however, to her happiness. She had noticed a slight coldness in Mrs. Hamilton's manner towards her. Of course, Norrie knew the cause. For it became apparent now to everyone that if Norrie Moore and Harry Brandford were not engaged, they soon would be. He never missed a day without seeing her.

The first of August was Norrie's birthday, and Lucy was to spend it with her. But word came in the morning that she was too ill to come, and a request that Norrie would spend the day with her instead. So she went, full of concern, for her friend. She met Mrs. Hamilton first and asked the cause of Lucy's illness.

"I don't think it ought to be necessary for you to ask that question, Norrie," answered Mrs. Hamilton, in a colder tone than she had ever before used to her. "She is unhappy, poor child, and not being overly strong, she cannot keep up her spirits and look happy at all times." Then, seeing the pained look on Norrie's face, she touched her cheek gently, saying, "Of course, I speak to you as I would to Lucy's sister, if she had one. I know it's not your fault, tho' you are the cause. She told me to send you up to her room immediately." Then, taking her in her arms, she kissed her warmly and said, "Oh, I had almost forgotten this is your birthday, Lucy being ill put it out of my head. I wish you many happy returns of the day."

When Norrie got to Lucy's room, the tears were running down her cheeks, and to all the latter's questions she only gave evasive answers.

"Never mind me, Lucy," she said. "I want to know what is making you ill."

"Nothing in particular," she answered, "and everything in general. I'm never strong, you know, and I don't think my life will be a long one."

"Hush, Lucy, you must not say such things, and you must get up and rouse yourself, and not give way to those morbid feelings." She succeeded in rousing her somewhat, and they spent the morning in the bright little flower garden. As Harry was passing on, in the evening, to Norrie's house, he saw the two girls in the window and went in. He told them he had just heard the unpleasant news that he must go some distance west of the island on business connected with the firm. He was to start that night in their own schooner. They had a few songs. The last one Norrie sang at Harry's request, "In the Gloaming";[85] he joined in at the last verse, and the sadness of the words, together with Norrie's expressive singing, seemed to affect them all:

In the gloaming, oh! my darling, think not bitterly of me,
Tho' I passed away in silence, left you lonely, set you free,
For my heart was crushed with longing, what had been, could never be,
It was best to leave you thus, dear, best for you and best for me.

To Norrie's oversensitive nature, the words seemed like a foreboding of coming sorrow. Shortly after, she arose to go. Harry accompanied her. When they reached the gate in front of Norrie's residence, they paused. Harry declined to go in, as he said the schooner was to start at ten, and consulting his watch found that it was past nine. "And besides, Norrie," he said, "I want my final answer from you tonight, here in the moonlight. I have waited long and patiently, and have kept my promise of not prying into this troublesome secret of yours, have I not, dear?" he asked, taking her hand in his.

"Yes, Harry," she answered, "you've been more than generous, but I ask one favour more. Wait for my answer 'til you return."

"But, why this delay? You've given me to understand from your manner that this trouble you spoke of last winter has all disappeared."

"It has not," she answered, "and there is something I wish to do before I give the promise you ask."

The fact was, she could not bear the thought of telling the news of her engagement to Lucy and Mrs. Hamilton without first speaking it over with them, and, in a way, preparing them for it, and this she might easily do during his absence. And then, Lucy's illness of the morning made her hesitate.

"I cannot imagine anything you wish to do interfering with the promise I expect from you, Norrie."

"I have a strong reason for this, Harry," she answered. "Wait 'til you return. It will be but two weeks you say."

"Very well, Norrie," he answered. "I'll consent to wait 'til I return for the words I had hoped to hear tonight, but I shall look upon you as my promised wife just the same as if you had told me."

"You hold promises of this kind very sacred, Harry, do you not?"

"Certainly, Norrie," he answered, "as sacred, almost, as a promise made to the dying."

"Almost," she echoed, as a sudden pang struck her. "Then you would keep a promise to the dying more faithfully?"

"Yes," he answered, "if the promise was a just one."

They remained silent for a time. How Norrie often looked back on that night: the quiet hush that pervaded everything; the August moon, shedding its soft, mellow light on the little white huts of the fishermen; the distant murmuring of the sea!

"Harry," she said, earnestly, "are you sure of your love for me? Do you think anything would ever change it?"

He looked at her with such a sad, reproachful gaze in his deep, grey eyes that she felt sorry she had asked the question.

"Norrie," he answered, after a moment's pause, "I'm a man of few words, and what I say I mean. No other love but yours has ever entered my heart, or ever will. If this trouble you speak of were to separate us forever, I should go unmarried to my grave."

"But, are you sure you love me for myself alone? People say I am pretty, but I should not like to be loved merely for that."

"Nor should any woman," he answered. "Beauty may be the means of attracting attention, but never of winning love, tho' I'm glad you are fair and talented, my Norrie. But if you lost all these tomorrow, you should still be the star of my life, for I love you for your own sweet self. When we see a beautiful flower," he went on, "we are naturally attracted towards it, but if we find it possesses no sweetness, besides its appearance, we do not love it."

"But your mother, Harry, she dislikes me."

He started first, at the words, then, raising his hat, he looked up to the moonlit sky. "My mother, Norrie," he said, "is amongst the angels in Heaven. Do not desecrate her name by applying it to Mrs. Brandford."

"Oh, forgive me," she said. "I spoke without thinking. Your stepmother, I mean."

"Mrs. Brandford's likes or dislikes," he said, "do not in the least affect me. When you are my wife, Norrie, I shall secure you from any unpleasantness from her, you may be sure of that. And now, dearest, are you not going to tell me anything of your love for me. Do you think it is as deep as mine for you?"

She looked up with a sweet, tender expression in her dark, brown eyes, a clear, candid, truthful gaze, as she answered, "Yes, Harry, just as deep, noble, generous and entire as yours for me." And he was content.

After a few minutes he took from his pocket a small parcel. "Norrie," he said, "this is a birthday gift. I intended to give it to you as my promised wife. You can look at it when you go in, and when I return, dear, you will give me your full promise and name our wedding day."

"How long will you be gone?" she asked.

"About two weeks," he answered. "I had hoped to put this journey off 'til your vacation was over, but found it was of too urgent a nature after all."

"Well, goodbye, Harry," she said. "I hope I shall be able to answer you, as you desire, upon your return."

"Goodbye, darling," he said, "pray for me 'til we meet again." And ever afterwards Norrie remembered how strange it was he should say "'til we meet again" instead of "'til I return," or "whilst I'm away." She remained leaning on the gate 'til the last sound of his footsteps died away, and such an unaccountable feeling of sadness overpowered her, a dread of something indefinite, that it was with difficulty she could keep from running after him. She roused[86] off the feeling at length and went into the house. Going to her room she lighted the lamp and examined Harry's gift. It was a gold locket with a chain attached, and on the inside was carved "from H.B. to his promised wife."

She did not retire for some hours and, when she did, she could not sleep. She was thinking how she would break the news of her prospective engagement to Lucy and her mother. At last, she fell asleep with such a troubled mind that she dreamed she saw Lucy in her coffin, and that Mrs. Hamilton came to her side and pointing towards it said, "But for you she would not be there." Then she began to tell her of the sacrifice she had tried to make, but, as it always happens in a dream, she could not utter a word. It seemed to her that Doctor Hamilton appeared in the doorway, and was looking at her, not reproachfully, but with a kindly smile, such as he always had for her. With a cry of joy she rushed towards him, then she awoke to find Mrs. Moore bending over her, and the bright sunlight streaming into the room.

"What ails you, Norrie?" she asked. "I heard you crying in your sleep."

"I was dreaming," she answered, rubbing her eyes. "What time is it, Aunt?"

"It is near nine now, but you need not get up yet if you feel sleepy."

"My! so late," she said, sitting up. "Yes, Aunt, I'll get up now."

When she had breakfasted and done a few light duties about the house, she went to see Lucy, and found her so pale and sad-looking, that not for worlds would she venture to tell her anything that day. She insisted on Norrie remaining with her and the latter consented to do so on condition that Lucy would go with her for a row on the harbour. She went, but somehow the sea air seemed too strong for her, and gave her a headache. After dinner they went for a short ramble through the woods, which fatigued Lucy so much that she had to retire early. Norrie sat by her, bathing her head and face, for she seemed quite feverish.

"I don't think I ever was intended for a long life, Norrie," she said. "It is better for people like me to die and not live to give trouble to everyone."

"Well, Lucy, I think it positively unkind of you to imply that I think anything which I do for you a trouble. The only trouble is knowing you are suffering. But anything which I can do to lessen that suffering is only pleasure to me and, besides, Lucy, you are going to be a strong woman yet. Take my word for it. You are not ill near as often as you used to be, and you know your dear father always said you would be perfectly healthy by the time you'd reach your twenty-first year, and you are nineteen now. It is only a slight cold you've got with the headache that is making you feverish." So she sat holding her hands and trying to soothe her 'til dusk, when, thinking she seemed inclined to sleep, she kissed her goodbye.

She intended to run into the drawing-room to bid Mrs. Hamilton good evening, but as she reached the door she heard the voice of no less a personage than Mrs. Brandford and, not feeling much disposed to meet that lady just then, she lingered for awhile at the outer door. At last, she thought she would steal up again just to see if Lucy had fallen asleep. She went quite noiselessly to the door, and heard her murmuring to herself. Whether she was sleeping or waking, she could not tell, but distinctly she heard the words, "Oh, Norrie, why did you not let me drown that day? I would be free now from all this pain and sorrow." Turning, she went down as noiselessly as she had come.

If Lucy was awake, the words were not intended for her ears, and not for anything would she let her know she had heard them.

She went into the garden and sat on one of the seats under the drawing-room window, forgetting for the moment the existence of Mrs. Brandford.

"No," she thought, "it's no use. I cannot do it. I was weak and cowardly to give Harry the encouragement I did for the last few weeks. How can I be happy with him when her heart is breaking?"

The drawing-room window was open and, as plainly as if she were inside, these words fell on her ear.

"Do not be offended, my dear Mrs. Hamilton, if I tell you that I know the cause of your child's illness. She loves my stepson, Harry, at which I'm not surprised, seeing how much he tried to make her do so last summer. And I'm certain he cared a great deal for her, too, 'til that girl Nora Moore came with her clever wiles and coquettish airs. Poor Lucy, of course, not being robust and of such a tender, sensitive disposition, has taken the betrayal of her false friend to heart."

"You are entirely mistaken, Mrs. Brandford," said Mrs. Hamilton, very coldly. "It would be an impossibility for Norrie to be a false friend to anyone, much less to Lucy."

"And you would not call stealing her lover from her being false to her?"

"Harry was never Lucy's lover, nor is he Norrie's accepted lover as yet."

"Ah, then, I see Miss Shrewdness is able to keep her own counsel. So she has not told you, who have done so much for her, of her engagement?"

"I am quite sure she would not form any engagement without first consulting me, or, at least, telling me of it."

"Then, she is not worthy of the trust you place in her, Mrs. Hamilton, for Harry, with his own lips, told me before he left last night that she is to be his wife."

"I think there is a mistake somewhere, Mrs. Brandford, and excuse me when I tell you I will doubt this statement, unless I hear it from Norrie herself."

"Mrs. Hamilton, I will overlook the implied insult and, for the sake of your child's happiness, will join you, if you will consent to make the compact with me, to separate them. He will be away for two weeks yet, and I will tell of a plan I've got to manage her."

But Mrs. Hamilton had risen to her feet, in her indignation.

"Mrs. Brandford," she said, "do my ears deceive me? Is it possible you think so little of me as to make such a proposition? I join you in any scheme to separate Norrie from the man she loves? The child whom my dead husband committed to my love and care, and who is almost as dear to me as my own, to save whose life she risked hers? Yes, and hear me further, Mrs. Brandford, for whose sake she would now forfeit her own happiness, if only I asked her? But I would not do it."

Mrs. Brandford saw she had gone too far, and so did not care to conceal her anger any longer. "Then, I wish you and your husband had let that fisher girl stay where she belonged. I suppose, then, my dutiful stepson would not stoop to take her from the fishing stage to reign as mistress in my elegant home. She might indeed be well proud of the education she has got; one half of the money paid for it came out of your pocket, and the other out of Harry's and mine."

"Why! What do you mean, Mrs. Brandford?"

"I mean that her father died head and ears indebted to my husband. When everything was sold to realize the amount, he, with his usual reckless generosity, presented it to the wife, whose lazy spendthrift habits were half the cause of the debt. Some of that went to pay for her education, and what John Moore refused to pay for had to come out of your pocket, as Doctor Hamilton so instructed before he died. Oh, yes, I know it was to be kept a profound secret from that mischief-making girl, and you are surprised at my finding it out, but I've done so. When you say she would forfeit her own happiness for your child's, if you asked her, you forget that she is only a fisherman's daughter and not capable of such a sacrifice."

A quick, firm step in the hallway, an abrupt opening of the door, and Norrie stood before them. Out there, in the twilight, her resolve was taken, and her noble, if mistaken, sacrifice made. Her face was very pale, with the exception of two bright spots on either cheek, the only sign of excitement which she exhibited; her large, wonderful, brown eyes had a solemn, mournful expression as she said, "I've heard every word you've spoken for the past five minutes."

"Ah," said Mrs. Brandford, triumphantly, "you've been listening. Well, those sort of people never hear anything good of themselves."

"Mrs. Hamilton knows me too well to believe that," she said, in slow, sorrowful tones. "What you may think does not interest me."

"Certainly, Norrie, my dear," said Mrs. Hamilton. "You do not need to tell me."

"Mrs. Brandford," said Norrie, fixing her eyes with such a calm, fearless expression on that lady's face, that they made her feel quite uncomfortable. "What harm have I ever done you that you've persecuted and hated me all my life?"

If she had answered truthfully, she would have said, "Because you are pretty and clever, and a perfect lady, in spite of all I said to the contrary, and because you never have, either as a child or woman, stood the least bit in awe of me."

"Understand, girl," she said, "that I've never taken the trouble to persecute or hate you. What I'm doing now is simply my duty, in trying to keep a headstrong young man from ruining his life, by marrying one who is in no way fitted to be his wife, and—"

"That will do," said Norrie, holding up her hand, and Mrs. Brandford was forced to admit that she was mistress of the situation.

"Now, why have you spoken falsely by saying that your stepson told you that I am to be his wife? He did not tell you that, for he would not say what is untrue, and," she said, turning to Mrs. Hamilton, "thank you, my good, more than mother, for your firm faith in your Norrie. It is true Mr. Brandford wished me to promise to marry him, when bidding me goodbye last night, but I did not do so, tho' I confessed my love for him, simply because I intended telling you and Lucy before I gave him that promise. And, oh! I know how much I owe you and your dear, dead husband; but all my debts shall be faithfully discharged. Will you be good enough, Mrs. Brandford, to name the sum which my father was indebted to your husband?"

Mrs. Brandford got pale with fright. If Harry ever heard of her speaking of such a thing, she dared not think where it would end.

"No," she said, "I'm not prepared to give you any answer on the subject. Besides what good would it do you to know, pray?"

"Because," answered Norrie, her eyes flashing for a moment, "every cent shall be paid back."

"By whom?" sneered her enemy.

"By me, his daughter. I would rather die than live and be indebted one cent to you. I would not be you, with your thousands, and have your spirit, were it to make me Queen of the Universe."

Then, kneeling by Mrs. Hamilton's side, she took her hand, and said, "I would not insult you, dear Mrs. Hamilton, by promising to pay you in money what you've so generously spent on me. I shall discharge my debt to you in another way."

"Hush, child," she answered, "do not ever let it trouble you, and do not speak of it again."

"I should not," went on Norrie, "have been kept in ignorance as to who was paying for my education. But I know why it was done, for much as I craved it, I would never have accepted it, had I known the truth." She arose to her feet and gave one lingering, affectionate glance at Mrs. Hamilton.

"Goodbye," she said, "dearest, best of friends; I must go now. Your trust in me is not misplaced, for I shall be true to it."

Then, standing very erect, with a proud light shining in her eyes, she faced Mrs. Brandford, saying, "When next we meet it may be under very different circumstances. I forgive you freely for all you've ever said to me, and I'm glad to know what I should have known before. I'm not ashamed of my humble birth, Mrs. Brandford. On the contrary, I feel quite proud, that, tho' *only a fisherman's daughter*, I can show you, a member of the charmed circle of the aristocracy, what proper pride and independence of spirit mean." She walked slowly from the room.

Mrs. Hamilton followed her to the outside door. "Why are you going so soon, Norrie dear?" she asked, taking her in her arms.

"I intended going some time ago," she answered, "as Lucy seemed inclined to sleep, and I have been away from home all day. I was only waiting for Mrs. Brandford to go, to bid you good evening and, chancing to sit near the open window, I heard what passed inside."

"Yes, I know, dear. What a mean, nasty spirit the woman has! Do not let anything she said trouble you, Norrie. I never enjoy her visits, and I heartily wish she would cease them, which I suppose she will do after this evening."

"Goodbye, Mrs. Hamilton," she said, throwing her arms around her neck, "kiss Lucy for me. Oh, I'm so glad you have such faith in me. I love you both, more than I can tell. Always believe this. I pray that she may get well and strong soon." And with a lingering kiss she left her.

Often afterwards Mrs. Hamilton remembered her words, and remarked that she had said goodbye instead of good evening.

CHAPTER FIFTEEN

When Norrie got some distance from the house she turned and gazed, oh, with such sorrowful eyes upon it. "Farewell, loved scene of my happiest hours," she murmured, then hurried on, not in the direction of home.

"It is nearly dark now," she thought, "and I've much to do before midnight. Yes, I know the steamer will reach here on her way to St. John's before daylight tomorrow. I must find out the exact hour, but, oh, have I strength for what I'm doing?" she wailed, clasping her hands over her heart. "Kind Heaven, direct me."

She reached the telegraph office, and inquired of the operator what she wanted to know.

"Tell you what hour the steamer is expected? Certainly, Miss Moore," he answered, going to the battery. Presently, he returned, saying, "She is due here at midnight. Pardon me, Miss Moore, but have you heard any bad news? You look a little frightened."

"Do I look frightened?" she said. "I do not feel so. I've had unpleasant news, and I'm going to town by the steamer tonight." She left the office and directed her steps towards the little cemetery. It was quite dark now, and many a maiden would very naturally have a superstitious fear of going to such a place at that hour, and alone. But fear of any kind was a thing foreign to Norrie's nature. She knelt by her mother's grave and rested her burning brow against the wooden cross. "Oh, Mother," she said, "would it have been wiser if Uncle John had persisted in refusing to give the money you left for me, to spend on my education? Harry and I would not then have met on equality. I would still be just the lowly little fisher maiden, and I would not be called upon to make the sacrifice that is now breaking my heart." She remained by the grave for some time, begging her mother's blessing and guidance on the task she was undertaking. Then, her thoughts went to Mrs. Brandford, and she stood erect. "That mean, selfish woman," she murmured, "shall know that the pride of a fisherman's daughter is of a nobler and higher order than hers. Oh, if Harry only knew what she said. I suppose he knows of my father's debt but he, like his father, in his noble generosity, would not accept it back; in fact, counts it cancelled. But I vow here tonight, in the spot where my mother's remains are laid, that I, her child, shall pay to Mrs. Brandford the money which her husband so generously gave to us."

Then going some distance further, she knelt by the white marble monument which marked the spot where, about five years before, Doctor Hamilton was laid to rest. "I wonder do you know, dear, kind friend," she thought, "what it is costing me to fulfill the promise I made you. I said I would give up my own life's happiness any time, if by so doing I could save Lucy pain, and I'm doing it now, tho' unfortunately, the sacrifice is not complete, as I cannot keep her from suffering, for, I fear, she will never be more to Harry than she is now. If I could only make her be to him what he told me I am, I would,"—but here she paused. Ah, human nature is only human after all. "Oh, could—could—I do it?" she asked herself. "Well, were it in my power to make her his wife and make them happy, I would do it." Then, with a quick, firm step, she hastened homewards. "What I've got to do I must do quickly," she thought, "or my courage will fail me. How fortunate Harry is away, for I could never do it otherwise. One look at his dear face, one reproachful gaze from his deep, grey eyes, and Doctor Hamilton, Lucy, and all else would be forgotten."

John and Bridget Moore were preparing to retire when she entered the house but she requested them to stay a few minutes longer as she had something to say to them. "I've had news," she said, "which compels me to return to St. John's by the steamer, which is due here tonight."

"Why, Norrie," said Bridget Moore. "What on earth is taking you off so soon? I thought you were going to stay 'til the first of September."

"I thought so, too," said Norrie, "but you see my time is not my own, and business comes before pleasure."

"So I suppose," said John, "but it's quite sudden, Norrie. Did you get a telegram?"

"No," she answered, evasively, "not a telegram. I got word, tho'. But, Uncle John, I want to ask you a few questions."

"Sartinly, Norrie. What are they, child?"

"Is it true that my father was indebted to Mr. Brandford at the time of his death?"

"It is, Norrie," said John, after thinking for a few moments, and removing a well-seasoned T.D.[87] from his mouth.

"Do you know how much?"

"Yes," he answered, rubbing his hand through his hair. "Four hundred dollars. But it's all right tho', Norrie. When your mother had everything sold off—such as skiffs, traps, cod-seines, house and ground, and so forth—it was a little over that amount, and when she offered the money to Mr. Brandford, he towld her he'd not take a penny of it, and never to trouble about the debt, and that's the money she left in care of us for you, Norrie. But 'tis nearly all gone now since you went away to the boardin' school."

"And why did Mr. Brandford allow the things to be sold, when he did not intend to take the money?" asked Norrie,

"He knew nothin' about that, for he was away when it happened. But, anyhow, your mother did not intend carryin' on the bisness since you were a girl instead of a boy. But I daresay she would have rented the place and not sold it, if it warn't for some remarks she heard that Mr. Brandford's wife passed about yer father's careless ways for gettin' in debt, and that the house of Brandford 'id soon be broke if every wan turned out like him. So, bein' like yourself, Norrie, a little bit too high-spirited, she right away sold off all, and Mr. Brandford had some trouble to make her keep the money. Only for your sake, I daresay, she never would."

"If I had known all this before," said Norrie, "I would know that Mrs. Hamilton was paying for part of my education; for, of course, it cost more than that."

"Why! How did ye hear that?" asked John, glancing suspiciously at his wife, who looked a trifle uneasy.

"I learned it this evening," said Norrie. "It doesn't matter how. But, Uncle John, I want to ask you about my mother. Was she idle or careless?"

"Idle or careless?" repeated John indignantly. "No, indeed, Norrie, just the opposite to that was yer mother."

"As industrious a woman as iver lived," said Bridget. "Wherever ye hard anything to the contrary, just tell me, and I'll talk to 'em."

"I did not mind it," said Norrie. "I felt it was untrue. Uncle John, will you mind giving me what is left of the four hundred dollars?"

"Sartinly not, if ye wants it, Norrie. It's only fifty dollars tho', but yer in a good way of earnin' money for yerself now, which I'm glad of, so I'll give ye the book and ye can draw it from the bank when ye get to town."

"Thank you, Uncle, and now, when I've my trunk packed, will you please carry it to the pier and then you can both go to bed, as I can manage the rest myself?"

"Do yet think I'd dream of goin' to bed and ye goin' away tonight, Norrie," said Bridget. "No, indeed, I'll sit up and get you some tay."

"I could not take anything, Aunt, thank you."

"Oh! But you must, child. You'll want something to keep up yer strength goin' on the water."

Which, Norrie felt, was true. She wanted strength, indeed: strength of mind and body. She hastily packed her trunk, and gathered all her treasured little mementoes into a satchel, all except one, which she pressed reverently to her lips, then laid it carefully aside, and sat down at a plain little table on which stood a small writing desk. Ah! here lay her hardest task; what words could she use to express her grief and despair, to ask his forgiveness for what she was doing and yet make him understand they must part forever. True, she would be far beyond his reach when he got it, for, if he could find her, all her resolutions would be utterly useless. Not one tear did she shed when, after nearly an hour, she arose from her task, with a small sealed packet in her hand. Her face was very pale, as she placed it in John Moore's hand, saying, "Uncle, I am going to entrust this to you, to give to Mr. Brandford when he returns. But, you must promise to let no one else see it."

"I give ye me promise niver to breathe a word about it to anywan but him. He is a good man, Norrie, a splendid fellow is Harry Brandford. I wish there were more like him in the world," and he placed it carefully in a large leathern pouch which he had taken from his pocket, thinking it was some love token and explanation of her sudden departure, for, of course, John Moore was not blind. Mrs. Moore then came with some tea, which she made her take. Shortly after midnight they heard the sound of the steamer's whistle, and then Norrie bade a sorrowful farewell to the home of her childhood. Her two guardians saw her on board and both wondered why she seemed to feel the parting more than she had ever done before. Tho' she never felt any extra amount of love for them, still they were her only relatives, and, as they disappeared in the midnight darkness, the poor girl felt a terrible sense of loneliness and desolation steal over her. She began to wonder if she were acting very wrongly. Quite suddenly the words of the Mother Superioress occurred to her: "You often act, my child, in very important matters, the moment an idea strikes you, without consulting, as you should, those older and wiser than yourself." But, ah, the circumstances now were quite different from what the good Mother had spoken of and, besides, who could advise her? Her best friend, Mrs. Hamilton, expected it of her; her relatives would not understand. Then she thought of Mrs. Dane; could she not consult her when she got to St. John's?

"No," she decided, "she would only try to stop me, and I must not let anyone do that now, for," the old proud light coming in her eyes, "that woman shall feel what it is to insult the memory of my father, if Lucy were never in the question."

"Yes," she said, looking up to the sky, "your daughter will avenge the insult offered to your memory, and to her." She went to her stateroom and lay down to try and sleep but that "blest barrier twixt day and day"[88] refused its much-needed balm to her tired brain.

Late as the hour was, there came stealing softly down to her from the music-room above, the words of an old song:

Good-bye, old home, sad is my heart;
To think that forever, to-night we must part,
Weeping, I leave thee, my heart is in pain,
I feel that I never shall see thee again.
Scenes of my childhood, forever adieu,
Oft' will my memory wander to you,
And to the loved ones wherever I roam,
But, oh, I must leave thee, good-bye, old home.

Then a number of voices joined in the chorus:

Home of my heart, home sweet home,
Oh! how I love thee wherever I roam;
But we must part, for the hour is nigh,
When weeping, I'll murmur, old home, good-bye.

She longed to find relief in tears, for her heart seemed bursting, but they would not come, and it was not 'til daylight that sleep came to her tired eyelids.

Wearily the days passed 'til they reached St. John's, and now her one idea was to escape observation from all who knew her. She walked timidly some distance up Water Street. It was near six in the evening, and soon the cry of the newsboys' *Evening Telegram*, *Evening Herald*[89] came to her ears. She bought one and, walking quickly 'til she reached one of the quiet streets, she entered a house, with board and lodging marked over the door. She was shown to a clean but poor-looking room, and opening the paper began looking over the steamer notes. Ah! here was one which seemed to please her. S.S. *Portia* sails for New York, via Halifax, at midnight tomorrow. A little girl then appeared at the door to know if the young lady would have tea in her own room, or come downstairs.

"I'll take it here, please," answered Norrie, "and then I will go to bed, for I feel very tired." She dreaded leaving this temporary seclusion, fearing she would meet someone to whom she should be supposed to give an explanation of her unexpected presence in town. An elderly woman appeared with a tray, bearing a substantial supper.

"You look quite tired, Miss," she said, sympathetically.

"I feel so, too," said Norrie. "I am going away in the *Portia* tomorrow night and I want to get all the rest I can."

"Ah! what a pity that so many of our young girls leave their native land to earn their bread. I hope you'll meet with success, Miss. Is there anything else I can do for you?"

"Yes," answered Norrie. "Could you go or send to Harvey's office[90] tomorrow and buy me a second-class ticket for New York, and also get my trunk from the coastal wharf, bring it to Harvey's, and get it labelled and checked?" and she gave her card.

"Certainly, Miss," she answered. "I'll see to it all tomorrow, as early as possible."

"I cannot give you the money 'til the morning," said Norrie. After bidding the woman good night, she ate a fairly good supper and went to bed.

Oh! how lonely she felt, how she longed for love and sympathy, which she might have had so easily, for those who loved and would help her were not more than one half hour's walk from her. But she dreaded opposition to her plans too much to risk a meeting with them, and, besides, she could not betray Lucy's secret, neither did she care to speak of that old debt of her father's, and how, then, could she account to them for her sudden determination to leave Newfoundland. No, she must bear her sorrow and burden alone. She had heard from May Weston and Lilian Roy while at St. Rose and rejoiced to learn that Frank Dane was so far keeping firm in his good resolutions.

At ten next morning, she dressed herself in her shabbiest clothes and, wearing a thick, black veil, went to draw (as she bitterly told herself) the few remaining dollars of Mr. Brandford's charity to her mother. She did not feel safe 'til she found herself again in the shelter of her room and, calling the landlady, gave her the money necessary for all her expenses. When it was quite dark, she dressed for her journey and walked quickly to the wharf. She felt uneasy 'til she stood in a secluded corner on the deck of the *Portia*. It was, as usual, crowded with passengers and their friends who had come to bid them a last farewell. At midnight the first whistle blew, and quite suddenly a terrible fear of the responsibility of the step she was taking came over Norrie, a dread of something, and a sense of such utter loneliness, that she made a step forward to leave the steamer and abandon her idea of leaving home. "It is not too late yet," she thought. The resolution became stronger as Harry's handsome, noble face rose before her, and she could see in imagination the pained, reproachful look in his dark, grey eyes as he read her letter. Much pain, sorrow, anger and resentment might have been spared had she acted on this impulse, but she paused, the word coward seemed to sound in her ears. Was it from a good or bad spirit? She could not tell, for she really did not know whether she was doing right or wrong. She was leaning against the rail, looking at the crowd on shore, when she saw, watching her intently, Will Roy. She drew hastily away and was soon lost to view in the crowd. She was thankful to see by the expression of his face that he was not quite sure of her identity. And, now, she found they were steaming slowly off. "Oh! Farewell, my darling," she murmured. "My own, dear love. So brave, good and true. If I could only bear the pain I am making you suffer as well as my own, I could even be happy, but I cannot. You must suffer also if you will deem me worth it. Perhaps it would be better if you could think of me as a fickle-hearted flirt, who does not know what constancy and truth are."

She remained on deck 'til the last glimpse of her native land faded from view. She then descended to her cabin and, although not troubled with seasickness, she did not appear again 'til they reached Halifax. She had no heart for anything and, now that the fear and anxiety of getting away without being seen by someone who knew her, was over, all she could do was to lie still, and try and picture her future without Harry Brandford, without all who loved her, and whom she loved. She wondered if she would always feel that dull, heavy pain in her heart.

Very unlike the Norrie of a month ago she looked, as she went on deck. She was thin and pale, with dark circles under her eyes, and did not feel equal even to thinking. But the bracing sea air revived her somewhat, and she began to get her brains into working order once more. The first fact which became apparent to her was this: here she was, a young girl in a strange land, without friend or protector, almost a child in the ways of the world, and about twenty dollars in her purse. The delay in Halifax was short, and once more she was "rocked in the cradle of the deep."[91] The passengers were all strangers to her and some eyed her curiously but, not being particularly attracted towards any of them, she made no acquaintance. She had heard such stories of the dangers of New York City for one unprotected like herself that, when they arrived there, she sought the captain, who remembered her quite well for he had seen her going and returning from school. She had travelled first-class then and had someone to take charge of her.

"It is not a very nice thing," he said, "for an attractive young lady like yourself to travel alone, going to a place like New York, but I suppose you have friends to whom you are going?"

"Yes," said Norrie, "I am going to a good friend."

He found her trunk and saw her safely in a second-class car, which he advised her was the best to take. The train was just leaving for the place of her destination. She arrived safely and, hiring a cab, directed the man to drive to — Convent.

Oh! how the familiar scenes recalled to her memory bygone, happy days. She wished with all her heart that she was still a school girl. It seemed but yesterday that she had last run up those steps and rung the bell.

The Sister who was portress[92] recognized her instantly and welcomed her cordially. "You wish to see the Mother Superioress. Certainly, my dear," she said, "I shall tell her immediately."

Soon, the dear and revered face of the guardian of her schooldays entered and, clasping in her arms her old pupil, said, "And it is indeed my own Norrie. You always said you would come and see us again if ever the chance offered. But, child, how changed you are! Where are all the bright roses gone, and the merry light from your eyes, and, oh, my dear, what is it? What is the matter?" For Norrie was weeping as if her heart were bursting, the first tears she had shed since before she left St. Rose. It was some time before she could calm herself enough to explain anything and then, with her head resting on the shoulder of that kind, motherly woman, she told her whole trouble. It did not seem like betraying Lucy's secret to tell it to her, for she knew it was as safe as it was with herself.

After some deliberation, she spoke. "Oh, Norrie, my dear child!" she said. "You've acted very wrongfully. Why did you leave your home and friends without consulting someone? Mrs. Hamilton would never dream of expecting such a sacrifice from you and, besides, what right had you to treat a good and noble man in such a manner? Heaven guides these things, Norrie, and even your own life cannot be ordered to your own ideas. The man whose promised wife you almost were had a right to your confidence and, unless he were satisfied to have you make this sacrifice, you should not have done so. And I fear, my child, that pride is the leading element which has influenced you in this step."

"And I suppose a fisherman's daughter has no business with pride," said Norrie bitterly.

"Oh! Norrie, I do not like to hear you speak in this way. You are too young yet to have the iron enter your soul.[93] Of course, a certain amount of pride of the proper nature is all right. I only warn you not to let it run away with you altogether."

"If I had one spark of independence in me, and heard that woman speak as she did of my parents and me, I could not do otherwise than I have done."

"Norrie, would it be quite useless for me to ask you to give up this idea, and go right back home again? If you marry this man, who you say is wealthy, could you not then pay to Mrs. Brandford the money your father owed her husband?"

"Go back?" said Norrie. "After all I've suffered in coming? Oh! dear Mother, you do not know me. Never will I go home until I have paid the last farthing[94] to Mrs. Brandford, and it is only certain circumstances that will permit me to go then, for, tho' you do not seem to credit it—were this money never in question—I would do what I have done for Lucy's sake, and to fulfill my promise to Doctor Hamilton. I will never accept happiness that would cause her pain."

"Were you alone the sufferer, Norrie," said the Mother, "your sacrifice would be a grand one, but you've no right to destroy the happiness of another. You do not know what harm it may do."

"It will not make him do wrong," said Norrie. "He is not a weak man; he is as firm as a rock where duty is concerned. But he will suffer, I know. I can judge of that by what I'm suffering myself."

"Poor child," said the Mother, fondly, stroking her brown curls.

"Well, since you are determined in your resolution, what would you wish me to do for you?"

"Oh, dear Mother, if you could only find me a situation as governess, besides giving private lessons. I do not mind how hard the work is; the more I get of it, the sooner I will earn the money required and, besides, it will keep me from thinking of the past."

"I will do my best for you, Norrie."

"Oh, thank you a thousand times," she murmured, "and now I must go and find some nice, quiet house where I can stay 'til I get work."

"No, indeed, my dear," answered her kind friend. "You shall stay here under the protection of the Convent 'til I see fit to let you go and, indeed, you look too ill to go anywhere at present."

Norrie took the hand of her benefactress and kissed it. It was indeed true, for she felt too ill to speak.

CHAPTER SIXTEEN

A week passed away, and Norrie was only able to sit up for the past two days. She had been confined to her bed with complete prostration of mind and body, and the doctor feared it would be a serious case. But her usually strong constitution triumphed at last, and she was once more herself, as far as health was concerned. But the bright, sunny spirits had gone; a look of calm determination had settled on her face, and her large, fearless, candid brown eyes had a sad, far-away expression in place of the bright light and mischievous laughter that once shone there. Today she ventured out into the bright, sunny little flower garden. The pupils had most all gone, as it was vacation time. The Mother Superioress was with her. They were sitting on one of the garden seats, and could see the road for some distance off. They soon noticed a fashionable coach coming in the direction of the Convent. It stopped in front, and the occupants got out.

"Some visitors, I expect," remarked the Mother.

A few moments after, a little Sister came smilingly into the garden, and said, "You would never guess, Mother, who has come."

"Someone who wants me, I suppose, Sister Clare?" she answered.

"Yes, and someone you will be glad to see, and whom you have not seen for, I think, six years."

"Not Ada?" said the Mother, brightening up.

"Yes," answered Sister Clare, "none other than Mrs. Erington and Maude."

"Is it possible?" murmured the Superioress, rising to her feet. "Excuse me, Norrie dear. Sister Clare, you may remain and tell her who Ada and Maude are," as she hastened away.

It was the first time Norrie had felt any amount of interest in anyone since leaving home, and now she turned with an eager face to Sister Clare.

"Ada, Mrs. Erington," explained Sister Clare, "is our dear Mother's half-sister, and it is six years since she has come to the North. Maude is her only child, who was but a girl of fourteen when last we saw her. They are very fond of our Mother, but Mrs. Erington is very unlike her sister. She is nice and kind, but very worldly, fond of gaiety and travelling, and Maude, I think, promises to be like her mother, but still a very generous girl. They are rather proud in their way, and do not care to mix with any but very high-toned society. Maude's father died when she was a baby, and a few years afterwards her mother married Mr. Erington, a rich widower from the South. He has a daughter also of his first wife, a very delicate child, I believe, and so cannot go into society as does Maude."

"And do they go and leave her?" said Norrie. "The poor child must feel it lonely."

"Maude is not the kind of girl to give up pleasure and devote her time to an invalid," said Sister Clare, "tho' yet not thoroughly selfish, unless she has changed a great deal in six years. Her name is Varley, tho' she is often called Miss Erington."

About an hour afterwards when Mrs. Erington was taking her leave, Norrie heard the words: "You will remember, dear, won't you, that she is to be thoroughly refined, a perfect lady, and of good family. Mr. Erington is very particular on these points as, of course, the most of her time must be spent with Alice."

"Let me sum up now what I've got to remember," the Superioress said. "She is to be kind-hearted, sympathetic, young and pretty, take the place of governess and companion, play and sing well, paint and read well, refined, well educated, of good family, and of a bright and sunny disposition, and you want her in three days' time."

"Yes, that's exactly it. I hope you will succeed, dear. It will be a great trouble off my mind."

"Very well! This is Tuesday. Come on Thursday, Ada, and I think I shall have found just the young lady that will suit you."

A few minutes after, she went to Norrie, with a beaming countenance. "My dear child," she said, taking her in her arms, "I expect I shall lose you. I had hoped to find something for you in some part of New York so that you might come sometime to see me, when, here comes right to the door the exact thing that will suit you. Did Sister Clare tell you all about my sister?"

"Yes, Mother, and about Alice, who is an invalid, and cannot go into society."

"Well, my sister's husband is a wealthy, southern gentleman. Perhaps, you do not exactly realize what a wealthy southern gentleman is. It means simply that there is no end to his money. The family are going on a twelve months' tour. They are to visit some of the most important cities of the world and they wish to take Alice with them. The doctors say she has not long to live, but the father, who idolizes her, will not believe it and wishes her to be better educated so as to take her place in society when she gets stronger. He will not have a stiff or middle-aged governess, but a nice young girl, bright and lively, who will keep Alice in good spirits. In fact, it is as much companion as governess she wants. Maude is a nice girl, but fond of gaiety, and so does not feel disposed to spend the most of her time with Alice. So Ada thought the best thing she could do, as Mr. Erington has business in New York just now, was to come to me, having so many young girls under my care, I might find one who would suit her. And, Norrie, I know of no one so well fitted for the situation as yourself. You will receive a good salary, my child, and, perhaps it will not take you long to cancel that debt, which troubles you so much."

"Oh! dear Mother!" exclaimed Norrie. "How thankful I am! But are you sure I will do? Would my humble birth interfere in any way? I heard Mrs. Erington say that the person should be of good family."

"They are rather proud in this way," answered the Mother, "but generous and nice. You are of honest parents, Norrie, and in my eyes that is good family enough. They will take you on my recommendation and ask no further questions. It often grieves me," she went on, "to see Maude and her mother so fond of the world and its pleasures, especially Maude. She is so young and impressionable, it will leave her with little taste for quiet home life, I fear. I've never seen Alice, but she is a sweet child, I think, from what I hear. And now, Norrie, my dear, will you be prepared on Thursday to give them an answer?"

"I am prepared now, dear Mother, and only thankful to accept the situation."

On Thursday Mrs. Erington came, accompanied by Maude. Norrie was led to their presence by the Superioress. She had dressed herself plainly and neatly, a black dress falling gracefully round her tall, stately form, a cluster of moss rosebuds[95] at her throat, her rich, brown hair, which would curl in little soft rings, in spite of all the brushing, needed no ornament. Her face was thinner, and a little paler than it was some four weeks ago; her sweet, brown eyes had a quiet, rather grave expression, which seemed capable of winning any heart. The look of resolution which had settled on her face had given to it a dignity which seemed to suit her. She felt not the slightest bit of nervousness as she approached the wife and daughter of a millionaire, and never for a moment lost her calm self-possession. Mrs. Erington was a tall, well-made woman, her face was handsome with a rather haughty, tho' not hard, expression. But it was on Maude that Norrie's eyes lingered. She was of middle height, slight figure, black hair and eyes, pale face but yet with a wonderful amount of animation in it. The lips were full and rich, nicely curved, and seemed made for smiling, her face beamed with pleasure, and a softened look shone from her large, black eyes as they rested on Norrie.

"And this is your favourite pupil, whom you've told us so much about?" said Mrs. Erington, rising and taking Norrie's hand, surveying her critically as she did so. "I am pleased to meet you, my dear, and hope you will consent to accompany us abroad."

"I am most happy to consent, Mrs. Erington," said Norrie, "and only hope I shall give satisfaction in whatever is expected of me."

"I think that will be an easy task for you, Miss Moore. It is simply to make pleasant the dull hours of a sweet girl of sixteen, who is in a delicate state of health. The lessons need not be daily, and only what she wishes to learn."

Then Maude came forward and, as they were introduced, they smiled into each other's eyes. "And you are all the way from Newfoundland?" said Maude. "You are the first young lady I've met from there."

"And you are the first Southern young lady I have met," answered Norrie.

"Then we shall be a curiosity to each other," laughed Maude Varley.

As they were leaving, she whispered to the Superioress, "Auntie, why did you not tell us she was a beauty?"

"What an eye you have for the beautiful, Maude, my child!" answered her aunt. "Norrie is beautiful, but she has truth and goodness, which are more worthy of admiration."

"I'm sure Alice shall fall in love with her at first sight," said Maude.

They were to come for Norrie on Saturday, then proceed to their Southern home for Alice, from whence they were to sail for the Old World.[96] Norrie went in charge of a lady friend of the Superioress to the city, where she added a little to her not extensive wardrobe, and on Saturday bid a tearful adieu to her kind friend and departed with Maude and her mother. She had left Mrs. Hamilton's address with the Superioress, who promised faithfully to write on the following week to her, and let her know that she (Norrie) was safe and well.

How Norrie's heart bounded with delight in anticipation of actually beholding what she had so often read and dreamed of. The old plantations, where years ago the slaves had served in bondage, the glowing clime and delicious odours of the sunny south, the magnolia, the grape vine and orange groves, the old historic scenes, which Harriet Stowe in her writings[97] so vividly brings to the mind of the reader.

It was only as they were leaving the hotel that Norrie was presented to Mr. Erington. "The real type of a haughty Southerner," she thought, as she bowed to him.

It was night when they arrived. Norrie felt just a little bit awed as the grand, stately, Erington carriage drew up near the depot. She was left to her own thoughts pretty well during the drive. Mr. and Mrs. Erington and Miss Varley kept up quite an animated conversation about places they had visited and people they had met. Presently, Maude said, "Look, Miss Moore, you say one of your highest ambitions is to see an old-time Southern home. We are just entering our grounds now. This place belonged to Alice's great-grandfather and here, previous to the Civil War, the darkey slaves hoed the cotton and the corn." How Norrie's ardent young soul drank in the beauty of the scene! The fireflies danced in the sparkling splendour amongst the immense forest trees. The drive was long and winding. Soon, the house came in sight. It was just what her imagination had often pictured: large and white, shaded by towering trees, surrounded by climbing vines, and flowers of gorgeous hues and sweetest odours, sparkling fountains sending their cooling sprays into the air.

Alice had waited up to meet them. She was lying on a small couch drawn near the window, as it was (even for that clime) an unusually sultry night, and a neat looking little quadroon[98] maid was sitting near, fanning her. Alice was not much like a Southern girl; her skin was very fair, almost to transparency, with that bright, hectic colour in her cheeks which tells its own sad tale. Her eyes were large and blue, with a wistful expression; a mass of pale, golden curls covered her small head. Norrie could have taken her in her arms then and there, she reminded her so much of her loved Lucy. She greeted her stepmother and sister affectionately, but threw her arms convulsively round her father's neck, who held her to his heart as if he would, in defiance of all the doctors and everyone else, keep the gentle spirit in its earthly prison, by the strength of his love alone. She then turned with a searching gaze to Norrie. "This is Miss Norrie Moore, Alice dear," said Maude, gaily. "She has come from the far North, the island of Newfoundland."

Norrie advanced with one of her sweetest, winning smiles, and took the two small white hands in hers. "I hope I shall please you, Miss Erington," she said gently.

"Norrie Moore," Alice murmured, softly. "What a musical name, and, oh! what a sweet face you've got. But do not call me Miss Erington any more. Will you call me Alice, and you will let me call you Norrie, will you not?"

"Most gladly, dear, if it pleases you."

Only one week passed before they left for their long tour, and Norrie felt as if an eternal separation lay between her and those she loved.

CHAPTER SEVENTEEN

John Moore had intended to keep faithfully the secret which Doctor Hamilton had entrusted to him, but it was not as easy as he thought. His wife, woman-like, was quick to suspect something when Norrie, while at school, made some allusion in one of her letters to her music and painting lessons.

"I thought," said Bridget, "that she was only to larn the sensible part of edication."

"If they chose to larn anything else to her, I can't help it," answered John.

But Bridget was not to be so easily put off. "'Tis no use, John Moore," she said, "tellin' stuff like that to me. They don't go larnin' girls complishments in schools like that for nothin'. Either you'r payin' for it onknowns't to me, or Mrs. Hamilton is, an' ye may as well tell me or I'll find it out for meself."

So John thought it safer to confide in her, with strict injunctions that she was to keep it to herself, which she promised to do, but of course she could not keep it from Jane Smith, her bosom friend and confidante, who was often engaged at Mrs. Brandford's when there was any extra work on. And Mrs. Brandford's housekeeper knew of the intimacy between her and Bridget Moore, and got around her in such a manner as to draw all she knew with regard to Norrie out of her, and then go with the gossip to her mistress. And on the night of Harry's departure for his business up west of the island, she went with a fresh piece of gossip to Mrs. Brandford, of how the girl Jane Smith had told her that she had heard from Bridget Moore only that day, that Norrie was as good as engaged, and that Harry Brandford was like her shadow, and she would not be at all surprised if they were married soon. This set Mrs. Brandford in a towering rage, and, when her stepson arrived home after bidding goodbye to Norrie, she met him with the words: "Are you aware, Harry Brandford of the gossip that's going on about you? You've been flirting with that girl, Nora Moore, 'til people are actually speaking of your engagement and possible marriage with her."

"And what if they are?" said Harry, quite coolly.

"What if they are?" she repeated. "Why, the end of it will be that her folks will think you are going to marry her, but I, of course, know you are not mad enough for that."

He smiled slightly as he said, "Then, I expect you'll entertain serious doubts as regards my sanity, when I tell you that I shall think myself a blessed and happy man when I win from Miss Moore the promise which I hope to win, that she will one day do me the honour of becoming my wife."

Rage kept her silent, and he left before she had time to speak again. So next evening she hurried to pour her tale into Mrs. Hamilton's ears, and hoped to enlist her on her side, by feigning a profound sympathy for her daughter. Next morning Lucy was feeling a little better, and rose early, thinking she would give Norrie a surprise, for she knew she would come to see her as early as possible, on account of her illness the night before. But the hours dragged on slowly 'til noon, and yet no Norrie. "It is strange, Mamma," she remarked, "Norrie always came early to see me if I was sick."

"Perhaps she is not well, herself," suggested Mrs. Hamilton, thinking of the words Norrie had heard from Mrs. Brandford the evening before; but she said nothing to her daughter concerning them.

When afternoon came, and still no sign of Norrie, a message was sent to know if she were ill.

The answer came that she had sailed at midnight for St. John's.

Lucy and her mother were dumbfounded. "Gone to St. John's, Mamma? Why, what does it mean? Norrie never did anything like this before."

"Let us go at once to John Moore's. I cannot understand it," said Mrs. Hamilton.

But they were no wiser from what they learned there, at least Lucy was not. John Moore expressed much surprise, as did his wife, at them not knowing all about it. "She towld us," said John, "she hard news that made her go to St. John's sooner than she expected."

"And she left no message for us?" said Lucy.

"No," he answered, "she said nothin' about ye at all."

"Oh, Mamma," said Lucy, as they walked home. "We have never deserved this from Norrie."

"We cannot judge her yet, my dear," said her mother. "Wait until we hear from her. Perhaps she may explain all satisfactorily." A suspicion had entered Mrs. Hamilton's mind, and some of Norrie's words began to return to her—"I will pay my debt in another way"— but she said nothing to Lucy. She wrote at the earliest opportunity to Mrs. Dane, telling of Norrie's sudden departure to town, in which she and Lucy enclosed a letter for the latter, fearing her former address might not find her. Lucy's was full of reproaches; Mrs. Hamilton's a request to know why she had acted so.

This threw their friends in town into some consternation. Why had Norrie come to town, and been there for over a week, and not go to see them, nor let them know of her presence there? May and her husband, and Mrs. Dane and Frank were holding a consultation over it when Lilian and Will Roy came in. When the latter heard the news, he said: "I'm blessed if I was mistaken after all. I would not say anything about it before, because I know you would all laugh at me, but I tell you this much now, for a certain fact, Norrie Moore sailed on the *Portia* one night last week."

"Will, you're crazy!" said his sister.

"I won't dispute that, Lil," he answered. "Perhaps there is a slate off my upper storey, but it does not deny the fact that I, with my own eyes, saw Miss Moore on the deck of the *Portia* the last time she sailed. It was about twelve o'clock. I was there to see a couple of chums off. Of course, I could not take my oath on it, tho' I feel just as sure as if I could. I noticed her move away amongst the crowd, too, as if she did not wish to be recognized, so I said if it is really Norrie we will soon know, and I'll hold my tongue for a while, which was no easy matter, I can tell you."

"And why did you not go on board and speak to her?" asked May.

"Because the steamer was just in the act of moving off when I saw her."

They went to the house where Norrie had kept her classrooms and found she had not been there. They then went to Harvey's office, and learned that a second-class ticket had been taken for Miss Moore to New York about a week ago. And Will turned to be out quite a hero.

They wired Mrs. Hamilton immediately. It was some days before she broke the news to her daughter. When she did so, it had such an effect on her that she feared a serious illness would be the result, and now she was no longer in doubt but that Norrie had made this sacrifice for Lucy's sake.

CHAPTER EIGHTEEN

The smart little schooner *Mermaid* is sailing swiftly before the wind towards St. Rose. On her deck stands Harry Brandford, watching the shore with longing eyes, for does it not contain the dearest treasure in the world to him, and soon he will see the sweet, brown eyes brighten with love for him. Ah! he knew she would give him her promise now. She was too loyal to let anything any longer stand between their happiness. He felt so light-hearted that he broke into the words of a gay song:—

> There's a pair of roguish dark-blue eyes waiting for
> me on shore.

"The eyes waiting for me are brown, tho'," he thought.

> And a pair of arms that will twine around and never
> loose me more,

"I'm not sure of this either; my darling is shy of caresses."

> And a smile that's like the sunshine, as it dances o'er
> the spray,
> Then sing yo ho, that the winds may blow,
> Which carry me home to-day.

"Ah! that is true," he said. "Like the sunshine indeed is her smile." They anchored out in the stream, and rowed ashore. The first one he met was Jerry Malone.

"Hallo, Jerry," he said. "How have you all been since? Any strange news?"

"Not much," said Jerry, grinning, and looking up and down. "She's gone away, dat's all."

"She—who?" asked Harry.

"Her," he said, nodding in the direction of John Moore's house. "Norrie Moore."

All the brightness died out of Harry's face. "Gone away," he echoed. "Where to? St. John's?"

"No! furder den dat," said Jerry, and the grin on his face broadened.

Harry said no more but walked in the direction of what was once Norrie's home. He found John and his wife out in the grounds and learned from them all they knew concerning Norrie's flight.

He turned and left them, with a heavy heart. John walked with him some distance 'til he knew he was out of sight of Bridget, then, taking from his pocket the little packet which Norrie had given him, said, "She gave me this to give ye, Mr. Brandford, and towld me to let no wan see it but you and me."

His heart felt a little lighter, as he reverently took it in his hand. "Perhaps," he thought, "this will explain matters." "I can hardly believe, Mr. Moore," he said, "that she has gone to New York."

"Oh, yes sir, that's sartin," said John. "Mrs. Hamilton heard it from the Danes." "I'll be bound she'll know nothin' about this," muttered John, as he walked back to his wife.

"What did ye give Mr. Brandford, John?" asked Bridget.

"What!" said he, looking spellbound, as he took his pipe from his mouth to stare at her.

"Look here, old man. It's no use tryin' to keep secrets from me. I wasen't born yisterday, an' I knew well enough ye diden't go out with him for nothin', so I went up the ladder and saw over the ruff."

"I'll be blowed!" said John. "If women don't bate banagher,[99] an' we all knows who he bates. Well, look here now, old woman. I towld ye somethin' afore, an' ye goes and prates about it to yer neighbours, 'til the next thing Norrie hears what poor Doctor Hamilton said she should never know. So don't let me ketch ye gossipin' about this, and have Norrie think 'tis I have the long tongue if iver she do come back."

"Well, den, what do ye be keepin' me in the dark about things for? The laws of God and man says husband an' wife should niver have no secrets between them, an' it's just as good to tell me for if ye don't I'll find it out like I did about the other."

"Well, it's only a little message Norrie gave me to give him when he came back, that's all. So I hope ye'll keep a quiet tongue about it!"

"I'll keep quiet this time all right," she said. "'Tis only to Jane Smith I ever spoke of the other but, since she's gone and gossiped about it, she'll get no more news out of me."

Harry walked on quickly, not daring to open the parcel 'til he was in the seclusion of his own room. When his eyes rested on the locket, his heart sank within him, for he knew then she intended that all must end between them. A short note was enclosed; it said:

DEAR HARRY,

The conditions under which I could have accepted this locket being an impossibility, I must return it to you. I am going far, far away, from all I know and love. That impediment to our happiness, instead of decreasing, has increased tenfold, as I learned the day after your departure. It would be useless for you to seek me, for I shall have left Newfoundland when you get this. I do not know what you will think of me but, no matter what you think, I must do what I'm doing. Try and forget me. Perhaps I am not worthy of the love you bear me, nor the trust you've placed in me. We will likely never meet again, but I will pray for you as long as I live, and I hope you will soon find one with whom you can be happy. Do not think that I suffer nothing in leaving you but, if I could only take your share of suffering along with my own, I would gladly do so. In deepest sorrow, I remain, ever 'til death,

Your faithful friend,
NORRIE

For the twentieth time he read those heartbreaking lines. Where had she gone, and why had she left him? These were the thoughts that racked his brain. "Oh, Norrie, my love," he murmured, "if you had felt one hundredth part of the pain I now suffer you would never have left me. Oh, are you truly cruel and heartless, or can it be possible that there is, known only to yourself, something of so serious a nature as to justify our lifelong separation? I cannot believe it," he concluded, "but whatever happens I will never lose my faith in your truth and goodness, and I will be true to your memory all my life."

He went to Mrs. Hamilton's that evening and heard all she had learned from the Danes, together with the account from Lucy of Norrie's last evening there, and her last words to her. Mrs. Hamilton mentioned nothing of what had passed between Mrs.

Brandford and Norrie, for how could she do so without betraying Lucy, and she must be excused if she shrank from letting Harry Brandford know the humiliating fact that her daughter had loved him unsought. Lucy felt for the first time in her life anger and resentment against her friend. "I did not deserve such treatment from her," she said to Harry.

"There is something behind it all," he said, "and I shall set myself to work to find it out, for there is heartbreak in every line she has written to me."

Harry went about his duties as usual, but his handsome face was paler, the lines of his mouth firmer, and in his deep, grey eyes lay such a pathetic sadness that a close observer would know that some heavy grief lay at his heart. Strange to say, a suspicion of his stepmother had taken possession of him from the first. "If I find out that she has anything to do with driving my dear one from me," he thought, "I will not answer for the consequences." During his leisure hours he devoted his time to his beloved violin and poured forth his sorrow in soft, mournful strains. He often played over the last song she had sung to him, "In the Gloaming," and an old song they both loved, "Golden Love."[100] Between himself and his stepmother, Norrie's name was never mentioned.

CHAPTER NINETEEN

And how fares it with our heroine? She is enjoying, as her heavy heart will let her, all the novelty of travel in foreign lands, drinking in the sublime beauties of nature, satisfying her artistic soul by gazing enraptured at rare paintings of the old masters, at the statues of famous sculptors. At old ruins and scenes that she had read of in history: she had seen Runnymede whilst in England, and the spot where John had signed Magna Charta. She had visited that fairyland Killarney, had sailed the Mediterranean, where the drooping trees mirror their branches in its waters. They had spent a year in travelling and, during that time, Alice Erington had become warmly attached to Norrie. She seemed happy only when in her company. But the poor child's health was not improved and on this account they could travel only by easy stages. Maude Varley and her mother were also much attached to Norrie, and Maude actually often remained a while from gay company to have a quiet chat with her and Alice. Mr. Erington admired her very much and was fond of her for his daughter's sake as well as for her own. There were times when Norrie thought of the past with such deep sadness that for a moment a keen regret for having left home took possession of her. How often she thought of Harry, how his sad reproachful gaze rose before her. At times she felt she would give the whole world for one look at his dear face, one clasp of his strong hand. She wondered if he ever thought of her, and did he hate her for what she had done? if he was learning to care for Lucy, and if the latter was stronger and happier?

She did not see a great deal of company; her whole time was devoted to Alice. The studies were only a few hours each day, and only on the days her young charge was well enough. So Norrie's duties were light. She was much admired by all who saw her, for her beauty, her perfect bearing, and her calm self-possession. She was not without gentlemen admirers, and not a few would wish to be something more, but the thought of another taking Harry Brandford's place in her heart seemed like sacrilege, and she firmly believed she would go unmarried to her grave. She sometimes wondered if there would ever be a chance of their being reunited. If, after she had cancelled that debt, which she would soon be enabled to do, she could hear that Lucy had got over her attachment to Harry and was happy, if she wrote to him, would he forgive her and love her just the same or had he put her entirely out of his mind and heart. It seemed an age, a whole year, without hearing one word from home. How many might be dead and almost forgotten in that time? She intended to write Lucy very soon; she could not well do so while travelling. She longed even to see a Newfoundland paper. She had a habit of searching in drawers and bookcases in every hotel they stayed in the hope of finding one, but only to meet always with disappointment.

Before they had visited all the places they had mapped out, Alice was seized with a longing for home and begged her father so earnestly to take her, that he had not the heart to refuse. They were now in Liverpool, waiting for the steamer which was to take them. Norrie and Alice were seated in a private drawing-room of a first-class hotel; they had been talking for some time. Alice had confided to her all the little secrets of her childhood, of her own dear mother, whom she remembered, of her father's love for her, and hers for him. "It makes me feel sad, Norrie," she said, "to think of his grief when I am gone, for I know I shall not live much longer."

"That is only because you are feeling depressed today," said Norrie, playing with her golden curls, which, she said, so often reminded her of the dear friend and companion of her far-off Newfoundland home-life. She had confided to Alice some of her history for, she, like all who are on the verge of eternity, was quick to read the heart, and she knew that the circumstance which had driven Norrie from her home was an unhappy one. Norrie had told her of the humble life to which she belonged, for she had no false shame at being known as the daughter of a poor fisherman and would just as soon have acknowledged it to a peer of the realm, were it necessary to do so. After talking for some time, Alice fell into a light slumber, and Norrie felt the old longing for news of home overpowering her. She saw several drawers of a cabinet which stood in a corner of the room. "I wonder would there be a paper in any of these?" she thought. She walked on tiptoe towards it, for fear of awakening Alice, noiselessly opened one and, to her intense joy, the pink shade[101] of an *Evening Telegram* greeted her eyes. She looked at the date: it was June, and this was September—three months' old. Well, it was from home, anyway. She pressed it to her lips, this welcome messenger from her native land, and soon was scanning over the local items. Then she turned to the births, deaths and marriages. Ah, poor Norrie! What made every particle of colour leave her face as her eyes were fixed in a stony, sightless stare on the paper? Simply this:—

Married, at St. Rose, at the residence of the bride's mother, Lucy, only daughter of the late Doctor Hamilton, to Harry Brandford.

At last, with a start, she came to herself. "And so it is all over," she said, "and my sacrifice is complete. Well! did I not wish for it? Did I not do all in my power to bring it about, and why am I not glad?" Ah! strange, mysterious, human nature, perhaps deep down in Norrie's heart, almost unknown to herself, there lingered a hope that, after all, Harry would be true to her, that Lucy would learn to be happy without him. "Yes," she told herself, "I am glad, but I did not think it would be so soon, not even one little year, and he can be happy with another. Ah! and perhaps he was even glad when his first disappointment was over, that he could marry one of his own class of life." Then she thought of the money which she must soon send. At first she intended to send it privately to Mrs. Brandford. Now she changed her mind. "It shall go to the firm of Brandford," she said, "for Harry must know that it is paid. He shall never have it to say that the money which should have been his was spent on my education."

She replaced the paper and, seeing that Alice was still sleeping, she crept away to her room, where she shed bitter tears of sorrow, and (tho' she would not acknowledge it to herself) of disappointment also. In an hour she had schooled herself to calmness and resignation. She tried to picture Lucy, with the light of happiness in her eyes and the bloom of health on her cheeks. "I wonder is Doctor Hamilton smiling at me now," she thought, looking up at the twilight sky, where the stars were just beginning to glimmer, in their setting of soft, azure blue, "and is he pleased? Oh!" she thought, "I can never, never see my home again, not for years, whatever. I could not trust myself, and I don't believe I can ever learn to forget him. I love him as much, nay, even more than when I left home, tho' it is wrong for me now. I must put him from my mind and heart forever, for he is another's." Two days after, they sailed for the home of the Eringtons, from whence Norrie sent to the firm of Brandford, a money order for the sum of four hundred dollars, with the accompanying little note:

This is the amount which the late Mr. Brandford refused to accept from the late Mrs. Moore, in payment of her husband's indebtedness to him, and which I, their daughter, now gladly pay, and so keep the promise I made over a year ago to Mrs. Brandford.

NORRIE MOORE.

CHAPTER TWENTY

Lucy Hamilton, contrary to her mother's expectations, bore up bravely against the loss of Norrie, and, strange to say, her love for Harry Brandford had merged into that of deep, sisterly affection. It must have been her sweet sympathy in his suffering that brought the change about, for she knew his whole heart was, and ever would be, Norrie's. They often talked of her; they knew she was travelling, for the letter of the Mother Superioress to Mrs. Hamilton had explained all. They went to town as usual for the winter months, and then a strange thing happened. The cousin and namesake of Harry, whose picture Norrie had seen in his locket, had come from the United States to his native land, and met Lucy. They fell in love with each other. He went to St. Rose with his cousin early in the month of May and there, one month later, he and Lucy were married, and Norrie's sacrifice need never have been made. Lucy's husband was like his cousin in features, but was of a lighter and gayer disposition.

Mrs. Hamilton rejoiced to see her daughter looking so well and happy, for she was fast attaining that perfect health which her father had prophesied for her. She felt she was in duty bound to explain to Harry the cause of Norrie's sudden flight and had resolved to do so when the year's tour was ended, even at the cost of betraying Lucy's secret. "Then," she thought, "he can easily communicate with her and all will be well."

She told the whole story to her daughter first, of all Mrs. Brandford had said on that evening, and what Norrie had found out and of how, without the slightest doubt, she had exiled herself from home and friends, in gratitude to them and for love of Lucy.

"Oh! Mamma," she said, "you should have told Harry long ago of this," as her tears fell fast, and her gentle heart was touched, at the noble sacrifice her friend had made in her behalf.

"I would have done so, Lucy, only for your sake, but now, as you are married, I don't mind, and I'm sure you won't either."

"Not at all," she answered. "And besides, you know, Mamma, I must not have cared as much as I fancied I did, or I never could have forgotten so quickly."

"Another thing troubles me," said Mrs. Hamilton. "I cannot tell him all without letting him know of his stepmother's share in it, for she was in reality the whole cause. It will make him have a bad feeling towards her."

"Well, Mamma, she deserves it, and it's not right to spare her at their expense. I hope they will be happy together yet. When Harry and I go on our tour, I won't come back 'til I find her."

That same day Mrs. Hamilton told all to Harry. She kept one thing back, and that was about his stepmother speaking of the old debt of her father's. She thought it wiser to leave this out. "The poor child," she said to him, "on learning what she would never have known but for your stepmother, that I had helped towards her education, felt she was justified in making this sacrifice. But I assure you, Harry, I would never have allowed her to go had I even a suspicion of her intention."

It was a great surprise to Harry to learn that Lucy had once cared for him with anything more than a friend's love and, if he thought it unjust that Mrs. Hamilton had not told him these things long before, he kept silent about it. "This," he said, thoughtfully, "must be the impediment to our happiness which she so often spoke of, and finding how much more she owed you than she thought at first, in the exaggerated idea she had of it, she said in her letter to me that it had increased tenfold. Oh, if I had only known!" he said, regretfully.

"Yes," said Mrs. Hamilton, "or even if Lucy had known, how much might have been spared you both." Lucy's husband thought it wiser to delay their wedding tour 'til the winter months, for he feared the heat of a warmer climate would not be good for his wife. So it was arranged for them to start at the end of December, and now his cousin Harry had decided to accompany them, his sole object being to find Norrie. Lucy's mother was to remain at Mrs. Dane's 'til their return.

One day, early in October, Harry was sitting busily engaged in his office, when the mail was brought in. As soon as he had finished what he was doing, he turned to the letters, when the sight of one sent a strange thrill through him, for which he could not account. He gazed at it for some time. The letter was registered, and bore many foreign postmarks. At last a joyous light broke over his face. "If she is alive," he said, "it is her writing," as he hastily tore it open. When his eyes had devoured the contents, and he looked at the money order, he arose to his feet, a dangerous gleam in his eyes. "May Heaven protect me from doing what I would regret all my life," he said. "She has taunted my poor darling with that old debt of her father's. Oh, Norrie, my love," he moaned, "why did you not confide all your troubles to me and let me shield you from her insults?" He had not spoken one word to Mrs. Brandford of what Mrs. Hamilton had told him. "She was not worth it," he told himself. But now he went straight to her and flung the note and money order towards her. "Read that," he said, "and see if there is woman enough left in you to feel ashamed." Never, before nor after, did Harry Brandford allow his passion to take such possession of him.

Mrs. Brandford grew white with fear; she had not counted on this. She thought that with Norrie's disappearance all danger of what she had said to her being known to Harry was past. "I know all you said to that poor child that evening at Mrs. Hamilton's. When she left her home, you drove her from it, but I did not know of this 'til now. For the future, woman, we are as strangers. I loathe and despise you, and the only thing I'm sorry for is, that I cannot take from you my father's name. At the end of the year I leave Newfoundland and will not return 'til I find and bring with me, Norrie Moore as my wife. In the meantime you must find another home for yourself; the same roof can shelter us no longer. The yearly allowance which my father left you will be sufficient for your needs. You are welcome to those four hundred dollars, and may the hard earnings of a poor orphan make you happy." With that, he turned and left her.

She had not uttered one word during the interview; she knew it was useless. She had overstepped herself, and her meanness, cowardice and uncharitableness had found her out when she least expected it. Rage, disappointment and mortification were now her portion. It was no small thing to an ambitious nature like hers to give up this elegant home where she had ruled for so many years, and had all her needs supplied, so that she had amassed quite a fortune by investing her yearly allowance in the bank. But she knew that the laws of the Medes and Persians[102] were not more inexorable than Harry Brandford when he was dealing out justice, and so she had to submit with as much grace as possible. "To think," she said to herself, "of that girl getting the better of me after all."

Norrie, of course, had given no address, and all they could make out from the letter was the state in which she resided, so, when Lucy and the two Harry Brandfords left St. John's in December, they decided to go first to the — Convent. The Superioress there, who was delighted at seeing Lucy, gave them all the particulars she knew regarding Norrie. She had received a letter from her since their return from abroad. She was well, she said, but not happy, she fancied from the tone of her letter. She had spoken of her young charge, Alice, as being far from well. The Superioress was at a loss to know if it were Norrie's Mr. Brandford to whom Lucy was married, 'til she heard her say to one of the Sisters: "My husband has lived for the past twelve years in a part of the States; he only went to Newfoundland a year ago."

They then set out for the South, and arrived at the home of the Eringtons only to find it shut up, and to learn from the servant who had charge that the family had gone travelling again for the winter and taken Miss Moore with them.

"And what of Miss Erington?" asked Lucy. "Was she well enough to travel again?"

"Ah," answered the woman, with a sorrowful face, "sure that is why the master would not remain at home. Poor dear Alice died about two months ago, and he was simply heartbroken after her."

"At what time do you expect the family home?" asked Harry, trying bravely to hide his disappointment.

"They did not state any definite time, sir," answered the servant. "They said they'd be away for the winter, that's all."

They turned away, discouraged.

"Well, all we can do now," said Lucy, "is to continue on our journey, stop at the most elegant and quiet hotels, which they will likely select on account of their late trouble, and, perhaps, when we are least expecting it, we shall meet them." And her advice was taken.

But when Lucy's husband got a chance of speaking to her alone, he said, "I fear, Lucy, there is little chance of finding them. The world is a big place, you know, and we have no clue to their whereabouts. The woman could not even tell us any particular place which they intended visiting."

"Nevertheless, Harry, with all those drawbacks, I feel confident we shall find her."

Lucy did not, of course, tell the exact circumstances to her husband of the estrangement between Harry and Norrie. It would not do. All she told him was that there had been a misunderstanding between them, of which his stepmother was the cause. So with hope and doubt mingled in their hearts, they sailed for Europe.

Yes, poor Alice had looked her last on this world sooner than anyone expected. It seemed as if she were only waiting to reach home 'ere she laid down the burden of her young life, for one week after she took to her bed. Norrie would not leave her except to take a few hours' sleep. One day whilst sitting by her bedside, Alice said to her, "Norrie, dear, I think since we've left England that you have been troubled more than usual about something."

"Why do you think this, Alice?"

"Because I've noticed a look in your eyes which was not there before—a kind of sadness without hope."

"What a keen sense of perception you have, Alice dear! Yes, you are right. I have learned something which has caused me some sorrow, and yet which I was pleased to learn."

"I do hope you will be very happy yet, Norrie. You are too good and brave to spend your life mourning over a hopeless sorrow. The world wants women like you."

"Ah, no, Alice, I'm not the perfect being you think me," said Norrie, smiling. "We all have our faults, and I can lay claim to a large share."

A few days after this, Alice passed quietly away, as if she were going to sleep. Just one hour before her spirit had departed, they were all standing near her, when she opened her large blue eyes and, gently disengaging one hand from her father's, she reached it towards Norrie, who drew near and took it in both of hers. "Norrie," she said, taking a breath after each word, "would you wish above all things to return to your native land and be happy again?"

"I would, darling," answered Norrie, "if it were possible. But it is not."

"Do not say that. I feel that it is not impossible and, you know, those on the verge of a brighter and better world can see with a clearer vision the things which are likely to happen to those whom they love, and must leave behind, and, if it is permitted, to work in Heaven for your dear ones on earth, my work there shall be to bring happiness to Papa and you." Those were the last words she spoke. Norrie shed some of the saddest tears of her life at gentle Alice's death. Mrs. Erington and Maude grieved for her also, but her father was inconsolable, so much so that a week after the funeral he said he could bear his life no longer there, where everything reminded him so much of his lost darling, and begged them to close the house for six months and go anywhere; he did not care where.

Norrie thought she should now look out for another situation, but Mr. Erington would not hear of her leaving them yet. So she accompanied them in the capacity of companion to Maude, and it was a great boon to this worldly but good-hearted girl. Their recent bereavement prevented them from going into gay company for a time, and Norrie's ideas and language were of such an elevating nature that they filled the hitherto worldly mind of the girl with thoughts and aspirations, far beyond the empty flattery and whirl of fashionable life, and made her remember there was something higher and nobler than mere pleasure, and gratifying one's every desire, to live for. They spent a month in Switzerland, another in Germany, then went to Italy, and from that to Florence. Here, Mr. Erington seemed to rest content. Alice had wished to visit these places, but when the sudden longing for home seized her, all interest in everything else faded. They had engaged a private and elegant suite of rooms in a suburban and first-class hotel, which was never overcrowded. They had spent nearly two months here, when Mr. Erington, the first sharp sting of his sorrow over, began to think of returning home.

Norrie and Maude had a habit of remaining up for a last chat after Mr. and Mrs. Erington had retired. Tonight they remained out on the balcony which led off the drawing-room. It was a beautiful night in the month of May; the moon shone brightly, and soft clouds of white, tinted with amber, with a background of blue, sailed slowly through the heavens, veiling now and then the twinkling stars.

"I shall never forget Florence," said Norrie. "I don't say its beauty is greater than that of other places I've seen, but somehow it seems to impress me more." She did not then dream what reason she should have for remembering Florence.

"Do you know, Norrie," said Maude, "I enjoy the beauties of nature more than I ever did before. In fact, I hardly gave them a thought 'til your description of them made me open my eyes and look." She lingered on the balcony some time after Norrie had returned to the drawing-room. Soon she entered, too, with a bound towards Norrie, who was touching softly the keys of the piano. "Oh! do come," she said, "and look at some new arrivals. They only came a few hours ago. I watched them as they walked the grounds, and saw their faces plainly in the moonlight, a lady and two gentlemen. Oh! you should see one of them, Norrie. I could not describe him. I think he must be like Romeo; his face is so sad and handsome." When they got to the balcony again, the trio had walked back to the house and so could not be seen by the girls.

"They're gone in," said Maude, disappointedly. "I wonder if they will come out again."

"Hardly," said Norrie. "It is getting late now, and it's likely they are tired after their journey. Are they English people, I wonder?"

"They are English-speaking people," said Maude, "because I heard their conversation." They then came in, but left the balcony doors open.

"Will you sing something for me before we go to our rooms?" asked Maude. "I feel quite musical tonight."

"Certainly, dear," assented Norrie, going to the piano. An unaccountable feeling had taken possession of her during the last half hour; memories of the past seemed to hover round, and would not leave her. As she sat at the piano, she thought of that last happy evening she had sung for him, the hero of her dreams, and almost unconsciously she broke into the same song, but, oh! with such sad pathos in her voice that, when she came to the second verse, Maude was moved to tears:

> In the gloaming, oh! my darling, think not bitterly of me,
> Tho' I passed away in silence, left you lonely, set you free,
> For my heart was crushed with longing, what had been, could never be,
> It was best to leave you thus, dear, best for you and best for me.[103]

As she finished the last verse, to their surprise the door opened and a voice which fell, ah! so familiarly on her ear, cried, "Norrie, Norrie, Norrie, oh! my darling, I felt I should be the first to find you." And, rising from the piano, she was clasped in the arms of Lucy Brandford.

"Oh! Lucy, my own dear Lucy," she murmured, resting the golden head on her shoulder. "What good angel has brought you here?" At this, Maude discreetly withdrew.

"Looking for you principally, and otherwise enjoying a tour with my husband, and, oh! Norrie," she said, looking fondly at her, "I know now all about what drove you from home. At first, I felt hard and bitter towards you, but now I know how much you love me, and what a noble self-sacrificing girl you are, but you shall be rewarded soon."

"I have all the reward I want, Lucy dear, when I see you looking so well and happy." She had grown a little pale when Lucy mentioned her husband. "I must prepare myself to meet him," she thought. "You did not tell me how you knew I was here."

"I lingered outside for a while, after the others went in," she explained, "and, when you began to sing, the balcony doors being open, every note and word could be distinctly heard. When I listened to the first few notes, I could not tell what was coming over me, I felt so strangely, but before you got to the end of the song, I knew to a certainty it was you. So I went in and told Harry I had found you, and made him come with me, tho' he said he was positive I was making a mistake."

Then some questions were asked and explanations followed, and finally Norrie said, "So you are strong now, Lucy, and perfectly happy?"

"Perfectly, Norrie!" she answered. "I have one of the kindest husbands in the world. When did you hear of my marriage, Norrie?"

"Not 'til last September. You know we were travelling all the time? I saw it then in an old paper."

"How proud I shall be introducing him to you," said Lucy.

Then a bewildered expression came over Norrie's face. "Introducing him to me?" she echoed. "Surely (with a smile) he is not changed so much that I shall need an introduction?"

Then it was Lucy's turn to look bewildered. But suddenly a light broke over her face and she dropped Norrie's hands, saying, "Tell me quickly, Norrie, where did you read of my marriage, and how was it stated?"

She told her.

"And you really believe I'm married to Harry Brandford of St. Rose, who is breaking his heart for love of you?"

"Of course, Lucy, what other Harry Brandford is there?"

"His cousin Harry, who went to Newfoundland the year after you left it; and we were married the following spring."

Norrie felt dazed. She saw herself for a moment by the side of a pond, and Harry near her, saying, "Only a cousin and namesake of mine, who has been for the past ten years in the United States."

But oh! the sudden rush of joy that came to her with the knowledge that he was true to her after all, and now there was no barrier to their happiness. Ah! surely Alice Erington had done her work well in Heaven.

"If you had happened to come across a later paper," went on Lucy, "you would have read a more correct account of our marriage. And now I must bring in my husband. He is waiting outside ever since. I would not allow him to come in with me, but I would not tell your Harry 'til I had the proof of my own eyes that it was really you, for if there should have been a mistake, the disappointment would have been terrible to him."

"Then he is with you also?" said Norrie, blushing, while a beautiful light shone in her eyes.

"Certainly," answered Lucy, smilingly. "He came to find you."

Then leaving Norrie for a moment, she returned, accompanied by a gentleman with a handsome, pleasant-looking face and smiling blue eyes, remarkably like the other Harry, Norrie mentally said, and the exact counterpart of the picture she had seen in his locket.

"My husband, Norrie," said Lucy.

"And this," he said, before his wife had time to say more, "is Miss Moore. You do not seem a stranger to me, for this little wife of mine has described you to me a hundred and one times, and I might safely say has talked of nothing else since we've met."

"Neither do you seem a stranger to me," said Norrie, as she gave him her hand. "You are so like your cousin, and it's enough for me to know you are dear to Lucy to make me like you."

They chatted on gaily for a few minutes, until Lucy interfered by saying, "We must leave her now, Harry. You know I've got the delightful task of telling the good news to your cousin yet."

They left her, and Norrie buried her face in her hands and actually wept tears of joy. It did not seem long 'til the door opened again and, taking a few steps forward, she was clasped in Harry Brandford's arms.

"Oh, Norrie, how could you do it?" was all he said.

"What else could I do, Harry? Tho' I should not have done it, I own, but I was bewildered, so many unpleasant things came to my knowledge together."

"You should have confided all to me, darling. What little faith you must have had in my constancy, Norrie, when you believed I had forgotten you enough to marry another?"

"Lucy has told you, then?"

"Yes, she has told me everything. I could never tell you what I suffered, Norrie, but the happiness of this night repays me for all."

"We will not talk of it now, Harry," she said. "We are happy, and let all the past be forgotten, but one thing I would say," smiling through happy tears, "if you had not been just a little cross that day at the pond when your cousin's picture fell from your locket, and told me more about him, and that you expected him in Newfoundland soon, and his name was exactly the same as yours, I might not have been so ready to take it for granted that it was you who had married Lucy."

"Yes," he said, "I plead guilty there. I own I was a bit jealous, where afterwards I found I had no reason to be."

When, some time after, Norrie went to their rooms, she found Maude almost breathless with suspense and curiosity, and the sight of Norrrie's radiantly happy face made her more curious still. Norrie satisfied her by telling the story of the last few years of her life, not, of course, entering into any details.

"And so, the handsome gentleman with the face like Romeo is your lover," said Maude. "I always thought you were too pretty not to have one somewhere."

The landlord was not a little surprised next day at hearing that both parties were leaving together in a couple of days, as they turned out to be old friends. The Erington and Brandford families grew very intimate during the journey.

Maude told Norrie that she almost envied her such a lover. They travelled all day by train as far as Calais,[104] passing through the famous Mount Cenis Tunnel,[105] then took the steamer to Dover,[106] and from that all land, travelling again 'til Liverpool[107] was reached. Then Maude and Norrie gazed at each other with sad faces, both with the one thought, "Here we must part." Mr. Erington had invited the whole party to go South with him and spend one month there, but they had to regretfully decline, as both the young gentlemen's business required their presence at home.

When bidding Norrie goodbye, Mr. Erington said, "I shall always associate you in my thoughts with my darling Alice, Miss Moore, and I am very, very sorry that our paths must lie so far apart."

"I shall never forget Alice, Mr. Erington," answered Norrie. "And I am glad I left my home just for the happiness of having known her."

Even Mrs. Erington, whose thoughts were chiefly, "I shall soon be able to mix in gay company again," felt a slight pang at parting with her.

Maude shed many tears at their separation.

They took different lines of steamers, of course, and two days before the Eringtons' departure, the Brandfords and Norrie sailed for Newfoundland, and so she, whose lot had been so unexpectedly cast amongst them, passed out of their lives.

Norrie and her lover enjoyed this ocean voyage immensely. Their past sorrows were forgotten during those blissful hours when they walked the deck by moonlight and told of each other's experiences since their parting. She told Harry of how, whenever she gazed at the moon to see her ideal, tho' not at all having any faith in the foolish superstition, his face in imagination always rose before her, and also of the promise she had made to Doctor Hamilton with regard to Lucy.

Harry had extracted from Norrie a promise that she would

marry him in St. John's, from whence he would take her to St. Rose as his bride. He told her that Mrs. Brandford had now found a home in the city, and would trouble them no more.

It was a beautiful morning in June when they reached St. John's. Frank Dane was at the wharf to meet them. The whole party went to Mrs. Dane's, where they were met by Mrs. Hamilton, Will and Jack Roy, also Lilian, and May and Philip Weston. Norrie had to answer endless questions, and good humouredly bore many reproaches from her friends, for, as Will Roy said, giving them the slip so cleverly.

Her marriage was set down for the morning of the sailing of the coastal steamer. Harry had telegraphed to John and Bridget Moore, informing them of it. It was very quiet. She was married early in the morning at Mrs. Dane's house. Very sweet she looked in her bridal robe of white, with veil and orange blossoms, her face wearing an angelic expression, as she solemnly and clearly pronounced her marriage vows. Lilian was bridesmaid and Frank best man.

Lucy's husband's place of business was in town, but they, together with Mrs. Hamilton, were to spend a month at St. Rose, and so accompanied the bride and groom to their future home. As Mrs. Dane said goodbye to Norrie, she whispered that Frank was again a model young man, and that he and Lilian were soon to be married, at which Norrie congratulated herself that her second attempt at match-making was a success, if the first had not been.

When they arrived at St. Rose, it was night; bonfires, rockets and guns saluted them on all sides, for Harry was a favourite with them, and Norrie quite a heroine in their eyes.

"I wishes ye much ji," said Jerry Malone, who was the first to greet them on entering their own grounds.

Next evening as the sun was setting amidst purple and gold in the western horizon, Harry asked his wife to sing one of his favourite songs. They went to the piano, Harry accompanying on the violin. She chose for her song one which she said suited them best: "Golden Love":—

Once more we meet beside the shining river,
    Not as we parted in the bye-gone days,
When storms of fate had torn our bonds asunder,
    And clouds obscured the golden love's dawn rays.
Once more we meet and cancel old regrets,
    Once more we meet and hand clasps hand again,
Never to ask if one of us forgets,
    Never to think of bye-gone hours of pain.

Once more we meet when sunset gilds the Heavens,
   Meet as we parted loyal, brave and true,
Only the hand of time has touched us gently,
   Changing perchance our hair to whiter hue.
Once more we meet the lonely hours are o'er,
   Once more we meet and own the past was best,
Never to part, oh, darling never more,
   Until the angels call us home to rest.[108]

And Harry Brandford, drawing his wife's head on his shoulder, murmured in low, happy accents, "never to part, oh, darling, never more, until the angels call us home to rest."

NOTES TO NOVEL

1. Original has "could cry."

2. Locally built schooners fishing on the Grand Banks of Newfoundland. In the 1880s and 1890s there was an extensive shipbuilding industry in the Grand Bank area. While the bank fishery decreased in other areas of Newfoundland in the 1880s, the south coast communities of Grand Bank and Burin maintained an impressive banking fleet.

3. Small or immature codfish.

4. In several parts of Newfoundland, and especially in the Grand Bank area where the beach extends for almost a mile along the coastline, fish was dried on the beach rather than on flakes. Flakes are open, elevated wooden platforms built of longers covered with spruce boughs on which the fish are laid to dry.

5. Carding is the process of cleaning, separating, and straightening the fibres of washed, sheared wool, usually by hand cards, a pair of wooden paddles, each with a short wooden handle, containing wire teeth. A small amount of the matted wool is placed on the toothed face of one card, and the other pulled across it several times, catching the fibres in its teeth. The carded wool is later spun into yarn by means of a spinning-wheel.

6. After grass was cut with a scythe, it was "made": it was scattered, allowed to dry for a day, then raked into rolls with long wooden rakes. The next evening it was raked and, with the aid of a hay prong, piled into "pooks" or stacks.

Men usually headed and split the fish, but women were involved in the final "making" or curing process: spreading the split fish to dry on flakes or on beach stones (although in some parts of Newfoundland, making fish meant splitting, gutting, and salting, as well as spreading and drying). The split fish was spread in the morning and taken up in the evening; and spread and taken up until sufficiently dried to be packed in a dry place, usually a store.

7. Short for "faith," a contraction from "in faith" or "i'faith"; a general exclamation among Irish.

8. A person who roves around from place to place.

9. Probably from the expression "Keep your wool on!" (c. 1880-1914) meaning "Don't get, or be, angry"; in this situation, it is equivalent to telling someone to "shut up."

10. A naughty or mischievous child. Between the sixteenth and the nineteenth

centuries this term was used pejoratively of women, often meaning an unpleasant woman.

11. A child's balancing board; a game of see-saw.

12. Probably an echo of British school language.

13. Pierced or impaled, especially in baiting a fishhook.

14. Vertiginous; dizzy.

15. Any variety of sticklebacks (*Gasterosteus* spp.); small fish found in fresh or brackish water.

16. Violin.

17. Unpleasant arguments or reactions; trouble.

18. Probably kept indoors and not allowed out to play.

19. Matthew 10:16 (KJV), "Behold I send you forth as sheep in the midst of wolves: be ye therefore wise as serpents, and harmless as doves."

20. Matthew 5:44 (KJV), "Love your enemies, bless them that curse you, do good to them that hate you, and pray for them which despitefully use you, and persecute you."

21. "The Harp that Once through Tara's Halls," poem by Thomas Moore (1779-1852).

22. Thomas Moore (1779-1852), Irish poet, singer, songwriter, and entertainer, author of "The Harp that Once through Tara's Halls." Moore is now best remembered for the lyrics of "The Minstrel Boy" and "The Last Rose of Summer." He intended many of his lyrics to be sung to the accompaniment of piano or harp. In the early twentieth century, Moore's songs were performed by John McCormack.

23. See n. 22.

24. See n. 4, a reference to the method of drying fish on beach stones rather than on flakes.

25. Put in the barn, where hay was stored for the winter.

26. "Dear," in the sense that it was costly to Norrie, as she was kept indoors for a week because of what she had done.

27. In the sense of arousing or capable of arousing sympathetic sadness and compassion (from *pathos* — a quality as of an experience or work of art, that arouses feelings of pity, sympathy, tenderness, or sorrow).

28. To propel a boat with a side to side motion by using an oar placed over the stern of the boat.

29. Device on a boat's gunwale, usually consisting of two thole-pins or a rounded fork, serving as a fulcrum for an oar and keeping it in place.

30. "Two girls and boys": the context suggests two boys and two girls.

31. In a noisy, lively mood.

32. A dory is a small flat-bottomed boat with flaring sides and a sharp bow and stern, providing both stability in the water and easy storage in stacks on deck, used especially in fishing with hand-lines and trawls. Cranky suggests that the boat did not respond well to maneuvering; uncooperative.

33. Close-lipped about money matters.

34. An echo of the common expression "ours is not to question why," which had its origins in Lord Alfred Tennyson's "The Charge of the Light Brigade" ("Theirs not to reason why" [stanza 2, line 6]).

35. Banking schooner.

36. Probably from folderols or falderals: foolishness, nonsense, trifles.

37. Stanch: to stop or check the flow of blood.

38. A large, partly decked fishing boat, propelled by oars or small sail and used in the coastal fishery to set and haul traps and for other purposes.

39. Steps or gaps in a fence or a wall that allow people to climb over.

40. Coastal steamship service began in the 1860s and provided transportation and mail service to Newfoundland's coastal communities.

41. French for seasickness; nausea caused by the motion of a boat.

42. A woman who acts as chief in a convent, abbey, or nunnery; a lady superior.

43. Sigismund Thalberg, born near Geneva 8 January 1812 (died 27 April 1871), was a composer and one of the most distinguished virtuoso pianists of the nineteenth century, and is remembered for his fantasias. On a tour of America in 1856, he enthralled his audiences with his flawless performances of his celebrated virtuoso showpieces. Like most visiting composers, he was compelled to write variations on tunes popular in America. Thalberg's "Home Sweet Home" (Air Anglais), Opus 72, is adapted from "Clari; or, Maid of Milan: an Opera" (1823). The song's text was written by John Howard Payne (1791-1852), an American author, actor, and playwright; Payne is best remembered for this song, which he wrote in 1822. The melody was composed by Sir Henry Bishop. While he was in the United States, Thalberg also wrote variations on "The Last Rose of Summer," the poem by Thomas Moore. His "Home Sweet Home" and "The Last Rose of Summer" were mainstays of popular concert programs and family musicales almost to the end of the nineteenth century.

44. From "Ye Banks and Braes o' Bonnie Doon" by Robert Burns (1759-1796).

45. "'Tis the Last Rose of Summer" by Irish poet Thomas Moore. This three-stanza poem was written in 1805 while Moore was at Jenkinstown Park in County Kilkenny, Ireland. Sir John Stevenson set the poem to its widely known melody.

46. A 732-ton schooner-rigged steamship of the Red Cross Line, owned by Bowring Company. It could reach New York from St. John's in five days, even with a Halifax stopover. The *Portia* was lost in 1899, wrecked on Big Fish Shoal on a voyage from New York to Halifax. The popular St. John's-New York service stimulated trade between these ports, as well as provided transport for many Newfoundlanders seeking employment and adventure off the island.

47. The entrance to the enclosed harbour of St. John's consists of a channel between the South Side and Signal Hill, with a depth of 11 metres. In the vicinity of Chain Rock, the Narrows is 61 metres wide. The channel, with high ground on either side, is exposed to strong easterly winds in early spring, and icebergs occasionally drift into the Narrows.

48. Affect negatively.

49. Scarlatina, or scarlet fever, an acute contagious disease caused by a haemolytic streptococcus, occurring predominately among children and characterized by a scarlet skin eruption and high fever.

50. Willingly; gladly; happily.

51. Getting.

52. Caroline Elizabeth Sarah (Sheridan) Norton (1808-1877) was a poet and novelist, born in London. She wrote songs, stories, and poems for periodicals, and also published long narrative poems.

53. Caroline Norton, "Bingen on the Rhine" (stanza 5). This touching poem

expresses the thoughts of a dying soldier stricken down in a foreign land (Germany), far from friends and home.

54. The words of this song were written by George Linley (1798-1865), who was born in Leeds; he was a verse writer and musical composer, and composed several hundred songs between 1830 and 1865. It was written and composed for Mr. Augustus Braham, and sung by him. It was probably written around 1830.

55. This epigraph (this is the only one in the novel) is the title of a song; the words are by Donald Reed Jr., and the music by Joseph Wheeler. It was one of the musical numbers in Charles H. Hoyt's musical comedy *A Trip to Chinatown*, which opened at Broadway's Madison Square Theatre 9 November 1891 and ran for 657 performances. It was the longest running Broadway musical in history to that time.

56. Having superior manners.

57. A soft thin muslin used in dresses and for trimmings.

58. Spinning already carded wool into yarn.

59. Even if.

60. *Evening Telegram*, started in 1879 by William James Herder, who apprenticed to *The Courier* as a printer; sixteen years later he bought out the paper, closed it down, and started his own daily newspaper, *The Evening Telegram*. The first issue appeared 3 April 1879 and consisted of a single sheet, folio format, of approximately 500 copies. Although there were eight other papers in St. John's at the time, none were dailies. Within weeks, the size of the paper doubled to two sheets, folio format.

61. Probably from the phrase (1815-1825) "spoil the sport," meaning to spoil the pleasures of others, in a game or in a social gathering.

62. Plenty of rain (British informal, an abundance).

63. Long tapering poles, usually conifers, with the bark left on them, used in the construction of roofs, floors, stages, flakes, and fence rails.

64. Fir, the balsam-fir (*Abies balsamea*).

65. Jerry Malone, already at the bottom of the social scale in St. Rose, loses rank even further.

66. From "jinx": to spoil, or to bring bad luck.

67. A small, temporary shelter in the woods, made of conifer branches made into a frame.

68. Probably a variant of "take the cake": to express incredulity.

69. Jibed: to utter mocking or scoffing words, to jeer, to taunt or deride.

70. A line from the poem "White Wings" (1884); words and music by Banks Winter.

71. See n. 45.

72. "Sweet Genevieve," a song by George Cooper, melody by Henry Tucker (1869).

73. One, two, or more small rings spaced along the top of a casting rod to hold and guide the line; or fittings on the end of a section of a sectional fishing rod, one fitting serving as a plug, and the other as a socket for fastening the sections together.

74. Fall hunting season.

75. A marriage to a person of a lower social class.

76. "A Life on the Ocean Wave," words by Epes Sargent (1813-1881), a nineteenth-century American poet, editor, and playwright, and set to music by Henry Russell

(1812-1900), a popular English pianist, baritone singer, and composer.

77. "I Heard the Bells on Christmas Day" (1864) by Henry Wadsworth Longfellow (1807-1882), which is based on Luke 2:13-14; music by John B. Calkin.

78. The spacious, four-storey Atlantic Hotel, with a superb view of St. John's harbour, opened in May 1885; it was destroyed by fire in 1892. Its main entrance was on Duckworth Street, opposite King's Road, with another entrance on Water Street. It catered to the wealthy, and its guests included Alexander Graham Bell, inventor of the telephone. It was steam heated, lighted through with gas, and had speaking tubes connecting rooms to the reception desk in the main entrance, as well as a passenger elevator and pneumatic bells. It also had a post office, telephone booth, hairdressing and laundry services, and a variety of small businesses on the ground floor (Water Street) including a watchmaker and a milliner. The hotel, which cost $70,000 to build, could accommodate 70 guests.

79. Paul O'Neill, *The Oldest City* (2003), includes a picture of the Pleasantville Hotel on page 274, which, according to the caption, was likely taken in the 1890s; the words "Pleasantville Hotel" are clearly recognizable on the transom window. *McAlpine's Newfoundland Directory* for 1894-1897 lists a Pleasantville Hotel on Quidivide [sic] Road.

80. The Benevolent Irish Society, the oldest charitable and social organization in Newfoundland, regularly held formal dances known as "Irish Balls."

81. A dance; a type of quadrille (historic dance by four couples in a square formation) for eight or sixteen pairs. The lancers quadrille, or the lancers, was probably invented about 1820, although it did not come into general vogue until the middle of the century. The dance begins after the first section (8 bars) of music has been played.

82. Some underhanded scheme; possibly a fraudulent scheme for obtaining money.

83. A domineering, violent, or bad-tempered woman.

84. "Love's Young Dream," poem by Thomas Moore, undated.

85. "In the Gloaming" by Meta Caroline Orred (c.1846-1925), English author and poet; set to music by Annie Fortescue Harrison (1851-1944), an English composer of songs and piano pieces. This popular song was composed in 1877.

86. To throw oneself with vigour and energy into an activity; to shake off.

87. Brand name of a type of clay tobacco-pipe.

88. From William Wordsworth's "To Sleep" (1806); last two lines, "Come, blessed barrier betwixt day and day, / Dear mother of fresh thoughts and joyous health."

89. *Evening Herald*, formerly known as the *Evening Mercury*, came into being in 1890 under the proprietorship of J.E.A. Furneaux. The first editor of the paper was H.E. Knight. Although the format of the *Herald* remained similar to that of the *Mercury*, its political support shifted in favour of the liberal politics of Sir Robert Bond. In 1912, it merged with the *Evening Chronicle*.

90. The Harvey Group of Companies operated under various partnerships and names. A. Harvey and Company Limited, established in 1865 by Alexander J. Harvey, was involved principally in manufacturing hard bread. It expanded into shipping and was the first to introduce steamships and steel-hulled vessels to the seal hunt. It acted as chief custodian of the Harvey's Group's shipping interests and in 1892 acted as terminal operators, charterers and brokers, and ship's agents.

91. From the poem of the same title, "Rocked in the Cradle of the Deep," by Emma (Hart) Willard (1787-1870), an American poet.

92. A woman in charge of the gate or door in a convent.

93. Anguish or annoyance felt most keenly; the allusion is to the ancient custom of torturing the flesh with instruments of iron. See Psalm 105:18 (KJV): "Whose feet they hurt with fetters: he was laid in iron." The Prayer Book version, "the iron entered into his soul," has established itself firmly among proverbial expressions. See also Laurence Sterne, *A Sentimental Journey* (1768): "I saw the iron enter into his soul, and felt what sort of pain it was that ariseth from hope deferred."

94. A farthing is a coin and monetary unit worth a quarter of an old penny; the least possible amount.

95. Moss roses (rose centrifolia) bear on their flower stems and sepals a mutation of the glands, making it appear as if a green or reddish-brown moss were growing there, adding a unique delicacy to the buds. The mossy fern-like lacy growth is totally unlike any other rosebud. The mosses are sports (naturally occurring mutations) of the Centrifolia. The moss covering is soft to the touch, slightly sticky, and so intensely fragrant that simply rubbing one's fingertips up the stalks leaves a strong and lasting rose fragrance on the hands. See Harriet Beecher Stowe, *Uncle Tom's Cabin* (ch. 27): "Eva's little table, covered with white, bore on it her favorite vase, with a single white moss rose-bud in it."

96. Europe.

97. Harriet Beecher Stowe (1811-1896), abolitionist, writer, whose novel *Uncle Tom's Cabin* (1852) attacked the cruelty of slavery. This novel, which was an immediate sensation, reached millions as a novel and play, and became influential in the United States and Britain. Her fame rests largely on this novel. The novel also displays women's ability to create positive social values and celebrates the peaceful order of a woman-dominated home.

98. The offspring of a white person and a mulatto; a person of one-quarter black ancestry.

99. Phrase used as a common reaction to something extraordinary or to describe something that surpasses everything. Banagher is a town in Ireland; its claim to fame is that it is the source of the well-known phrase "Well, that beats Banagher!" This phrase is possibly the origin of the expression "to beat the band."

100. The song which English labels "Golden Love" is actually "Once More We Meet" by Mary Mark Lemon, music by Milton Wellings (date unknown).

101. The St. John's *Evening Telegram* used pink paper from 1882 to 1942. In 1880 the *Telegram* received by accident pink paper which was supposed to be sent to the Toronto *Evening Telegram*. This look was maintained by the *Evening Telegram* until 7 February 1942 when World War II interrupted shipments (the Toronto *Telegram* printed on pink paper until the 1960s).

102. Unalterable laws. See Daniel 6:8 (KJV): "Now, O King, establish the decree, and sign the writing, that it be not changed, according to the law of the Medes and Persians, which altereth not."

103. See n. 85.

104. Town in northern France overlooking the Strait of Dover, the narrowest point in the English Channel; it is the closest French town to England.

105. The first great Alpine tunnel, Mount Cenis Tunnel was 8.5 miles long; the first long-distance rock tunnel driven from two headings with no intervening shaft, from Modane, France, to Bardonècchia, Italy, and took from 1857 to 1871 to build. On its completion, it was labelled the most enduring work ever accomplished by human hands.

106. Town and major ferry port in Kent, in southeast England. It faces France across the narrowest part of the English Channel.

107. Major port of England; by the nineteenth century, 40 percent of the world's trade passed through Liverpool's docks.

108. See n. 100.

AFTERWORD

Anastasia Mary English: "The Lady Novelist of Newfoundland"

Anastasia English, probably "Newfoundland's first published woman author,"[1] is the author of *Only a Fisherman's Daughter: A Tale of Newfoundland*[2] (1899), probably the first novel published in Newfoundland,[3] and likely self-published.[4] The *Encyclopedia of Newfoundland and Labrador* (*ENL*) lists Anastasia as "author" and the *Dictionary of Newfoundland Biography* (*DNB*) calls her a "prolific writer of escapist fiction." Patrick O'Flaherty describes her as a writer of escapist,[5] romance[6] fiction. English was a native-born Newfoundlander, yet her novels, long out of print, have received little attention in studies of Newfoundland literature.

I was introduced to Anastasia English's *Only a Fisherman's Daughter* in 1991 by Dr. Elizabeth Miller in a graduate course in Newfoundland literature. I was excited to learn of a "new" Newfoundland writer, but when I began to research English's life, I was dismayed by the lacunae in biographical information. My search for Anastasia English grew and her novels became the subject of a master's thesis.[7] I wanted to rescue English from obscurity and make her books available to be read by another generation of readers.[8] Extensive archival research, however, has revealed little about her life.

Since June 2007 *Only a Fisherman's Daughter* has been available in digital format[9] through Memorial University's Digital Archive Initiative. While this is a significant move to make a neglected writer available, it does not, however, make her text or details of her life available to the general reading public.

******

Anastasia Mary English was born in St. John's in 1862 (or 1863[10])
into a respected family.[11] She was the daughter of Joseph English
(1832-1909) and Elizabeth Born (1833-1921), who were married 7
August 1860 at the Basilica of Saint John the Baptist in St. John's. Her
paternal grandmother, Anastasia Kinsella (for whom, undoubtedly,
she was named), arrived in the colony of Newfoundland in the
1830s from Tintern, Co. Wexford, Ireland, where she had probably
been one of the tenants dispossessed of their homes when Lord
Colclough of Tintern Abbey razed the town.[12] Joseph English's
family originally lived in Job's Cove, Conception Bay, where he was
born, but moved to St. John's when he was four years old. Joseph
likely received his education from a paternal relative, Patrick
Doutney, and apprenticed as a newspaperman. In 1880 Joseph
English founded the *Terra Nova Advocate*,[13] a paper established as
a voice for Catholics to counteract the pro-Protestant bias of the
press of the day. He eventually left the newspaper business for a
position with the government.[14] Anastasia's mother, Elizabeth Born,
was the daughter of Valentine Born (1798-1860) and Mary Doutney
(1808-1887) of St. John's. Valentine Born, a civil servant, was from
England and a convert to Catholicism, while Mary Doutney was
Irish and most likely a native of St. John's.

Anastasia was one of six children born to Joseph and Elizabeth
English. Her brother William J. (1861-1917) founded the *Bell Island
Miner* in 1913; Valentine emigrated from Newfoundland to the
United States; and Joseph F. (1867-1945) obtained a bailiff's job
through social connections.[15] Anastasia's sister Mary J. (1869-1946)
married John Fagan, and her sister Annie (1874-1963) worked at
the East End Post Office on Water Street in St. John's and never
married. Anastasia and Annie lived with their brother Joseph until
his death on 29 August 1945.[16]

It is likely that Anastasia was educated by the Sisters of Mercy[17]
or the Presentation Sisters. Her poem, "To the Memory of a Loved
Cousin and Friend," in *Yuletide Bells* (1945) recalls "The happiness
of those golden hours, / Hours spent within convent walls." The
lines, "When schooltime came, together we went / ... Wending our
way to the hallowed spot / Where our Alma Mater stood," suggest
that the school she attended was within walking distance. The
heroine in *Only a Fisherman's Daughter* learns "domestic economy,
and a certain amount of house-keeping ... [and] a good, solid,
English education, and other ornamental requisites, such as music,
drawing, painting ... nothing but what is good, useful, and
beautiful" (36) at an American convent school. Was this curriculum
modelled on Anastasia's own convent education? The curriculum
advertised for "the first Catholic pension or pay school in the

country [Newfoundland]," opened by the Sisters of Mercy in 1843, was likely similar to that which Anastasia studied:

A school for the Education of Young Ladies under the direction of the Sisters of Mercy, opened at the Convent of Mercy, Cathedral Place, on Monday, the 1st., May 1843. The general school course comprises Reading, Writing, Arithmetic, English, Grammar, Geography, use of the Globes, History, etc., Needlework (plain and ornamental), etc. Terms — Five pounds per annum. [*The Newfoundland Indicator* 1: LXXXX, March 30, 1844, p. 3][18]

Two pounds per annum were added for "The French or Italian language"; for Music, eight pounds per annum—all to be paid quarterly, in advance. Music, as O'Flaherty notes, "was a major emphasis of the Mercy and Presentation orders of nuns."[19] Whatever else Anastasia studied, she likely received music training; she later taught music.

Anastasia likely lived with her parents and paid room and board after she started working. Information culled from city directories, census reports, and electoral records offers a broad picture of the family's various domiciles. City directories were not issued annually, and the details included in them often varied from directory to directory. From 1885 to 1890 Joseph English and his family lived at 277 Duckworth Street.[20] For the latter part of the 1890s, their address was 71 Queen's Road,[21] and Joseph listed as a printer. Around 1904, the family home was located at 50 Long's Hill, and Joseph now listed as caretaker of a government building, his son Joseph, a clerk, and daughter Mary, a clerk at Garrett Byrne's bookstore on Water Street, with Joseph and Mary listed as boarders.[22] Their next recorded residence is 15 Monkstown Road, where they lived from approximately 1908 until at least 1915.[23] Joseph English died in 1909, and his son Joseph is now listed as the head of the household. In the 1911 Census of Newfoundland, Anastasia's occupation is a music teacher. In 1913 she is still a music teacher, boarding at 15 Monkstown Road, the English residence.[24] In 1915 she is listed only as boarding at 15 Monkstown Road.[25] For the next few years, city directories provide little information about the English family: for 1919, Joseph English resided at 30 William Street; for 1924, 126 Water Street;[26] and for 1928, 329 Water Street.[27] It is likely that his mother and sisters continued to live with him at these addresses. When the 1928 List of Electors was compiled, Anastasia, Annie, and Joseph were listed as living at 327 Water Street.[28] According to the 1935 Census, Joseph, Anastasia, and

Annie lived at 6 Wood Street; at that time, Anastasia's occupation is a journalist.[29] With the 1945 Census, they are still at Wood Street, and Anastasia the head of the household. Joseph English died in 1945, and, according to the 1948 List of Electors, Anastasia and Annie continued to live at 6 Wood Street. How long is unclear. Anastasia's residence at Wood Street is also confirmed by Paul O'Neill, who remembered that Anastasia "lived next door but one to my mother, who was born at 10 Wood Street."[30]

In the 1880s Newfoundland was a self-governing outpost of the British Empire, and St. John's, with a population of approximately 30,000 people, mainly of English and Irish origin, controlled the island's social and economic life. The period of 1879-1920 was especially exciting musically. Music lovers could choose from the music of local amateur operatic troupes and community choirs or performances by visiting troupes and musicians, often on their way to engagements in Europe or the U.S. The world-famous Newfoundland-born opera singer Georgina Sterling performed in concerts in St. John's during the 1890s; civilian bands were popular; St. John's had an Orchestral Society as well as a Choral Society; and, with the installation of pipe organs in churches during the second half of the nineteenth century, performances of sacred choral music by church choirs were popular.[31] Not only did Anastasia grow up in a musical heyday, but this period was also an exciting literary time. As Patrick O'Flaherty notes, the closing decades of the nineteenth century were important for "an outburst of scholarly and patriotic writing by resident authors anxious to prop up Newfoundland's faltering nationhood. [It] was possibly the most fertile in the colony's literary history, although, as in earlier decades, the bulk of the writing was descriptive and topical rather than imaginative." He mentions, among other writers (both male and female), "Anastasia M. English [who] wrote romances loosely based on Newfoundland life and history."[32] Anastasia also grew up with the *Terra Nova Advocate*, a "small and unpretentious" paper, of which her father was the proprietor, and one which was

> very newsy for the time ... well edited and the contents ... emanations of the most gifted minds of the city. It was the rendezvous for the cream of the legal and literary lights of St. John's. Its columns not infrequently scintillated with original local wit and humour, and its criticisms of public men or things were keen, caustic and biting in the political sense.[33]

Literary and musical references[34] abound in *Only a Fisherman's*

Daughter—poetry by Thomas Moore, Caroline Norton, Robert Burns, Henry Wadsworth Longfellow, William Wordsworth; music by Chopin and Sigismund Thalberg; songs by Thomas Linley, John Howard Payne, Epes Sargent, Emma (Hart) Willard, and Mary Mark Lemon; a reference to the novelist Harriet Beecher Stowe; as well as many Biblical allusions. These varied references probably reflect the author's own preferences in music and literature. As the daughter of a newspaper proprietor, and with a brother in the business, it is not surprising that Anastasia's poems and stories appeared in print. Poems and stories by Anastasia's nieces Leona, Kathleen, and Bessie—daughters of William J. English—were printed in periodicals and newspapers of the day. After her father's death, Bessie continued to publish the *Bell Island Miner* until the 1940s, and, after her marriage to Thomas Foote, she edited *The Christmas Annual*,[35] which often featured Anastasia's fiction and poetry. Kathleen, a poet and the author of the novel *"Lovers Meetings," or Monica's Destiny* (1937),[36] edited the *Christmas Greeting*,[37] which also featured Anastasia's writing. Anastasia's cousins included L.E.F. English (1887-1971), a prominent writer and curator of the Newfoundland Museum, who was, according to *Newfoundland Who's Who for 1952*, "the best living authority on Newfoundland tradition, [and] author of school textbooks"; Arthur Stanislaus English (1878-1940), a farmer, journalist, and scientist;[38] and Mary Theresa (Sister Mary Clare) English (1878-1940), a Presentation Sister who played a significant role in the founding of St. Clare's Mercy Hospital. From her father's side of the family, Anastasia was surrounded by writers, editors, and publishers. From her mother's side of the family—all strong, independent women and positive role models—she gained social position in the Catholic community.

Although Anastasia English reportedly began writing at an early age,[39] her first novel, which is the first extant piece of her writing, was published in 1899 when she was either 36 or 37. Anastasia published four novels—*Only a Fisherman's Daughter* (1899), *Faithless* (1901),[40] *Alice Lester* (1904), *When the Dumb Speak* (1938)—and a collection of short stories, *"The Queen of Fairy Dell" and Other Tales* (1912).[41] In four of her books the pseudonym "Maria" appears on the title page—*Only a Fisherman's Daughter* lists Maria (Statia M. English) as the author; *Faithless*, Maria; *Alice Lester*, Maria; *"The Queen of Fairy Dell" and Other Tales*, as Maria; while her last novel, *When the Dumb Speak*, published in 1938, lists the author as Statia M. English.

Most of Anastasia's stories published in Christmas annuals[42] include the byline Statia M. English.[43] As stories in nineteenth-century periodicals frequently did not include bylines, we may never determine her complete oeuvre. In the following discussion, I mention works without a byline if corroborated with the appearance of the same work in another periodical, with her byline, or in her short story collection. Anastasia wrote her last story in 1958 for that year's edition of the "Christmas Number."[44]

As editor of the Christmas annual *Yuletide Bells*[45] for 40 years, Anastasia likely wrote many of the editorials herself. Many read like homilies; others address war and its atrocities, World War I as a threat to Christianity, and the impact of modernism. The 1944 editorial writer castigated schools for not allowing "anything pertaining to God to be voiced," lamented the absence of God in social gatherings, called divorce courts "an insidious poison sapping all that is sacred and holy, all that is loyal and beautiful from the family life," and anticipated "a new era for Newfoundland when it had shaken off the yoke of Commission of Government which for the last ten years had oppressed [them]." The 1947 editorial is an impassioned plea for the return of Responsible Government:

> The love of home and country is deeply planted in the soul of every Newfoundlander, and the hearts within us beat with joy and pride, our pulses throb, our whole being glows with the warmth of our devotion, our imagination is fired whilst listening to the thrilling tales of our immortal and romantic history. The Responsible Government League has espoused a noble and holy cause, which is to foster in the younger generation that pride in their Country's charms, to kindle in their spirit that immortal fire, which is Godlike, for "next to God comes our Country."
>
> We loved her in the days of freedom and prosperity, in the days of her many sorrows, in her joyous days, and now, in the days of her bondage our hearts cry out, louder and stronger, "We love thee Newfoundland." How best can we prove the sincerity of our words, how best show that the words are not empty, meaningless? The answer is this, when the time is ripe, when the opportunity is ours, let every loyal son and daughter of Terra Nova mark their ballot for "Responsible Government" for which generations, yet unborn, will bless them.

"Matters Political," a short, unsigned article in the 1948 issue, inveighed against those who betrayed Newfoundland by supporting confederation with Canada:

> We Newfoundlanders are the victims of those in whose

hands is welded [sic] the sceptre of power. The year, now drawing to a close, is certainly the blackest in our history. It has been said that we mortals do not value highly enough treasures which we've always possessed. Alas; we must acknowledge it to be so in our case, for did we truly value the grand heritage which was ours we would never have allowed it to slip from our grasp[;] we would have put up a strong fight against such a disaster.

Even though we cannot state definitively if Anastasia wrote the editorials for *Yuletide Bells*, we know that she, like her father, had a keen interest in politics. Her patriotic appeal in the confederation debate, printed as a letter to the editor of the *Daily News*,[46] expressed sentiments that echo *Yuletide Bells* editorials. In this appeal, signed Statia M. English, she offers her credentials as "one of Newfoundland's oldest residents, [who] can remember as far back as seventy years ago." Her appeal is direct: "For myself, I may not live very long to enjoy our freedom; but, as next to God comes one's country, I would die happy to see the land of my birth freed from the shackles, which for fourteen years have held it, and have it still identified as England's Oldest Colony, the corner stone of the British Empire and not as the smallest pawn of the Dominion of Canada." A similar metaphor appeared in *Only a Fisherman's Daughter* in 1899: the heroine, the daughter of a fisherman, must fight for recognition and acceptance in a society of a few (the elite) who refuse to forgive her "for breaking the fetters that bound [her] to the life of [her] ancestors" (63). Anastasia points out that her early years had been spent in "a fishing village, amongst fisher-folk," but she does not include when or where: "I love them, and I love them still—I love their bright little homes, their trim gardens, their honest, sincere hearts, their kind hospitality—I love them too well to see them sacrifice their little homes, which are now all their own, to taxes which shall make such a demand upon their earnings that they'll run the risk of losing what they now possess." Her appeal ends with two imperatives:

Remember, Canada wants us, just to get her hands on Labrador which we propose to hand "Unshackled in freedom grand / To the sons and daughters of Newfoundland." So fishermen and sons of fishermen, mark your ballot on Referendum day for Responsible Government so that your children's children may bless you in the years to come.

The inclusion of her own poems and stories (with bylines) in

Yuletide Bells indicates that this annual was a forum for Anastasia's own writing.[47] Extant issues contain stories, poems, and articles by either Maria or Statia M. English. The 1916 issue contains the poem "Somewhere in France" by Maria; the remaining extant issues, listed below in chronological order, use the byline Statia M. English, if one was included. "The Passing of the Year" (1923, poem); "At the Ship's Side" (1928, story); "Christ the King" (1940, poem); "Farewell Old Year" (1943, poem) and "The Shadow Fell" (1943, story, no byline, written for *Yuletide Bells*; reprinted, with byline, in 1953 *Christmas Greeting*); "Babes in the Woods" (1944, story, no byline, written for *Yuletide Bells*; reprinted, with byline, in 1953 *Christmas Annual*), "In Memory of M.F. Aylward" and "When the Year is Closing In" (1944, poems); "To the Memory of a Loved Cousin and Friend" and "In Memory of Jos. F. English" (1945, poems); "The Other Side of the Sun" (1946, poem); "To His Grace Archbishop Roche (In the Year of His Golden Jubilee)" and "The Old Chapel Bell" (1947, poems).

The Christmas Annual, edited by Anastasia's niece, Elizabeth Foote, printed Anastasia's writing, all with the byline Statia M. English:[48] "Death of the Old Year" (1949, poem) and "A Little Bit of Evergreen" (1949, story); "The Parades of the Past" (1951, article on various annual St. John's parades) and "Reminiscence: Regattas of the Hallowed Past" (1951, article); "Just Around the Corner" (1952, poem) and "That Camera" (1952, story); "Babes in the Woods" (1953, story); "A Master Mind" (1954, article honouring Roman Catholic Bishop J. Thomas Mullock (1807-1869) for his eloquent message on a "notable date in the political history of Newfoundland" [13 May 1861, the riot at the foot of McBride's Hill, stopped when soldiers opened fire on the crowd]: "What food for reflection! A people whose hearts could then be swayed in the right direction, by strong reasoning and touching language, must surely have left implanted the same field for labour in the hearts that beat today within the breast of their offspring"[49]); "Shorty Wins" (1958, story, from 1947 *Yuletide Bells*), "When the Year is Closing In" (1958, poem, written in 1944), and "At Midnight Mass" (1958, poem).

Christmas Greeting, edited by Kathleen English, contained the following stories by Anastasia, all with the byline Statia M. English: "A Hundredfold Repaid" (1947); "A Serious Blunder" (1948); "Snow Maid" and "The Shadow Fell" (1953, from 1943 *Yuletide Bells*); and "At the Ship's Side" (1954, from 1928 *Yuletide Bells*).

The foregoing list of Anastasia English's writings from the extant issues of the three Christmas annuals edited by the English women suggests that Anastasia's stories were indeed popular, but, as her stories were published and re-published, it also might indicate that her oeuvre was relatively small. Her popularity as a writer is also endorsed by local papers. The first extant story, "A Harmless Deception," appeared in the 1904 *Christmas Bells*; it had no byline, but written beneath the title was, "By the author of 'Only a Fisherman's Daughter,' 'Faithless,' 'Alice Lester,' &c." This story was later included in her short story collection. "A Harmless Deception" is the only one of Anastasia's stories to have been reprinted in twentieth- and twenty-first-century anthologies—it was included in *Tempered Days* in 1998[50] and in *Land, Sea & Time* in 2001.[51] In 1907 Anastasia won second prize ($3.00) in a Christmas short story competition for "Snowed in at Tickle Harbour; or, Granny Hunt's Prediction." The *Free Press*,[52] which ran the competition, noted that English, a writer of fiction, had won, with this prize, "a well-merited position in local literary circles."[53] The next year she received first prize ($5.00) for "Looking for Santa Claus." The *Free Press* praised Anastasia as "one of our best-known local writers, [who] always has an interesting story for Christmas. Many of her short stories have been more pretentious than that we published last week [the winning story, 15 December 1908], but none have excelled in its tone, easy diction and wholesome influence. We would greatly miss Miss English, were her name not to appear amongst our prize winners."[54] This reference to "many of her short stories" is tantalizing—had she written many stories and/or had she already published many stories? We will likely never know. These two prize-winning stories are included in *"The Queen of Fairy Dell" and Other Tales*.

Anastasia's productivity is emphasized in "Local Authoress Dies at 97; A. English, Novelist, Poet,"[55] a short piece that appeared in the *Evening Telegram* two days after her obituary notice,[56] and remembered as "a prolific writer of short stories, magazine articles, poetry, and novels." Was Anastasia popular only in St. John's, or were her works disseminated further afield? In 1900, one year after it was printed, *Only a Fisherman's Daughter* was advertised as "a tale of Newfoundland founded on fact" (by "Marie [sic]") in *Newfoundland Illustrated*,[57] an American book, first published in 1894,[58] that contained photographs of Newfoundland by S.H. Parsons,[59] among others. *Only a Fisherman's Daughter* was included under the heading "A List of Books Relating to Newfoundland: Novels and Stories, Scenes of Which are Laid in Newfoundland." Was *Only a Fisherman's Daughter* actually founded on a true story? Which part of the novel is true? Anastasia does not assuage our curiosity. In her own introduction to *Faithless: A Newfoundland Romance*, her second novel, Anastasia addresses the book's reception and forestalls her critics. None of her other novels contains such an introduction. I quote it here in its entirety:

> To the readers of "Faithless," who may be inclined to think that the picture of the heroine, in actual want, is overdrawn, I would say that the writer has known, not only this one, but several other instances, where persons living in affluence previous to the Bank crash of '94, were reduced to most extreme poverty afterwards. It was not the poorer class who suffered most, but those whose pride, or delicacy, forbade them seeking that relief which kind and charitable hearts provided for those who needed it.
>
> Of the merits of this, my second work, its readers must judge. I have endeavored to make it a book which all may read, young and old, grave or gay, and in its pages I trust nothing shall be found that would wound the feelings of the most sensitive.
>
> As the events which are supposed to have transpired in the story, must have occurred at such a recent date, great care has been taken to place them where they cannot be identified with the originals.
>
> The name "Faithless," may be thought, by a great many, to be misapplied to the story, but, though being faithful in her love for Alan Horten, Eva Carlen was, in a degree, faithless, when she failed to keep her appointment with him at the end of the two years.
>
> Most sincerely do I thank the many kind friends whose patronage helped me through, in my last work as well as in this one, with the financial difficulty of publication. In my former venture I more than realized my expectations, and should I meet with the same success in this effort, I shall feel amply rewarded for the months of labor which must be given to a work of this kind.
>
> Should this book help to pass pleasantly a few spare hours for its readers, I shall feel that my time has not been given in vain.

When her third novel, *Alice Lester,* was published in 1904, the *Evening Telegram* (1 August 1904) announced that the book by Maria was for sale in local bookstores, and an advertisement noted that her two previous novels—*Only a Fisherman's Daughter* and *Faithless*—had local scenes and plots. Does "local ... plots" equal "founded on fact" as it was promoted in *Newfoundland Illustrated*? Special circumstances surrounding the publication of *Alice Lester* are inscribed on the title page, immediately after the title, in fairly large font: "Especially Dedicated to the 'Old Home Week.'" In a brief notice entitled "Latest Local Novel," the 1 August 1904 *Evening Telegram* informed its readers that *Alice Lester* had been published and was dedicated to "Old Home Week" visitors. Old Home Week[60] welcomed hundreds of Newfoundlanders who had left the island to seek their fortunes in the United States and Canada back to their native land. *Alice Lester* contained, the paper asserted, "all local [scenes] and one with which all Newfoundlanders are thoroughly acquainted, and this should make the story doubly interesting." The *Evening Telegram* also carried an advertisement for this "latest Newfoundland Novel," which was for sale at bookstores[61] and 50 Long's Hill[62] (price 50 cents). Seven days later, a lengthier write-up on *Alice Lester* and "the lady novelist of Newfoundland" appeared in the *Evening Telegram* (the full text appears below):

[*Alice Lester*] from the pen of a talented local writer, who is already known to the public under the pseudonym of Maria, author of "Only a Fisherman's Daughter" and "Faithless". Miss English is the daughter of our fellow-citizen, Mr. Joseph English. She knows how to tell a good story, and in her latest venture, "Alice Lester," has woven a thrilling tale of love and madness, of incident and adventure. From the earliest chapters the interest of the reader is assured. Her characters are not sentimental impossibilities, but very man and very woman—neither all bad nor all perfect, but such as the world knows and has known from the days of Eden to these latter days, when even amid the stress and strain of the strenuous life, there remains time for mystery, for generosity and love. At times the tale is one of absorbing interest, and to Newfoundlanders it will appeal with especial force on account of the delightful local touches with which the book abounds.

The scene is placed on the western coast of the island, whence it shifts to the city of St. John's and other parts of the mighty, and yet, little world, in which humanity lives, and moves, and has its being. The book is dedicated to the wanderer who has been "compelled by circumstances to bid adieu to home and friends, and seek a fortune 'neath a foreign sky; to the wayward roamer, whom love of adventure and a yearning for a wider sphere of action have wooed from his native soil; to the stranger, who bent on pleasure and wholesome enjoyment, comes in our midst in all good fellowship." Printed attractively on thick paper, it presents a pleasing appearance and does credit to the typographers of the *Free Press* office, who have been working night and day during the past three weeks to have it ready in time to greet our visitors.

At the modest sum of fifty cents it should meet a ready sale. Miss English wrote for the love of her art, but the public cannot express their appreciation more truly than by promptly exhausting the edition. The carping critic may find defects and blemishes in her work, but the "tout ensemble" does credit, not only to the gifted writer, but to the city, of which she is a resident and a native. Those who have read her previous books will notice that in facility of description and vividness of narrative, Miss English has excelled, and will unite with us in warmly congratulating the lady novelist of Newfoundland.[63]

In the absence of reviews, in the twenty-first-century sense of the word, such a write-up offers readers a glimpse of Anastasia's popularity and stature as *"the* lady novelist of Newfoundland" (my emphasis). The quotation in paragraph two is taken from "L'Envoi"[64] at the end of *Alice Lester*; this is the only novel to have such a concluding address from the author (I quote it here in its entirety):

To the Wanderer, who has been compelled by circumstances to bid adieu to home and friends, and seek his fortune 'neath a foreign sky;

To the wayward Roamer, whom love of adventure, and a yearning for a wider sphere of action, have wooed from his native soil;

To the Stranger, who, bent on pleasure and wholesome enjoyment, comes in our midst in all good fellowship;

This little book is dedicated.

Facts, that have come to the writer's knowledge, linked and interwoven, form the story of Alice Lester. Strange and startling though some of the incidents may seem, none are either overdrawn or exaggerated. The only alterations are the changing of dates, and the suppression of the real names of persons or places. That fact is often stranger than fiction is every day becoming more apparent. The pages of romance are no longer regarded as the home of impossibilities, or as the stage on which strut heroes and heroines, too perfect to exist, in this faulty and imperfect age.

The ALL, who, during "OLD HOME WEEK," visit the shores of TERRA NOVA, the Author, on behalf of her fellow-country-women, extends a hearty WELCOME. May each hour of their stay be filled to the brim with pleasure and happiness; and may they take away with them pleasant memories of days long-looked for, which may never come again!

THE AUTHOR

Anastasia English's next publication, the short story collection *"The Queen of Fairy Dell" and Other Tales*, appeared in 1912. Curiously, *Faithless*, her second novel, which had been published in 1901, now became the focus of advertising by Dicks and Co. Limited in the *Evening Telegram*. It first appeared on 13 June 1912 and ran on 17, 18, 20, 21, 24, 25, 26, 27, and 28 June, and 1 and 2 July 1912. Why the focus on this novel, and only this novel, now? Was this a strategy to reacquaint the reading public with Anastasia English prior to the release of her next book? to raise awareness of her as a writer? to increase sales of her books? *"The Queen of Fairy Dell" and Other Tales* was published in 1912 (exact date unknown) and mentioned (accompanied by a picture of the author) in the 14 October 1912 *Daily News*:

> ... Miss English, our local novelist, whose works, "Only a Fisherman's Daughter," "Faithless," and "Alice Lester," are well known to our readers. The new volume consists of a number of short stories, most of which have appeared in the Christmas editions of the Free Press from year to year, Miss English having been a successful competitor, and generally the leading one in the story competition in successive years. The book is one that all lovers of Newfoundland should have on their bookshelves. The stories are racy of the soil, and will be read with general interest. The price is one dollar. The book, which is neatly printed at the Herald office, and nicely bound by Dicks and Co., is on sale at the bookstores. Miss English is the eldest daughter of the late Mr. Joseph English, for many years Editor and proprietor of the Terra Nova Advocate. The old Advocate press is still in existence, and is still in use as a jobbing proof press in the Daily News office. We congratulate Miss English on the publication, which, we hope, may prove the forerunner of even more pretentious efforts in the future.

Anastasia's last novel, *When the Dumb Speak*, was advertised by Dicks and Co. Limited in the 14 October 1939 *Daily News* as "A Newfoundland Novelist's Absorbing Tale of Newfoundland Life."

The advertisement contained this quotation: "Her fine exactness of detail enables us to see every incident that she sets before us … From her first page to her last she builds a character with the most minute and delicate craftsmanship" (quotation marks and ellipsis in original). Were quotation marks and ellipses a stylistic feature of copy writing, or is the *Daily News* reprinting a blurb from elsewhere and omitting some of the text? Two weeks later, the 28 October 1939 *Evening Telegram* printed, at the bottom of the extreme right-hand column on page 6, a notice headed "When the Dumb Speak":

> The *Telegram* acknowledges receipt of a copy of the book "When the Dumb Speak" by the Newfoundland writer Statia M. English.
> Centred in the little Newfoundland village of "Flowervilla," 100 years ago, the novel is replete with local colour, which should serve to make it of particular interest locally.
> The author of "When the Dumb Speak" has also written "Only a Fisherman's Daughter," "Faithless," "Alice Lester," "Queen of Fairy Dell," and other tales.[65]

The title page of *When the Dumb Speak*, however, lists 1938 as the copyright date. Why, then, did the *Evening Telegram* announce this book in the fall of 1939? Could it have been in time to rival Margaret Duley's *Cold Pastoral*, also published in 1939?

In the 1949 *Christmas Annual*, in a farewell to Anastasia and her 40-year editorship of *Yuletide Bells*, Elizabeth Foote celebrates Anastasia English the popular writer, but, curiously, *Only a Fisherman's Daughter* is listed as her magnum opus, not her last, and more recent, *When the Dumb Speak*. This farewell is the only write-up to measure all of her works:

> After a continuous publication of forty years, this estimable little volume [*Yuletide Bells*] has closed its useful career. It brought into the hearts of its readers refreshing moments at Christmas time, with its thoughtful editorials, its pleasing tales of Newfoundland life, its charming pieces of poetry, and its choice selections from the world's literature….
> Words fail to covey our full appreciation of Miss English, who has become a household name to thousands of Newfoundlanders through her books. There is scarcely a home in the country which has not had a copy of "The Fisherman's Daughter," a master piece written in a style at once simple and charming; it has portrayed life in our

island outports as indeed no other book has even attempted. Then there was "Alice Lester," another entrancing story wherein history was written and interwoven. There was the absorbing love tale of "Faithless"; we saw it in a true romance of actual persons well known in the social scale of our capital. The author herself confessed with a twinkle in her eye that she was somewhat grieved by capitalising on the weakness of human hearts. Another production from the pen of "Statia" was that absorbing tale "When the Dumb Speaks [sic]" and a collection of children's stories[66] under the caption of "Fairy Dell." This literary effort, though not so well and widely known as her larger works, deserves more than passing tribute. In fact, in other lands and with wider sphere of readers, we believe that Miss English could have achieved fame as a writer of this kind of fiction. We have seen on the continent children's books, illustrated by outstanding artists and made as attractive as the printer's art can attain, yet in actual content beneath the standard of "Fairy Dell."

... this grand old lady, now in her eighty-seventh year, is still in excellent health at her home on Wood Street in St. John's ... May we assure her that generations yet unborn in Newfoundland will thrill with pleasure and pride when they read her works, and indeed if these were only "A Fisherman's Daughter" her place in our literary Hall of Fame rests secure.[67]

If in 1949 Anastasia English's novel *Only a Fisherman's Daughter* had been in almost every home in Newfoundland, had it and its author already fallen into obscurity by 1956 when Margaret Duley's literary essay, "Glimpses into Local Literature [of Newfoundland]," appeared in *Atlantic Guardian* (July 1956)? In this essay Duley devoted two paragraphs to "The Novelists" of Newfoundland—Erle Spencer and herself:

Amongst the records Newfoundland novelists show the smallest output of all. But heresay [sic] memory turns immediately to Earl [sic] Spencer, born in Fortune, and who by a magical turn of destiny went to England, as a protege of Lord Beaverbrook, to work on the staff of the *Daily Express*....

The writer of this article [Duley] has published in London, New York, and Toronto, and acclaims

Newfoundland as a magnificent and dramatic background
for any novel ...

And at the end of "The Poets" section, Duley adds: "And let us not
forget the women." These are represented by Florence Miller: "One
calls to memory Florence Miller's folksy poems and acclaims her
faculty for seeing magic in the near and far view of 'Topsail Bay.'"[68]
Anastasia English is not included in either of these categories.

Anastasia English and her nieces were not the only women
writers being published in St. John's at the turn of the century
and into the twentieth century. Rose M. Greene, Phoebe Florence
Miller, Bertille Tobin, and Ellen Carberry were popular female
poets who published in newspapers, Christmas annuals, and other
publications. But it is Margaret Duley (1894-1968), though, who
is perhaps Newfoundland's most well-known (female) literary
figure and generally considered the first female novelist of any
import. Duley was, according to the *ENL*, "one of Newfoundland's
first native-born professional novelists"[69] and "Newfoundland's
first significant female novelist," according to Elizabeth Miller.[70]
In a review of Duley's third novel, *Highway to Valor* (1941), Linda
Whalen notes that Duley "represents a double phenomenon in the
admittedly short history of Newfoundland-lit, being not only our
first successful novelist, but a woman to boot."[71] Duley's first novel,
The Eyes of the Gull (1936), which made "a small splash in her native
waters,"[72] was published just two years before the copyright date of
1938, listed on the title page of *When the Dumb Speak*, Anastasia's last
novel. Duley's novels, more feminist in nature than English's, were
published outside Newfoundland and were circulated in the U.S.,
Canada, Britain, and Newfoundland. In the forties, Alison Feder
asserts, "all books in Canada were published either in the United
States or Great Britain."[73] Duley's writing might differ from English's,
but the question remains, why did English, who was so popular in
her lifetime, disappear from the annals of Newfoundland history
and literature so soon after her death? Why is Duley remembered
today and not English? Is it because English self-published and
her novels, following "the old patterns for local production[,] ...
[were] published by newspaper firms in St. John's"?[74] Paul O'Neill
suggests that Anastasia has probably not had "the same recognition
as Margaret Duley[,] whose works were published in New York,"[75]
because she published her books independently. Or does the lack
of recognition result from Anastasia being a writer of romance
and sentiment? Or is it contingent on class, with Margaret Duley
belonging to a higher social class than Anastasia English? Duley,
unlike Anastasia, grew up "amid the snobbery and comforts of the

St. John's East merchant class. She knew the outports only from a distance, from the perspective of an occasional summer visitor."[76]

Duley's biographer, Alison Feder, points out that Duley wanted to be "a bell-wether for Newfoundland writers." In 1940, Duley said in a letter: "One of the things regarding a Newfoundland novel is that there are no writers from this country and I feel we must emerge sometime ..."[77] What about Anastasia English, a writer who grew up and lived in the same town as Duley and whose novels appeared in the same decade as Duley's own? Anastasia was the only Newfoundland-born female novelist to have had her novels in print in Newfoundland before Margaret Duley began publishing. Had Anastasia's popularity waned to the point of extinction by 1940 when Duley wrote this letter, or is her non-inclusion in Duley's essay ("Glimpses into Local Literature") and letter due to another factor? Feder adds, in an endnote: "Two native Newfoundlanders, Anastasia English (1864-1959) and Erle Spencer (1897-1937), had some success with fiction. The one wrote innocuous romances; the other, whom Margaret Duley knew through 'hearsay memory,' focused on sea stories. They were not known on the Canadian mainland."

Carole Gerson, writing about the literary culture of Atlantic women between World War I and II, includes Anastasia English, along with Kathleen English, Phoebe Florence Miller, and Margaret Duley, in a list of more than three dozen women writers associated with the Atlantic region (including Newfoundland) who published at least one book in the period bounded by the world wars. Gerson points to "[the] multiple marginalization of Atlantic women writers: as women in a masculinist society, as Atlantic authors during an era when national Canadian culture was largely defined from a centralist Western outlook, and as recounters of women's experiences when 'virility' was the mode most acceptable to the academic modernists (male chromosomes and taste) who guided the institutionalization of Canadian literature between the wars and whose judgements still linger."[78] Has Anastasia English been marginalized within Newfoundland by gender and/or by genre?

Anastasia English died 30 May 1959 at St. Patrick's Mercy Home at the age of 97.[79] According to the obituary notice, she retained a clear and intelligent mind right up to the time of her death. She never married, nor did her sister Annie, with whom she lived all her life. Her name is a vague memory for even those who have heard of her. Where then—in the pages of Newfoundland's literary history—is the writer whose book *When the Dumb Speak* had so absorbed well-known Newfoundland writer Paul O'Neill[80] when he was in Grade 7 at St. Bon's College that he was "completely fascinated by

it and … totally swept away by the story." It was "one of the early
books that influenced [him] to become a writer":[81] "it showed [him]
the way."[82] Where is the writer who so captivated her readers with
Only a Fisherman's Daughter, the writer whose name has already
been inscribed in Newfoundland's "Literary Hall of Fame"[83]?

******

Within 20 chapters, *Only a Fisherman's Daughter* encompasses a wide
geographical landscape, which the heroine moves through—the
fictional village of St. Rose somewhere on the coast of Newfoundland;
the capital city of St. John's; the United States (the New York area
and the South); England; and the Old Country (Europe)—within a
time period of 15 or 20 years. The title, with the placement of the
adverb "only," connotes class tensions, condescension, deficiency—
the label is an insult (and the intonation is supplied by the reader).
The opening dialogue catapults the reader into the tensions
inherent in the stratified society of St. Rose, that of merchant versus
fisherman. The heroine, Norrie Moore, an impoverished orphan
and the daughter of a fisherman, is the object of the "aristocratic" (1)
Mrs. Brandford's hatred and scorn. Mrs. Brandford, the widow of
St. Rose's merchant and the self-appointed social conscience of the
community, is ruthless in her monomania to ensure that the upper
class is not contaminated by the vulgarity of the lower class. She is
sensitive to the ill-breeding, lowness, and vulgarity of the fisherfolk,
as she deems it. She dispenses her venom into the ears of St. Rose's
doctor and his wife, the Hamiltons, and her stepson, Harry—the
only other members of the elite in St. Rose to appear in the novel.
To malign Norrie is, it seems, her raison d'être, as she flicks in and
out of the narrative, frequently branding Norrie as a temptress and
a betrayer, among other vices. Mrs. Brandford regards herself far
above even members of her own class, and it comes as no surprise to
the reader that her downfall results from hubris. After undergoing
a series of trials severe enough to try a saint, the self-sacrificing
Norrie triumphs over the greedy, ruthless Mrs. Brandford. At the
end of the novel, Norrie, now the wife of Harry Brandford, has
become "a member of the charmed circle of the aristocracy" (125)
from which she was barred at the beginning, and Mrs. Brandford
has been banished from the ancestral home, and the circle over
which she had so long held power, to the geographically distant
city. Norrie has come full circle; she has moved from a simple to an
enriched life, moved outward and away from her roots, and only
after achieving refinement and triumph over adversity does she
finally reintegrate into her first community.

Is this novel "founded on fact" as the advertisement in

Newfoundland Illustrated suggests? The outport locale of the novel is fictional—St. Rose is somewhere on the coast of Newfoundland. Where, is not clear, but it is a coastal steamer port.[84] Places and landmarks in St. John's are named (the Narrows, Quidi Vidi Gut, the Atlantic Hotel), but although the topography of St. Rose is given names such as Fir Cove, Rocky Falls, and Beach Bay, the landscape is vague and mythical, a landscape where the sea is benign rather than threatening as it is in Norman Duncan's *The Way of the Sea*—it lacks verisimilitude. Outside St. John's, the landscape is a stock, idyllic, romantic landscape. Even in St. John's, the landscape is more imaginative rather than realistic. English uses Newfoundland as a backdrop on which to paint her own romantic landscapes. For her reader, an authentic landscape was subordinate to the "story."

******

Anastasia English's novels are similar in narrative technique, plot construction, character, and theme to those of numerous American, British, and Canadian novels of her time. While these novels are of a particular genre, they are more than "escapist fiction" and "innocuous romances." Literary critics have been biased against the type of fiction written (and read) in the nineteenth century by women, referred to pejoratively as the genre of "women's fiction," "sentimental fiction," "domestic fiction," or "domestic sentimentalism." Anastasia's novels fit this genre of fiction. As a result of this bias, these novels and their authors have fallen into the literary rubbish heap of oblivion, and the myth of the dreadful nineteenth-century woman writer has become entrenched. While not claiming that these women writers are outstanding writers, feminist critics now insist that these women wrote valuable fiction, more complex than originally thought, and that it needs to be studied and contextualized.

One criticism of this fiction is its overt didacticism. Nineteenth-century novelists often wrote in a tradition of piety and moral commitment for a reading public steeped in a religious and moral discourse. Fictional characters faced trials as the means of strengthening character, and young women readers learned about submission to the will of God, endurance, resignation, fulfilment of duty, self-sacrifice,[85] and what behaviour to emulate or shun. In *Only a Fisherman's Daughter* the highest calling is to give one's life for another.[86] The heroine of this novel puts her childhood friend (Lucy Hamilton) before her romantic love relationship (with Harry Brandford); she is loyal to Lucy even at the cost of sacrificing her love with Harry, a much-desired ideal.[87]

"Women's fiction" has also been denigrated for its structural shortcomings: its frequent digressions, an intrusive narrative voice (often in parenthetical asides) telling, rather than showing, the reader how to read. Being addressed as "dear reader" and having plot action stopped for tedious lecturing, philosophizing, and sermonizing is often annoying to a twenty-first-century reader. In the nineteenth century, the textual strategy of direct authorial approach, often in a confidential, conversational tone, enhanced the sentimental potential in the plot. The narrator, guiding the reader by using the plural personal pronoun ("we"), lessened the distance between the author and the reader. In the beginning of *Only a Fisherman's Daughter*, the ubiquitous narrator makes her presence known on the first page by announcing the locale as "the village *we* will call St. Rose" (1, emphasis added). The narrator reports, explains, moralizes, makes pointed references to the future, and is opinionated (though obviously sympathetic with Norrie, not Mrs. Brandford). By modern standards, the narrator's intrusion interrupts the story line, destroys the climactic build-up, and is, in short, a clumsy device.

Today's "carping critic" might find other "defects and blemishes"[88] in *Only a Fisherman's Daughter*: it is rife with improbability, melodramatic, and formulaic. Coincidences abound (a ready-made governess position for Norrie in the U.S.; a newspaper found in a Liverpool hotel contained the marriage announcement of Harry Brandford and Lucy Hamilton in Newfoundland); conversations are overheard; and mystery followed by revelation is the order of the day. Other stock devices include a deathbed pledge; a complicated love triangle; many character doublings (two blonde, invalid girls—Lucy Hamilton, St. Rose; Alice Erington, U.S.); multiple mother figures (the good: Mrs. Hamilton, her sister Mrs. Dane, and the Mother Superioress; the wicked [stepmother], Mrs. Brandford); and two men with the same name (Harry Brandford). With its emphasis on plot rather than on character development, such a narrative is often intricate and multi-threaded. One critic has argued that such fiction is linked by participation in one overplot in its chronicling of "the 'trials and triumphs' of a heroine":[89] the heroine, most frequently an orphan (as Norrie Moore is), begins as a poor and friendless child; or, she is a pampered heiress who becomes poor. In both, the heroine develops the capacity to survive and surmount her troubles; in both, the heroine is deprived of all the external aids she had (rightly or wrongly) depended on to sustain her throughout her life, and to make her success in life entirely a function of her own efforts and character, forcing her to win her own way in the world. And this, in a nutshell, is the plot of *Only a Fisherman's Daughter*. The basic plot of all "women's fiction" is the "woman's achievement of happiness and success through self-discipline, with the aid of teachers and examples, and sometimes in the teeth of determined opposition."[90] Before a happy ending can be realized in *Only a Fisherman's Daughter*, Norrie undergoes many trials in her efforts to abide by her principles, and she has to discharge her pride and her responsibilities to the upper-class Hamiltons and Brandfords, as well as achieve an integration of culture and self, before a new identity of self can be forged.

On the technical side, the plot of this fiction is constructed of a series of events or repetitive scenes taking the form of "five or six confrontations with heavy emotional content" and the plot machinery needed to get from one to the other is "rapidly narrated and inconclusively imagined."[91] The central focus is the heroine's emotions; information about other characters is developed only to the extent that it will make the heroine's emotional confrontation possible. Time is often telescoped: the action is condensed, and great chunks of time are jumped over, leaving out details that would often aid plot development. In *Only a Fisherman's Daughter*, English often uses the first sentence of each new chapter to situate the time frame for the reader: "Norrie is in her twelfth year" (ch. 3); or, "four years have flown quickly by" (ch. 5). The sharp delineation into chapters and the clumsy manipulation of time causes displacement and may often be tiresome for the modern reader. Often antecedents are summarized in one sentence; and, once the heroine has received a proper education, she is ready to embark on her adventures or trials.

The type of prose fiction referred to as "women's fiction" was popular in late nineteenth-century St. John's newspapers. In that time, the newspaper was

> a place for serialization of books or as a place for essays, poems, and other materials that were to be gathered later into a book. The newspapers are testing grounds for fledging writers. And they are also the place where pieces by well-established writers are also found. In one issue of a newspaper, one might find a local poet and, two columns over, a short poem, lifted from an English or American poet, even someone quite famous like Tennyson or Browning. The relationship between books and newspapers goes further: the newspaper firm served as the printer and publisher of most 19th and early 20th-century books.[92]

The *Evening Telegram* in the 1890s, for example, ran unsigned serials with such titles as "The Lovers' Quarrel"; "Life or Death:

Love's Dangerous Compromise"; "The Double Secret; or a Terrible Retribution"; "Love Wins; or Mabel Carew's Victory"; "His Heart's Idol; or The Fatal Message"; and "Gracia Tempest's Triumph; or, The Conspirators Foiled: A Thrilling Story of Love, Jealousy, Revenge and Final Triumph"—all women's fiction. Popular female writers of the day being read in St. John's, according to bookstore advertisements in the same newspaper, included Mrs. Humphrey Ward, Marie Corelli, Rhoda Broughton, Amelia E. Barr, Lily Dougall, Mrs. Inchbald, Mrs. Oliphant—all writers of popular fiction similar to that written by Anastasia English. In the bookstore lists[93] of their latest shipments of books from July to December 1891, we encounter such authors and novels as Countess de Bremont, Marie Corelli, Olive Schreiner (*Dreams*), and Alcott's *Little Women*. This is what many women of St. John's were reading when *Only a Fisherman's Daughter* was published.

******

The language of the characters and the intrusive narrative voice is a central issue in *Only a Fisherman's Daughter*: language is an important marker of class. Even though the novel is set in the coastal village of St. Rose, the spoken language is that of the St. John's elite, not the rough dialect of the fishermen. Dialect is spoken only by Norrie's guardians (her aunt and uncle) and a few locals who make brief appearances. When Norrie is introduced, she speaks the language of the Hamiltons and the Brandfords, but, the narrator reminds the reader, Norrie is not a natural member of the upper class: "(Norrie's grammar was often at fault)" (10). A clear distinction exists between Norrie and her guardians: their dialect marks them as lower class and less intelligent, but, Norrie, frequently referred to as being bright and intelligent, has the potential to rise above her status. Her guardians view education ("larnin'") as madness, "idle habits" which take Norrie from her duties (carding and spinning wool, milking cows, and making butter, etc.) and "notions not fit for her" (35). Because of Dr. Hamilton's financial generosity, Norrie receives "a good, solid English education, and other ornamental requisites, such as music, drawing, painting" (36) at an American Convent, where Lucy, his daughter, is being educated. Dr. Hamilton secures Norrie's education by telling her uncle that she is "fit … for a different sphere of life" (36) than St. Rose. When Norrie tells Lucy Hamilton what her uncle has said, she uses his vernacular, but then explains, "but I always try to speak the way Miss Bryant [the teacher at St. Rose] tells us, and the way you and your father and mother speak" (13). In this exchange, Norrie acknowledges her awareness of contrasting languages—the language of power is that spoken by the elite, the Brandfords and the Hamiltons, not the dialect of her guardians. Norrie's choices about her life and future are predominantly choices about these languages. As the novel unfolds, the tension resident in Norrie, a tension between her Newfoundland heritage and the world of the elite, becomes more apparent. The novel's dialogue reveals that Norrie consciously adopts the language of the upper class. The "aristocratic" Mrs. Brandford is at the top of the social scale and Norrie, the child of fisherfolk and an orphan, is at the bottom. Although Mrs. Brandford expounds on Norrie's "ill-breeding"— "[t]he utter absence of refinement and education makes them [the fisher people] ill-bred" (3)—later, when Norrie is no longer "the terror of St. Rose" (1), as Mrs. Brandford labels her, but thoroughly educated and refined, Mrs. Brandford, whose notions of caste and class are rigid, still considers her ill-bred.

In an early scene, a teasing dialogue between the town's children (including Norrie) and one which develops into a snowball fight, Norrie's appropriated language differs markedly from Tommy Brown's vernacular. He speaks phonetically; she, more formally. She has not yet fully mastered the language spoken by the Hamiltons and Brandfords, as the narrator informs the reader (apologetically and parenthetically) that "(Norrie's grammar was often at fault)" (10). Her "faulty" grammar is an indicator of her struggle for social ascendancy. In utilizing language to convince her playmates to play truancy from hay making, not only does Norrie distance herself linguistically from them, but she distances herself physically, "so as the eloquence of her persuasive powers might have the desired effect on her auditors" (12). Despite this facile use of language, Norrie's silence before the accusatory Mrs. Brandford reveals a sharp power differential.

The fisherman's daughter not only has to appropriate the language of the upper classes to rise above her lowly position (she has to speak "properly" and be educated), she must also change her manner, her dress, and lose her brown tan before she is fully refined and ladylike. As Norrie ascends from fisherman's daughter to perfect lady, her skin loses its natural tan: "the coat of tan, which exposure to sun and wind had given her, had entirely disappeared, and her skin was soft and white" (48). Even her brown curls, after long training, are tamed and "straight enough to allow them to be dressed after the fashion of the day" (48). When she and Harry meet after she had been in the U.S. for four years, her "tangled brown curls [once] hanging about her head" are now "gathered in a large coil at the back of her head" (64). Her hands, "once brown and somewhat hardened," are now "soft and white" (64). Norrie, now educated and accomplished, is finally refined and ladylike, yet she still does not qualify as such in Mrs. Brandford's eyes. She does, however, pass as a lady to the exacting Mrs. Erington, the wife of a "wealthy Southern gentleman," who engages Norrie to be a governess to her stepdaughter. Mrs. Erington demanded that the governess be "kind-hearted, sympathetic, young and pretty, take the place of governess and companion, play and sing well, paint and read well, [be] refined, well educated, of good family, and of a bright and sunny disposition" (136)—in short, a paragon. Mrs. Erington's list of qualifications rival Mrs. Brandford's rigid notions, yet Norrie not only meets but surpasses them. Norrie's accomplishments in music and painting—"foll-dolls" as her Uncle John regards the ornamental areas of education—ultimately have cash value. Norrie, who opens a music and painting school in St. John's on her return from the United States, has pupils who pay well, perhaps because such accomplishments were markers of upper-class refinement. These accomplishments are influential in her being hired as governess for the wealthy American Eringtons.

Only a Fisherman's Daughter points to class stratification in the colony of Newfoundland and the interdependence of language and identity: "you are the way you speak."[94] The different dialects in the novel mark the aspirations of the characters and determine their eligibility to enter varied social strata. Language, according to M.M. Bakhtin, "lies on the borderline between oneself and the other." It is not "a neutral medium that passes freely and easily into the private property of the speaker's intentions," but language "is populated—overpopulated—with the intentions of others. Expropriating it, forcing it to submit to one's own intentions and accents, is a difficult and complicated *process*"[95] (my emphasis). After an encounter with a local, Jerry Malone, Norrie, the narrator reveals, "suddenly remembered she was relapsing into her slang ways again" (22). For Norrie, the fear of relapsing into her slang ways "again"—as if by speaking the language of the lower class will cause her to fall back into that lower status—is always present. However, to Maude Varley, the wealthy and sophisticated young American girl whom she accompanies on a tour of the Continent, Norrie's "ideas and language [are] of such an elevating nature that they filled the hitherto worldly mind of the girl with thoughts and aspirations, far beyond the empty flattery and whirl of fashionable life" (157). Norrie has successfully appropriated the language of the elite, and her language now has the power to elevate.

At the end of the novel, "indigene and exile, language

and place"[96] are merged. Norrie and Harry are not married in Florence, where they re-unite, but in St. John's, in their home country. They return to St. Rose and "their own grounds" to be greeted in dialect by Jerry Malone, who wishes them "much ji," and by the "bonfires, rockets and guns" of the happy fisherfolk, as if they are the returning gentry (162). The last scene in the novel reveals the happy couple making harmony with the song "Golden Love." The fetters that had bound Norrie to her ancestors have been broken and she is now integrated into the social sphere of the elite; her words fuse with Harry's "happy accents" (163).

******

Literature is not simply words on a page but "a complex, social, political, and material process of cultural production."[97] History and the author cannot be divorced from each other, as authors and books exist within historical moments as "junctures of ideas, controversies, and tensions in a society."[98] Fiction reveals an author's experience, reading tastes, obsessions, and social and moral values. Even though we know few details about Anastasia English's life, we know that her own reading influenced and shaped her writing of *Only a Fisherman's Daughter*; it was, clearly, her knowledge of life in the colony of Newfoundland that gave shape to the novel. Within her worldview, duty, discipline, self-control, and sacrifice (within limits) were not only moral but strategies for survival.

Feminist critics have re-discovered "women's fiction." New readings of this fiction attest to its depth and complexity and offset any justification for its wholesale dismissal. Neglected novels such as *Only a Fisherman's Daughter* "offer powerful examples of the way a culture thinks about itself, articulating and proposing solutions for the problems that shape a particular historical moment."[99]

Anastasia English's novels have not been included in the canon of Newfoundland literature—itself on the margins of the Canadian mainstream canon. Commenting on canonicity, Helen Porter, a well-known Newfoundland writer, lamented the non-inclusion of women writers in anthologies of Newfoundland literature: "We felt then, as we've often felt before and since, that women writers in Newfoundland have not been actively discriminated against as overlooked, which sometimes can be a far worse insult."[100]

This silence reverberates throughout the history of book publishing in Newfoundland in general—"Where, one might ask, are the Newfoundland books themselves? Who are the writers? the editors? publishers? Here we suddenly encounter a remarkable silence"[101]—but it is especially pertinent to women writers and "[t]he first novelist ... to attempt local publication,"[102] whose name is hardly remembered, and who had not, until 1998, been included in any anthology of Newfoundland literature.[103] However, three of her works—*Only a Fisherman's Daughter*, *"The Queen of Fairy Dell" and Other Tales*, and *When the Dumb Speak*—were source-texts for the *Dictionary of Newfoundland English*.[104] Although Anastasia English is now included in two anthologies of Newfoundland writings, in one she is placed in context but, in the other, she remains marginalized.

Despite its melodramatic plot, thin characterizations, and many pedestrian coincidences, *Only a Fisherman's Daughter* remains, 110 years after its publication, a surprisingly readable book. This first work of fiction written and published in Newfoundland by a native-born Newfoundlander is an important cultural artifact. Its particular significance is its revealing exploration of the manners and morals that reflect the way of life of a distinctive society. *Only a Fisherman's Daughter* may not appeal to all twenty-first-century reading tastes, but it is an important "historical text as it reflects, in various ways, the life and times of colonial Newfoundland" and, through a reading of it, we can learn about "inter-community relations at the turn of the nineteenth century."[105] Margaret Duley deplored the "little Newfoundland literature on library shelves," adding that "[i]n spite of frustration, voices have been heard and stars of varying lustre have illumined the Newfoundland sky." Yet her roster of Newfoundland novelists included only herself and Erle Spencer.[106] George Story also lamented that "Newfoundland has not been a happy haunt of the learned Muses."[107] Anastasia English, who remains "unheralded for her contribution to Newfoundland literature, for leading the way for the many Newfoundland women writers [and men] who have become worthy successors to her legacy,"[108] is an uncelebrated Muse. *Only a Fisherman's Daughter* has languished in the margins too long. With this edited text, Anastasia English's first novel is once again available to "thrill [her readers] with pleasure and pride"[109] and to be enjoyed by another generation of readers.

— Iona Bulgin

NOTES TO AFTERWORD

1. Kathleen Winter, "Writers Guild: Promoting Creative Writing in the Province," *The Newfoundland Herald*, 12 February 1983.

2. This subtitle appears on the cover of the novel, not on the title page. Similarly, the title page of *Faithless* lists "A Newfoundland Romance" as the subtitle; and *Alice Lester*, "A Newfoundland Story."

3. *Encyclopedia of Newfoundland and Labrador (ENL)*, s.v. "Printing and Publishing."

4. English's own introduction to her second novel, *Faithless*, suggests that she paid for the printing of *Only a Fisherman's Daughter* and *Faithless* herself, with help from friends (see full text, p. 180).

5. In *The Rock Observed: Studies in the Literature of Newfoundland* (Toronto: University of Toronto Press, 1979), Patrick O'Flaherty notes that "Newfoundland and Labrador continued to serve as a backdrop to … escapist fiction well into the twentieth century, in, for example, the Billy Topsail stories of Norman Duncan … and the various performances of the Newfoundland-born novelists, Anastasia M. English (1864-1959) and Erle R. Spencer (1897-1937)" (84). A footnote leads the reader to the 3 June 1959 *Evening Telegram* ("Local Authoress, Dies at 97; A. English, Novelist, Poet") for an account of English. This brief piece appeared two days after an obituary notice (1 June 1959 *Evening Telegram*), and noted: "A local author better remembered today by those of the older generation … a prolific writer of short stories, magazine articles, poetry and novels … Her early novels were popular when they appeared in local bookstores years ago."

6. Patrick O'Flaherty, "Writing in Newfoundland," *The Oxford Companion to Canadian Literature*, ed. William Toye (Toronto: Oxford University Press, 1983), 548-552, see 550.

7. Iona Bulgin, "'Trials and Triumphs': The Heroine in Selected Novels of Anastasia English," MA thesis, Memorial University of Newfoundland, 1994. See also Bulgin, "Anastasia M. English," WORD (March 1993), 4-5.

8. In her PhD dissertation, "'Acts of Brief Authority': Entrapment, Escape and Narrative Strategy in Selected Twentieth-Century Newfoundland Novels" (University of Ottawa, 1993), Joan Strong examined two of English's novels; this dissertation was published by Breakwater Books in 1994 as *Acts of Brief Authority: A Critical Assessment of Selected Twentieth-Century Newfoundland Novels*. In 2005, *Only a Fisherman's Daughter* was the focus of an essay by Heather C. O'Brien entitled "Interethnic Folklore and Representations of Outport Life in Anastasia

M. English's *Only a Fisherman's Daughter: A Tale of Newfoundland"* (*Culture and Tradition* 7 [2005], 140-149).

9. *Faithless* and *"The Queen of Fairy Dell" and Other Tales* are also available in this format.

10. I have not located a specific birth date (day/month/year) for Anastasia English. *ENL* lists her birth date as 1862 (?), *DNB* as 1864. According to the Parish Records Collections for the Basilica of Saint John the Baptist, 1861-1864, held at the Provincial Archives, Anastasia English was baptized 22 February 1863. While this does not necessarily substantiate a birth date of 1863, it does, at least, eliminate the 1864 birth date used in the *DNB* and cited by O'Flaherty (see n. 5). There is no consensus on her age at the time of her death: according to 1 June 1959 *Evening Telegram*, she died at the age of 96; 3 June 1959 *Evening Telegram* states that she passed away at the age of 97 years; and 1 June 1959 *Daily News* notes that she was in her ninety-seventh year. In the 1949 *Christmas Annual*, Anastasia's niece, editor Elizabeth (English) Foote, announced her aunt's retirement as editor of *Yuletide Bells*, and noted that "this grand old lady [is] now in her eighty-seventh year."

11. See Obituary [Mrs. Joseph English], *Evening Telegram*, 14 January 1921: the obituary writer notes that she was "a member of one of the oldest and most respected families in the country."

12. Most of the biographical information in this Afterword was provided by Edward-Vincent Chafe. I am indebted to him for sharing his research on the genealogy of the English family (letters to author, 21 January & 20 May 1994).

13. See source, n. 11: he "founded and edited the *Advocate*." In the obituary notice of 19 July 1909 *Evening Telegram*, he is listed as the proprietor of the *Advocate*. The office of the *Advocate* was located at 279 Duckworth Street, and English, its proprietor, lived next door at 277 Duckworth (*Sharpe's Directory* 1885-1886). In "Journalism in Newfoundland," T.D. Carew notes that the *Advocate* "issued from the proprietor's residence at the head of McBride's Hill" (*Book of Newfoundland*, vol. I [St. John's: Newfoundland Book Publishers Ltd., 1937], 157-161, see 157)—277 Duckworth is at the top of McBride's Hill. English was still at this address in 1890 (*Might & Co.'s Directory* 1890).

14. Obituary [Joseph English], *Evening Telegram* 19 July 1909 notes: "About thirteen years ago [~1896] he resigned from the printing business and accepted a position as keeper in the Bank Dept. Building under the Morine Government."

15. See also *Free Press* 8 September 1908: "Mr. Joseph English has been appointed as Sheriff of the Magistrate's Court, and took up duty on the first instant."

16. The date of his death is from the poem, "In Memory of Jos. F. English," by Statia M. English, *Yuletide Bells* (1945), 33.

17. Chafe suggests that she was probably educated by the Sisters of Mercy.

18. Quoted in Sister Mary Basil McCormack, "The Educational Work of the Sisters of Mercy in Newfoundland 1842-1955," MA thesis, Catholic University of America, 1955; see also http://www.heritage.nf.ca/society/rel_orders_edu.html.

19. Patrick O'Flaherty, *Lost Country: The Rise and Fall of Newfoundland 1843-1933* (St. John's: Long Beach Press), 2005, 196.

20. See n. 13.

21. *Devine & O'Mara's St. John's City Directory* 1897; *McAlpine's Newfoundland Directory* 1898.

22. *McAlpine's Newfoundland Directory* 1904.

23. *McAlpine's St. John's Directory* for 1908-1909 lists Joseph English as a caretaker

at "Deptal. Bldg.," and his son Joseph, a bailiff, as boarding at this address. See also *St. John's Newfoundland Directory* 1913; *McAlpine's St. John's City Directory* 1915.

24. Obituary [Joseph English], *Evening Telegram,* 19 July 1909. In *St. John's Newfoundland Directory* 1913, Joseph jr., a bailiff at the Central District Court, is now the head of the household, and Anastasia and her mother, Elizabeth English, listed as boarders.

25. *McAlpine's St. John's City Directory* 1915 lists Anastasia (no occupation listed), her sister Annie, and her mother as boarding at 15 Monkstown Road, and Joseph, a bailiff at the Central District Court, the head of the household.

26. Chafe notes that "[a]t the time of her death in 1921, Anastasia's mother, Elizabeth Born English, resided at 136 Water Street." This is likely the same as 126 listed in the Directory (possibly a transcription error).

27. *St. John's City Directory* 1919 and 1924; *Newfoundland Directory* 1928.

28. According to the *Newfoundland Directory* 1928, Joseph English, bailiff at Central District Court, lived at 329 Water Street. It is unclear if 327 Water (from the List of Electors) is actually the same as 329 listed in the Directory, or if this is a clerical error.

29. *Newfoundland Directory* 1936 lists Annie, retired official of East End post office, as the head of the household at 6 Wood Street. Anastasia is not listed.

30. O'Neill, letter to author, 4 April 1994.

31. *ENL,* s.v. "Music."

32. O'Flaherty, "Writing in Newfoundland," 550.

33. Carew, "Journalism in Newfoundland," 157.

34. These are glossed within the text of *Only a Fisherman's Daughter.*

35. Elizabeth Foote is listed on the masthead.

36. This story, set in Nova Scotia, was published by Manning & Rabbitts (47 pages).

37. St. John's printers William English and William Cullen officially registered the *Christmas Greeting* in 1895, but it probably began around 1893 and was printed by the *Daily News* office in St. John's. It probably ceased publication shortly after 1913. In 1933 it was revived by Kathleen Mary English, and appeared until 1947, at least (*ENL,* s.v. "Christmas Issues").

38. L.E.F English and Arthur S. English were regular contributors to the *Newfoundland Quarterly.* This journal did not publish any of Anastasia's writings.

39. *ENL,* s.v. "English, Anastasia Mary." Bibliographical sources for this entry do not substantiate this statement.

40. On 11 May 1901 a note headed "Writing a Novel" appeared in the *Evening Telegram*'s personal column. It announced: "We are informed that one of our outharbour lady teachers is spending her spare moments writing a novel, the plot of which is founded on fact. She has it well started and hopes to have it published in the fall." Whether this refers to Anastasia English is unclear, but the date does coincide with the publication of *Faithless* in 1901, a book which, it is clear from her own introduction to the book, is based on fact. It raises the question, however, whether Anastasia was ever a teacher in a Newfoundland outharbour (and what geographical locale is deemed "outharbour"). Extant *Reports of the Roman Catholic Schools of Newfoundland* (1886, 1889, & 1898) do not list her. I could not find any documentation of another women novelist in Newfoundland at that time. *ENL,* however, omits *Faithless* (1901) from her oeuvre.

41. Both *ENL* and *DNB* credit English with a book entitled *Book of Short Stories* (n.d.). I have not located such a book. It is likely an incorrect reference to her short story collection, *"The Queen of Fairy Dell" and Other Tales* (1912).

42. Christmas annuals were supplements to regular newspapers or independent Christmas issues. Early annuals include *Holly Branch* (~1891); *Christmas Bells* (~1892); *Christmas Greeting* (~1893); *Christmas Chimes* (1909); *Holly Leaves* (1909); *The Christmas Annual* (~1910), and *Yuletide Bells* (~1910). *The Christmas Annual* and *Yuletide Bells* were two of the longest running Christmas issues (*ENL*, s.v. "Christmas Issues"). These annuals are an "absolutely crucial source of evidence for the literary life in the country from 1893 onwards" as "a gathering place for highly heterogeneous material—short historical essays, reminiscences, stories, poems, dialect sketches, photography, drawings, accounts of dramatic productions, and so on. All very civilized, and clearly a product of genteel classes, in these journals temporarily insulated from the more rough and tumble world of the newspaper. They mediate between the timeliness of the newspaper and the timelessness of the book. Yet they are so grounded in the literary activity of the community that they serve as a very important index of taste" (William Barker and Sandra Hannaford, "Towards a History of the Book in Newfoundland" [1996], http://www.hbic.library.utoronto.ca/fconfnfld_en.htm). See also Peter Churchill and Jeff Monk, *Newfoundland Christmas Annuals: A Preliminary Index Guide*, A Research Project supervised by William Barker (1989).

43. I base this on those stories that I did find. Several list Marie (a typo of Maria?) as author, and there is also one poem by A.E. I have not included these.

44. *Evening Telegram*, 3 June 1959. This is likely a reference to *The Christmas Annual*. The *Telegram* reference notes that as Bessie Foote, the editor, died in 1958, the issue was never published. The 1958 *Christmas Annual* published Anastasia's story, "Shorty Wins," which had been taken from *Yuletide Bells* (1947).

45. The Centre for Newfoundland Studies, Queen Elizabeth II Library, has 1910, 1913, 1916, 1928, 1943, 1944, and 1948 on microfilm, and she is listed as editor on the masthead of each of these extant issues. I also examined 1940, 1945, 1946, and 1947 at the Provincial Archives of Newfoundland. I am indebted to Bert Riggs for providing me with a copy of the 1948 issue. According to *ENL*, *Yuletide Bells*, started by Miss A. English, began in 1910 and was still being published in 1947. Is this date correct? In the 1949 *Christmas Annual*, the editor, Elizabeth Foote, says goodbye to *Yuletide Bells* and its editor, Anastasia English, and notes that *Yuletide Bells* had run for 40 years—this would give it a starting date of 1908. This is corroborated by internal references: the 1923 edition celebrates its fifteenth year; the 1928 edition, its twentieth edition; and the 1943 edition, the thirty-fifth edition.

46. *DN* 22 July 1948. See http://www.heritage.nf.ca/confederation/letter4.html. I am indebted to Dr. Valerie Legge for bringing this to my attention.

47. "A Man and A Dog" (unsigned story, *Yuletide Bells* 1910), "Queer Story—An Affair of 'Honor'" (unsigned story, *Yuletide Bells* 1916), and "A Cent, Missus" (unsigned story, *Yuletide Bells* 1923), likely were written by Anastasia, but this cannot be corroborated.

48. These are the only issues of *The Christmas Annual* I located.

49. Paul O'Neill notes that "Between eight and nine o'clock the ringing of the Roman Catholic cathedral bells summoned the multitude to the church, where Bishop Mullock rose in the pulpit and denounced the riot and rioters, sending them all scurrying home to wash their wounds and bury their dead" (*The Oldest City: The Story of St. John's, Newfoundland* [Boulder Publications, 2003], 321).

50. *Tempered Days: A Century of Newfoundland Short Fiction*, ed. G.J. Casey and Elizabeth Miller (St. John's: Killick Press, 1998), 25-41.

51. *Land, Sea & Time*, volume 2, ed. Edward A. Jones, Shannon M. Lewis, Pat Byrne, Boyd W. Chubbs, and Clyde Rose (St. John's: Breakwater), 2001, 138-147. This is one of a three-volume high school text used in Newfoundland and Labrador. While the note to the volume states that the series "offers a blend of previously neglected voices, new voices, and those often found in anthologies," the absence of biographical sketches of the authors and artists behind each work homogenize the "previously neglected" with the rest.

52. This weekly newspaper, which began printing 1 May 1901, contained foreign news, editorials, news from the outports as well as the city, and a children's section. By 1907 the circulation had reached approximately 12,000 and the Christmas edition sold a record 7,000 copies. It ceased publication in the 1930s (*ENL*, s.v. "Free Press"). The *Free Press* was instrumental in promoting English as a writer: publication of her stories in this paper assured her a wide readership, and two of her novels were printed by the *Free Press* office.

53. "Prize Competitions," *Free Press*, 17 December 1907, 4.

54. "Prize Competition No. 7," *Free Press*, 22 December 1908, 4.

55. *Evening Telegram* 3 June 1959.

56. Obituary [Anastasia English], *Evening Telegram*, 1 June 1959.

57. 2nd ed. (Grand Rapids, Michigan: James Bayne Co. [1900]). http://www.national.gallery.ca/sva/nf/new_01/pg_74e.htm. The advertisement section also listed *Faithless* (by Marie [sic], author of "Only a Fisherman's Daughter") under the same heading, as well as "By Way of the Sea" [sic] by Norman Duncan. I am indebted to Dr. Maudie Whelan for this reference.

58. O'Flaherty, *Lost Country*, 197.

59. S.H. Parsons (1844-1908), originally from Harbour Grace, "photographed many of the leading figures of Newfoundland society of his day and is recognized as having been a pioneer in his profession" (*DNB*, s.v. "Parsons, Simeon H.").

60. The June 1904 issue of the *Newfoundland Quarterly* was devoted to the visit of exiled Newfoundlanders during Old Home Week. According to James J. McAuliffe, of Everett, Massachusetts, in "Old Home Week in Newfoundland," "the footsteps of absent sons and daughters of the ancient Colony will be turned in the direction of their dear old Island Home, to participate in the grand re-union known as 'Old Home Week.'" The object of this reunion (3-10 August) was to promote "a spirit of patriotism and love for the land of their birth" (19). Low travel rates were offered to encourage expatriates to return home to Newfoundland.

61. *McAlpine's Newfoundland Directory* for 1904 lists twelve booksellers in St. John's, all concentrated on Water Street: Atlantic Book Store, 138 Water; Barnes & Co., 421 Water; Garrett Byrne, 357 Water; John F. Chisholm, 201 Water; Dicks & Co., 253 Water; Gray & Goodland, 206 Water; Hon. Geo. Knowling, 387-391 Water; Charles L. March, 299 Water; and George Milligan, 375 Water.

62. The English residence; see n. 22.

63. *Evening Telegram*, 8 August 1904.

64. L'envoi, a convention of in old French poetry, is traditionally one or more detached verses at the end of a literary composition, seeking to convey the moral, or to address the poem to a particular person.

65. I am indebted to Dr. Roberta Buchanan for both of these references.

66. These stories are of the same genre as her novels.

67. *The Christmas Annual* 1949, 19.

68. Margaret Duley, "Glimpses into Local Literature," *Atlantic Guardian* (July 1956), 20-27.

69. *ENL*, s.v. "Duley, Margaret." Edith M. Manuel also notes that "Our first native born professional writer was Margaret Iris Duley" (Newfoundland Historical Society Lecture, "Women in Newfoundland History," 24 February 1976).

70. "Newfoundland Literature in the 'Dirty Thirties,'" *Myth & Milieu: Atlantic Literature and Culture 1918-1939*, ed. Gwendolyn Davies (Fredericton: Acadiensis Press, 1993), 71-76.

71. *Quill & Quire* 43.17 (December 1977), 30; from the Margaret Duley Book Review file in the Centre for Newfoundland Studies, Queen Elizabeth II Library, Memorial University of Newfoundland.

72. Alison Feder, *Margaret Duley, Newfoundland Novelist: A Biographical and Critical Study* (St. John's, NL: Harry Cuff, 1983), 41.

73. Feder, *Margaret Duley, Newfoundland Novelist*, 41.

74. Quotation from Barker and Hannaford, "Towards the History of the Book in Newfoundland." The title pages of English's books list publication information: *Only a Fisherman's Daughter*, Entered according to the Act of the Legislature of Newfoundland, in the year 1899, on behalf of the author, at the Colonial Secretary's Office, Manning & Rabbitts, Printers; *Faithless: A Newfoundland Romance*, Entered according to Act of the Legislature of Newfoundland, in the year 1901, on behalf of the author, at the Colonial Secretary's Office, St. John's, Newfoundland, "Free Press" Publishing Co. 1901; *Alice Lester: A Newfoundland Story*, Free Press Print, 1904; *"The Queen of Fairy Dell" and Other Tales*, Printed at The Evening Herald Office, 1912; *When the Dumb Speak*, Copyright, 1938, Entered according to the Act, on behalf of the Author, at the Department of Home Affairs, Newfoundland, All rights reserved. The title pages adhered to the legislation pertaining to book publishing: "The first Newfoundland legislation pertaining to newspapers and books was passed 6 May 1836 (6 William IV), 'An Act for preventing the mischiefs arising from the printing and publishing books, newspapers, and papers of a like nature, by persons unknown, and to regulate the printing and publishing the same.' See Newfoundland Acts 1833-45, Department of Justice, Government of Newfoundland" (Maudie Whelan, "The Newspaper Press in Nineteenth-Century Newfoundland: Politics, Religion and Personal Journalism," PhD dissertation, Memorial University of Newfoundland, 2003, p. 27, n. 11).

75. O'Neill, letter to author, 4 April 1994.

76. O'Flaherty, "Writing in Newfoundland," 550.

77. Feder, *Margaret Duley, Newfoundland Novelist*, 59.

78. "The Literary Culture of Atlantic Women between the Wars," *Myth & Milieu*, 62-70, see 65.

79. See n. 8.

80. "How I Discovered the Prose of Anastasia English," *Telegram* 17 June 2000. O'Neill was responding to Bert Riggs's "The Lost Prose of Anastasia English" (subtitled "The first woman to publish a novel in Newfoundland is scarcely known today") in 30 May 2000 *Telegram*.

81. O'Neill, letter to author, 4 April 1994.

82. "How I Discovered."

83. *The Christmas Annual* (1949), 19.

84. The location of St. Rose is a fictional (Newfoundland) community. The length

of time to get from St. Rose to St. John's by steamer is not clearly delineated; and although the reference to making fish on the beach is specific to the topography of certain areas of Newfoundland and might seem to restrict the locale, neither of these details provides clues as to the whereabouts of the community of St. Rose on a map of Newfoundland. These details, however, add a modicum of authenticity.

85. A character in *Florimel Jones: A Novel*, by T.U. [W.B. Stabb] (London, 1876), offers a definition of "True Love": "True Love is founded upon the principle of self-sacrifice. True Love, in a word, is simply, purely, *self-abnegation*" (101, emphasis in original). W.B. Stabb's *Florimel Jones* appears to be the first novel written by a native Newfoundlander (O'Flaherty, "Writing in Newfoundland," 550).

86. John 15:13 (KJV): "Greater love hath no man than this, that a man lay down his life for his friends."

87. The concept of the ideal, one which figures prominently in *Only a Fisherman's Daughter*, especially in chs. 6 and 7, is the focus of an unsigned story in *Yuletide Bells* (1910, 7), entitled "An Ideal Husband." It was the last article of a series which showed what a girl looked for at seventeen, and what, as a wife, she wanted at twenty-five. It concludes: "And now I look back over several happy years of married life, I know that I had learnt even then the most necessary lesson for the woman who wants to be happy, and that is to love her husband for himself, faults and all, for the ideal husband is or should be to every wife, her own."

88. Quotations from the write-up on *Alice Lester*, 8 August 1904 *Evening Telegram*.

89. Nina Baym, *Women's Fiction: A Guide to Novels by and about Women in America, 1820-70* (Ithaca: Cornell University Press, 1978), 22.

90. Baym, "Portrayal of Women in American Literature 1790-1870," *What Manner of Woman — Essays on English and American Life and Literature*, ed. Marlene Springer (New York: New York University Press, 1977), 211-234, see 229.

91. Sally Mitchell, "Sentiment and Suffering: Women's Recreational Reading in the 1860s," *Victorian Studies* 21 (1977): 29-45, see 33.

92. Barker and Hannaford, "Towards the History of the Book in Newfoundland."

93. Sandra Hannaford, "An Index of Book Advertisements Appearing in the *Evening Telegram*, St. John's Newfoundland, for the year 1890," unpublished essay, Memorial University, 1990; and "An Analysis of Books Offered for Sale in 1890 as Recorded in the *Evening Telegram*, St. John's, Newfoundland," unpublished essay, Memorial University, 1991. These essays are in the possession of Sandra Hannaford.

94. Bill Ashcroft, Gareth Griffiths, and Helen Tiffin, *The Empire Writes Back: Theory and Practice in Post-Colonial Literatures* (London: Routledge, 1989), 54.

95. M.M. Bakhtin, *The Dialogic Imagination*, trans. Caryl Emerson and Michael Holquist (Austin: University of Texas Press, 1981), 293, 294.

96. Ashcroft et al., *The Empire Writes Back*, 173.

97. Cathy N. Davidson, *The Rise of the Novel in America* (New York: Oxford University Press, 1986), viii.

98. Davidson, *The Rise of the Novel*, 123.

99. Jane Tompkins, *Sensational Designs: The Cultural Work of American Fiction 1790-1860* (New York: Oxford University Press, 1985), xi.

100. Helen Porter, "Women and Newfoundland Literature," paper presented at the Annual Conference, Canadian Council of Teachers, Memorial University of Newfoundland, 1973, 1.

101. Barker and Hannaford, "Towards the History of the Book in Newfoundland."

102. Barker and Hannaford, "Towards the History of the Book in Newfoundland."

103. Miller and Casey, in *Tempered Days,* were the first editors to include a story by Anastasia English.

104. *Dictionary of Newfoundland English,* ed. G.M. Story, W.J. Kirwin, and J.D.A. Widdowson (Toronto: University of Toronto Press, 1982): "prickleys" (*OFD,* source for second entry); "wady-buckety" (under "weigh-de-buckedy," *OFD,* source for first entry); "bough house" (*OFD,* source for first entry); and "jink," v. (*OFD,* source for first entry).

105. O'Brien, "Interethnic Folklore and Representation," 141.

106. Duley, "Glimpses into Local Literature," 20.

107. "Notes from a Berry Patch," *People of the Landwash: Essays on Newfoundland and Labrador,* ed. Melvin Baker, Helen Peters, and Shannon Ryan (St. John's: Harry Cuff, 1997), 101-115, see 102.

108. Riggs, "The Lost Prose of Anastasia English."

109. *The Christmas Annual* (1949), 19.

ACKNOWLEDGEMENTS

I am indebted to Dr. Elizabeth Miller for introducing me to *Only a Fisherman's Daughter* and Anastasia English, for supervising my Master's thesis on English's novels, and especially for encouraging and advising me in this current project.

I would like to thank Dr. William Kirwin of the English Language Research Centre, Memorial University, for answering my questions about obscure terminology, and Dr. Valerie Legge, also of the English Department at Memorial University, for her encouragement at an early stage of this project.

I am grateful to Dr. Maudie Whelan, Lloydetta Quaicoe, and Glenda Dawe, who read drafts and offered many valuable suggestions.

Thanks to Jackie Hillier and Carl White, Centre for Newfoundland Studies, Queen Elizabeth II Library, Memorial University, for their patient and good-natured assistance.

— Iona Bulgin